Samuel Francis Smith

Poems of home and country

Also, sacred and miscellaneous verse

Samuel Francis Smith

Poems of home and country
Also, sacred and miscellaneous verse

ISBN/EAN: 9783337234317

Printed in Europe, USA, Canada, Australia, Japan

Cover: Foto ©Andreas Hilbeck / pixelio.de

More available books at **www.hansebooks.com**

POEMS

OF

HOME AND COUNTRY.

ALSO,

Sacred and Miscellaneous Verse.

BY

REV. SAMUEL FRANCIS SMITH, D.D.

EDITED BY

GEN. HENRY B. CARRINGTON, LL.D.

" My Country, 'tis of thee,
Sweet land of Liberty,
Of thee I sing."

SILVER, BURDETT AND COMPANY,

BOSTON . . . NEW YORK . . . CHICAGO.

1895.

𝔘niversity 𝔓ress:

JOHN WILSON AND SON, CAMBRIDGE, U.S.A.

TO

Mg Dear Wife,

WHOSE LOVE HAS BEEN THE INSPIRATION OF MY VERSE
AND HER APPROVAL ITS BEST REWARD,

THIS BOOK

IS AFFECTIONATELY DEDICATED.

EDITOR'S PREFACE.

IT is an esteemed privilege to have been entrusted by
the author of our national hymn, "America," with
the original manuscript of his poetical writings, which
cover a period of nearly seventy years, for the purpose
of presenting them in durable form, as a legacy to his
countrymen and the Christian world.

As an ardent student of comparative philology, the
poet prosecuted its congenial pursuit until he mastered
fifteen languages, and rarely found himself at loss for
words by which to convey his thoughts and wishes, the
wide world over, without the aid of an interpreter.

An intense appreciation of Nature and country was
stimulated by a rare religious spirituality; and this
imbued his life and writings with a sympathy for
others which embraced all mankind. A vein of quiet
humor, hardly less delicate than that of his congenial
classmate Oliver Wendell Holmes, brightened all contributions to social and literary entertainments; but he
never failed to season such playful sallies and apt
allusions with the charity that "thinketh no evil," and
seeks only how best to impart happiness to others.

It rarely falls to the lot of man to reach the advanced age of Dr. Smith with intellectual vigor, youth-

ful sympathies, physical vitality, and an accurate memory in full and healthy exercise. His poems illustrate his life; and old and young alike, of whatever section, party, or creed, can find wholesome stimulant as well as a bright example in the pleasing, harmonious record.

The selections, their arrangement, and their relation to each other and to his life, have had his cordial sanction. Among the nearly three hundred and fifty odes and poems thus grouped or distributed, is represented nearly every possible phase of domestic, social, religious, and civic life. Nearly sixty patriotic hymns, or odes, supplement "America;" and one of these, "Patriot Sons of Patriot Sires," or, "A Song for Young America," written on Washington's birthday, 1894, shows how tenderly his heart sympathizes with the youth of his native land. Another, bearing as its title, "My Native Land," was composed immediately after his return from a two-years' absence in India and other remote foreign countries.

Sacred Psalmody has been equally enriched by his contributions. One of these, "The morning light is breaking," was contemporaneous in origin with "My country, 't is of thee," both having been written while he was a student at Andover Theological Seminary, in 1832. Another, "The Lone Star," has a record that will endear his name to the countless millions of India so long as time endures. As his classmate's "Old Ironside" rescued the frigate "Constitution" from demolition, so did this poem preserve in more enduring form than oak or bronze the mission altar at Telugu, India, in the year 1868.

Equally to be prized are others which have blessed many who never associated his name with the precious lines. A few are noted : —

"Blest be the sacred tie that binds;"
"Morn of Zion's glory;"
"As fades the light of closing day;"
"When shall we meet again, meet ne'er to sever?"
"The Prince of Salvation in triumph is riding;" and,
"Sister, thou wast mild and lovely."

It has been a prompting incentive in this compilation to present the poet's life and work while he might be able to have some recognition of his good service for God and country. It should incite others to seek the assurance of a happy old age, through acceptance of the same lofty aims and unselfish methods which have crowned his career, and that of his lovely companion, with purity and lustre.

Occasional notes indicate the special conditions under which many of the poems were written; and yet their breadth of thought and sympathetic expression enlarge their sphere of happy influence. A costly jewelled badge from the veterans of the Nineteenth Illinois Infantry, and a magnificent banner from the Grand Army Corps of Chicago, are among the many gifts, from all sections and from many lands, which remind him, and those who visit his modest home, that he is both loved and honored wherever he had contact with the world.

The selection made from his miscellaneous poems to close the volume, indicates his early conception of the grandeur of our destiny as a Republic; and in the mingled grave and light the reader will find that a mature patriotism and a ripe piety have uniformly characterized his life.

The tributes of his friends, Whittier and Holmes, who have so recently passed from earth, and of Washburn, who, at the age of eighty, gives to the world his "Vacant Chair and Other Poems," are fitly associated with this greeting to the public.

The following is the poet WHITTIER's letter: —

MY DEAR FRIEND, — I am thinking that thy birthday occurs about this time, and I cannot let the occasion pass without a word of kindly remembrance. I wish to give thee a hearty welcome to the octogenarian circle which everybody desires to reach, but is in no haste to do so.

The historian George Bancroft has been there for some time; and my dear friend and thy genial classmate Dr. Holmes is ready to join us, though I fancy he is willing to remain outside as long as possible. We shall all be proud of the acquisition of the Christian teacher and patriot poet, whose song of " Our Country " has been adopted by sixty millions of freemen. It has kept time to the march of Freedom. It has been sung around camp-fires, and the sick and wounded have forgotten their pain in listening to it. It has followed the American flag around the world.

I am sure, my dear friend, that we can both say that we are grateful to the Divine Providence which has blessed us in so many ways, and enabled us to feel, even at our age, that life is well worth living.

With love to thy dear wife, who, I do not forget, was my schoolmate in the old Haverhill Academy, and with every good wish for thyself, I am thy old and affectionate friend,

John G. Whittier

"OAK KNOLL," DANVERS, Oct. 18, 1888.

The letter from Dr. HOLMES is next in order.

DEAR MRS. SMITH, — I enclose a few lines for your husband's coming birthday, which I hope will be a pleasant reminder to him of an old classmate who holds him in great regard and honor. You will know how to present this, with the far more important offerings which will greet him on the coming most interesting anniversary.

Very truly yours,

OLIVER WENDELL HOLMES.

To the Reverend S. F. SMITH, D.D., Author of "My Country, 't is of thee," on his eightieth birthday, Oct. 21, 1888.

> While through the land the strains resound,
>   What added fame can love impart
> To him who touched the string that found
>   Its echoes in a nation's heart?
>
> No stormy ode, no fiery march,
>   His gentle memory shall prolong;
> But on fair Freedom's climbing arch,
>   He shed the light of hallowed song.
>
> Full many a poet's labored lines
>   A country's creeping waves will hide;
> The verse a people's love enshrines
>   Stands like the rock that breasts the tide.
>
> Time wrecks the proudest piles we raise:
>   The towers, the domes, the temples fall;
> The fortress ever crumbles and decays, —
>   One breath of song outlasts them all.

Oliver Wendell Holmes

The third tribute which belongs to this honored group is the following: —

To Rev. Samuel F. Smith, D.D., Author of "America."   1808–1888.

> Dear friend of well-remembered years,
>   When youth was on thy brow and mine,
> Thy smoothly flowing numbers seemed
>   A well-spring from a source divine.
>
> With undiminished affluence still,
>   From the same fountain calm and clear,
> Flow melodies as musical
>   As dropped upon my boyhood's ear.
>
> Aye, holier are their undertones,
>   And richer with the lore of age;
> The opening vista down the vale
>   Grows broader to the saint and sage.
>
> As friends beloved reach, one by one,
>   Life's limit, three-score years and ten,
> Thy fingers touch the old-time chords,
>   Responsive with their sweet Amen.
>
> For never fairer is the vine
>   Than when its purpling grapes hang low;
> And life's divinest hour is when
>   'T is radiant in its sunset glow.
>
> And thou dost stay the fleeting hours
>   To paint the blush ere it depart,
> And weave thy benedictions round
>   The holiest tendrils of the heart.

O heavenly gift of poesy!
   And beautiful, when it doth bless,
As thine hath done, its fellow-man
   In its embracing tenderness.

As oft a harp will murmur on
   When the sweet song we sang is o'er,
And charm us with its memories when
   The hand that swept it is no more, —

So will remembrance of thy life,
   Its four-score years of song and cheer,
Like music, linger when we miss
   Thy presence from the pathways here.

Henry S. Washburn.

A letter from Rev. W. E. Towson, dated Osaka, Japan, March 13, 1895, was received April 8, just as these pages were going to press. He wrote that "the native Christians of Japan have adopted the music of 'America,' to be sung with words equivalent to 'God save our Native Land,' on all national days;" and that "selections from 'Beacon Lights of Patriotism' have been translated and distributed, in tract form, to the Japanese army." He also desired that Dr. Smith be advised of the following: — "On a recent visit of two American lady missionaries to one of our men-of-war, after eight years of isolation in the interior of India and Japan, they heard the band play 'America.' At the welcome sound of our national hymn, one wept for joy, the other fainted."

The author's immediate response is given on the following page.

ECHOES OF "AMERICA."

"What are these notes of melody that float around me here, —
The tones of love that in my youth broke on my ravished ear,
The swelling notes from infant lips, the anthem of the free,
When childish voices trilled the song, 'My country, 't is of
    thee'?

"My fate has led me far from home; new scenes salute my
    eyes;
New climes and seasons greet me here, new flowers, fruits,
    and skies, —
But still my heart, untravelled, turns, dear native land to
    thee;
I sing again the old refrain, 'Sweet land of liberty'!"

She spoke in sweet and gentle tones, her cheeks with tears
    were wet;
"Dear native land, its light, its love, how can I e'er forget?"
She heard the strain; her bounding heart longed for the
    brave and free;
She breathed in ecstasy of love, "Sweet land of Liberty!"

Another pilgrim, far from home, heard the same echoing
    strain;
Her throbbing heart grew wild with joy to greet the thrill
    again.
She fainted as the glorious sound along the gamut ran,
"Is this the land of liberty?"   "Alas, 't is but Japan!"

But Freedom stooped to wipe the tears, to kiss the dead to
    life, —
Freedom that speaks the words of peace, healer of human
    strife.
Visions of love came o'er the soul; in faith, they rose to see
The tribes of all the peopled earth made, through the Gos-
    pel, free.

Newton Centre, Mass., April 9, 1895.

AUTOBIOGRAPHY OF THE AUTHOR OF "AMERICA."

THE following letter from Dr. SMITH illustrates many elements which have made his life so greatly a blessing to others: —

In accordance with your request for a familiar outline of my life, noting its chief events and the trend of my poetical writings, I send the enclosed, as the experience of one who courted the Muse partly for personal satisfaction, but chiefly from an earnest desire to promote patriotic sentiment and Christian living as he had opportunity. It has been a source of enjoyment, and, I hope, has been a comfort to others.

Sincerely your friend,

S. F. SMITH.

SKETCH.

I count it to have been a happy lot, and, possibly, an inspiration to my choice of a profession, that I was born under the sound of the Old North Church chimes, in Boston. I understand, from veritable family records, that the modest event occurred on the 21st day of October, 1808. I confess to a little touch of satisfaction that I am permitted, in my social retirement, to count "Discovery Day," as we now style the arrival of Columbus in America, as my own birthday; but I have never claimed that the coincidence was worthy of note, outside of the immediate Smith household.

Three years at the Eliot School, Boston, were followed by preparation for college at the Boston Latin School, from which I graduated to enter Harvard University. It certainly was a grateful experience of that preparatory training, that, in 1825, I was permitted to call the " Franklin Medal " my own, as well as a gold " Prize Medal " for an English poem.

My Harvard Class, 1829, brought me into intimacy with that congenial and beloved classmate, Dr. Holmes, and the friendship never abated; nor, in the progress of seventy years lacking one, was our tender fellowship ever lessened. Widely separated in our special lines of study, we were of " the boys " when together; and his playful reference to my being "disguised under the universal name of Smith," never hurt my sensibilities, but was one of the merry things of which we made sport together.

College days too quickly sped. I then pursued a three years' course at Andover Theological Seminary, from which I graduated September, 1832. I had meddled with verses from childhood, and, before leaving Andover, wrote the hymn, " My Country, 't is of thee," " The Morning Light is breaking," and many others.

I had "on the brain," a penchant for comparative philology; and, in my theological course, added four languages to my repertoire, besides accomplishing the pleasing task of reading every word of Mr. Marshman's Chinese grammar, — a vast quarto, nearly as large as a family Bible.

After the close of my course at Andover, I spent a year in editorial labor in Boston. Then I became village pastor in Waterville, Maine; was ordained February 12, 1834, and at the same time became Professor of Modern Languages in Waterville College, afterwards known as Colby University. During the course of eight years, on account of a vacancy in the Department of Latin and Greek Languages (for one whole year) all the Greek taught in the college was added to my department of instruction.

On the 16th of September, 1834, I was married to Miss Mary White Smith, of Haverhill, Massachusetts, grand-daughter of Dr. Hezekiah Smith, chaplain for six years in the Revolutionary Army, and an intimate friend of Washington, also one of the founders of Brown University, in the State of Rhode Island.

My double service in Waterville continued until January, 1842, when I became editor of the Christian Review (Quarterly), and took up my life residence at Newton Centre, Massachusetts. Becoming pastor of the First Baptist Church, I still retained my editorial chair till 1848 (seven years), and filled the pastorate for twelve years and a half. Meanwhile I fitted my children for college, — the two elder, a son and a daughter, for the sophomore grade of college study. After resigning the pastorate, I served as the editorial secretary of the Missionary Union, fifteen years, still preaching almost constantly as a stated supply.

In 1875, accompanied by my wife, I spent a year in Europe.

In 1880, we undertook a second journey, which included Southern Asia in its itinerary, being absent from the United States more than two years. This trip included England, Scotland, Sweden, Norway, Denmark, Germany, Switzerland, France, Spain, Italy, Austria, Turkey, Greece, India, Ceylon, and Burmah. We visited the missions of various Church Societies, — English, Scotch, French, German, and American, so far as time and circumstances would permit. Various correspondence had suggested the points in the field-service of the Master where labor was needed. I endeavored to learn as exactly as possible the actualities of the mission-work, its methods, its personelle, its needs, its trials, and its successes.

Literary work has been the natural result of my tastes and my studies. Articles for reviews, magazines, and newspapers have been almost without number. Among books, may be mentioned the "Life of Rev. Joseph Grafton;" "Lyric Gems" (publisher's title), "Rock of Ages," the two latter containing many of my own composition; "The Psalmist," in connection with Baron Stow, the current Hymn Book of the Baptist Churches throughout the United States for thirty years, from 1843; "Missionary Sketches," and "Rambles in Mission Fields." These were followed by "The History of Newton," Massachusetts, 950 pp. octavo; several books edited; and various translations for the Encyclopædia Americana, from the "German Conversations Lexicon," amounting to fully one thousand printed pages. Not far from one hundred and fifty of my hymns have, in various ways, been contributed to our Psalmody.

A strong poetical bias took hold of me when I was a boy of eight years. An "Elegy on a Cat," then written, disappeared long since, as well as the cat. The first poem published, was four years later; but if you do not find it among the old papers, I cannot supply it.   I have never bidden farewell to the lyre, simply because it was a part of myself.

The hymn, "America," was the fruit of examining a number of music books and songs for German public schools, placed in my hands by Lowell Mason, Esq. Falling in with the tune in one of them, now called "America," and being pleased with its simple and easy movement, I glanced at the German words, and, seeing that they were patriotic, instantly felt the impulse to write a patriotic hymn of my own, to the same tune. Seizing a scrap of waste paper, I put upon it, within half an hour, the verses substantially as they stand to-day. I did not propose to write a national hymn.   I did not know that I had done so.   The whole matter passed out of my mind.   A few weeks afterwards I sent to Mr. Mason some translations and other poems; this must have chanced to be among them.   This occurred in February, 1832.   To my surprise, I found later that he had incorporated it into a programme for the celebration of July 4, 1832, in Park St. Church, Boston.   I have since heard it sung in many languages, more than half-way round the world, the latest translation of it which I have seen being into the Hebrew.   When it was composed, I was profoundly impressed with the necessary relation between love of God and love of country; and I rejoice if the expression of my own sentiments and convictions still finds an answering chord in the hearts of my countrymen.

I pray that the spirit of the simple verses may be the spirit of our people evermore.

Samuel Francis Smith.

CONTENTS.

Part I. — HOME.

FAMILY PICTURES.

𝔓art II. — COUNTRY.

PATRIOTIC INCENTIVES AND EXAMPLES.

The Fathers and their Struggles.

The Sons and their Struggles.

𝔓art III. — SACRED AND RELIGIOUS.

INCENTIVES TO EARLY PIETY.

THE GOSPEL MINISTRY.

From Earth to Heaven.

A Redeemed World.

Part IV. — MISCELLANEOUS HYMNS AND ODES.

INTERVIEWS WITH NATURE.

RUSTIC SCENES. (*From the German.*)

VERSES FOR SPECIAL OCCASIONS.

Part I.

POEMS OF HOME.

Part I. — HOME.

FAMILY PICTURES.

———•———

I. DOMESTIC BEGINNINGS.

———

CHILDHOOD MEMORIES.

OH, no, they shall not be forgot,
  Those days of simple truth, —
The harmless sports and noisy joys
  Of boyhood and of youth;

CHORUS.

But when upon those early scenes
  We suffer thought to dwell,
We 'll drink to their dear memory from
  The pure, the pure deep well.

We wander o'er each scene anew,
  We tread each hallowed spot
Where time in giddy gladness flew, —
  Oh, can they be forgot!
              CHORUS.

Roll back, roll back the tide of cares,
  Roll back the swelling sea;
An hour we 'll give to think upon
  Our days of youthful glee;
              CHORUS.

But ah! those cheerful scenes are gone,
   Their joys fled fast away;
The friends of our bright boyhood's morn, —
   Oh, tell me, where are they!

CHORUS.

Bereaved, but bowing to our lot,
   Our onward path we tread,
As mournfully we gather up
   The mantles of the dead.

CHORUS.

The places where our youth was spent;
   The friends who now are not;
The scenes we loved, those joyous hours, —
   They shall not be forgot.

CHORUS.

———oo§o§oo———

TO LITTLE MARY WHITE.

"OUR FIRST-BORN."

THOU precious pledge of love,
   Of ties that bind two kindred hearts in one,
Dear infant Mary; 't is with joy we hail
Thy coming; and with joy we both shall strive
To make thee happy, useful, thro' the scenes
Of mortal life. Heaven watch o'er thee, my child,
Thro' all thy infant slumbers; guard thee well
In youth's most tempting perils; spare thy life,
To us as precious as our own, and give,
When life shall end, a crown of joy.

                         But know,
My child, this is a world of grief and change;
And 't is a high behest, beyond the lot
Of changeful earthliness and worldly pride,
Which thou art sent to finish.   When the day
That brings the power of knowing right and wrong
Shall be to thee, whate'er thou art, and where,
Know this, and 'grave it on thy memory,
Thy father and thy mother, fearing God,
Did, on this day which gave thee life and light,
To Him that life and light devote.   Know, then,
Thou must not think thyself thine own on earth,
For thou art wholly consecrate to God,
Born for His service, given for His praise.
So live that thou mayst honor Him, and then
Sit down in heaven with all the glorified.

WATERVILLE, Aug. 5, 1835.

CRADLE SONG.

FROM THE GERMAN.

SLEEP, baby, sleep!
     Our cottage vale is deep;
The little lamb is on the green,
His snowy fleece is soft and clean,
     Sleep, baby, sleep!

     Sleep, baby, sleep!
   I would not, would not weep;
The little lamb — he never cries —
How bright and happy are his eyes,
     Sleep, baby, sleep!

Sleep, baby, sleep!
Thy rest shall angels keep;
The lamb before the doors shall feed,
And suffer neither want nor need.
Sleep, baby, sleep!

Sleep, baby, sleep!
Near where the woodbines creep;
Be like the lamb so meek and mild,
A sweet and kind and gentle child.
Sleep, baby, sleep!

———oo⁘oo———

SALLIE.

THUS comes another; may she stand
   Among the saints in light,
Blest Saviour, at thy own right hand,
   And walk with thee in white.

And should her pilgrimage be long,
   And sharp affliction's rod,
Or short her pathway to the skies,
   Oh, may it end in God!

OCTOBER 18, 1838.

TO MY BLESSED WIFE.

ON THE BIRTH OF OUR "FIRST-BORN."

'TWAS an eventful day that made thee feel
  The breath of thy first-born. There are on earth
A thousand pleasant sounds, but none like that
In which the little babe, by slender cries,
Its earliest wants, else all unknown, reveals.
There is no sight to the young mother's eye
So full of sweet attractiveness, in all the scenes,
Tho' grand or beautiful in every part,
Of the Creator's works, as in the form
Of infant feebleness, and the first ray
In which its opening eye, unknowingly,
Looks up.

          Well, 't is a holy gift.   To us
The God we worship hath entrusted now
One of His jewels, to be trained on earth
For heaven's bright treasure-house. Oh, may He spare
The life so sweet and young, and ours, so full
Of weal or woe to her condition.   And may He,
Who heard the prayer of Hannah, list to ours,
And take this dedicated child, to serve
And glorify Him here — then shine above,
A star of matchless radiance, in the crown
Of our Redeemer.

AUGUST 6, 1835.

OUR FRANK.

A T first, a sickly babe, with angel face
        And gentle heart, and meek, fond, clinging ways,
O'er whom the tearful eye and careful hand
Watched long and faithful, half in hope, and half
Too near despair, dreaming that thy young life,
Like flickering taper, would ere long go out,
And early blight assail thy slight weak frame.
Now thou art grown a strong and noble boy;
Health flushes thy young cheek, and from thy mouth
Pour shouts of childish joy.   What hopes in thee
Lie treasured, child of our prayers, our eldest son !

God keep thee, Frank, firm in temptation's hour !
'T will come on thee; it has on all the earth.
God be thy shield, and God thy comforter;
We yield thee up to Him.   Be thou His child,
Prompt to obey His will; His messenger,
To bear to darkened men the light of life;
His loving, loved disciple.   May thy head
Rest on the Saviour's bosom, fitting place
For one whom earthly rest can never fill;
For gentle souls, for spirits born to be
Immortal as their author.

                              Live, fair boy,
A pillar of the truth on earth, and then
A gem, to shine with living, glowing light
Bright in the Saviour's coronet.

September 5, 1836.

TO LITTLE ANN.

OUR babe, escaping from life's woes
    Ere one brief day was given,
Just gleamed on earth, a fitful ray,
    Then shone, a star in heaven.

At sunset's mild and chastened hour
    We laid her 'neath the sod, —
Our earliest representative
    Before the throne of God.

September 15, 1837.

DANIEL APPLETON WHITE.[1]

ANOTHER bantling! lo, he comes,
    Not Miss, but Mr., Fudge;
A master-spirit, born to be
    Surnamed "the little judge"!

A portly personage, and fair,
    In wit and knowledge big;
Fat as an alderman, and decked,
    Judge-like, in his white wig.

[1] It was understood from the beginning that he was to be a lawyer, like his great-uncle whose name he bore; but he became a minister and a Doctor of Divinity.

Off! Puss and Frank and Sallie, off!
  The Master bids you trudge!
For I, in all these parts, am made
  His Majesty, the Judge!

"Tin plate and mug are mine, — who dares
  My rank of power to grudge?
I 'll have my way; I know I 'm right,
  Left-handed, but a judge!

"Off from the staircase! children, off!"
  (Why don't the babies budge?)
"I 'm coming down at one broad leap!"
  There sprawling lies the judge.

Whatever mighty man has done,
  Another, doubtless, can;
Now don't you think this wondrous judge
  Will make a wondrous man?

June 18, 1840.

II. ANNIVERSARIES.

TO MY DAUGHTER MARY, ON HER EIGHTEENTH BIRTH-DAY.

SO! leap the limit now that parts
    The woman from the child:
Enter life's great career at last, —
    No more with toys beguiled.

Earth spreads its pageant at thy feet,
    The bright world opens wide, —
Go, be a woman, glad assume
    The toils which thee abide!

Or joy, or woe, — no tongue can tell
    What fate thy lot may be;
But meet it bravely, strong in faith,
    God rules thy destiny.

Like breezes o'er the bending grain,
    Like sunlight on the wave,
Earth's rapid joys and trials pass;
    Jehovah lives to save.

Go, be a woman; round thy path
    Make love and gladness spring;
Reap in all fields; from every task
    Some sheaves of goodness bring.

So shall life's current cheerful flow;
    So bright shall be thy days;
No flattering words shall make thy fame;
    Thy works shall be thy praise.

TO MY DAUGHTER MARY, ON HER
WEDDING DAY.

FORTH from the sheltering wing of home,
  Forth from its sunlit bowers,
Fly like the bird, intent to roam,
  And try her new fledged powers.

Peace spread its gentle pinions o'er
  The nest so warm and fair;
And nature's glories round her pour,
  When free in upper air.

O'er broad, sweet fields, on joyous wings,
  With warbling throat, she flies;
She sings and soars, and soars and sings,
  Plumed for the distant skies.

So from thy dear, delightful home,
  With trusting faith aspire;
Life's beckoning labors bid thee come;
  The high behest desire.

Like evening sunlight on the hill,
  Like verdure on the sod,
Love, pure and ardent, lingers still
  Where'er thy steps have trod.

APRIL 27, 1858.

TO MY DAUGHTER, MARY W. JONES,

ON HER TWENTY-FIFTH MARRIAGE ANNIVERSARY.
APRIL 27, 1883.

BACKWARD, to-day, my sunny thoughts are turn-
ing,
Speeding through happy years, loving and learning,
So gently led through flowery paths of blessing,
Life's truest joys in all their wealth possessing.

What was my wish, — my young heart's early craving,
What forms of bliss, before my fancy waving,
Still lured me on, — life's pathway scarcely broken,
And love's first lisping utterance scarcely spoken ?

I hoped, I sang, so happy in my dreaming, —
Would the reality be like the seeming ?
Have I life's choicest pleasures overstated ?
Have I its Paradises antedated ?

Or will the birds of bliss be ever winging
Their joyous flight around, soaring and singing ;
Day feel no chill of twilight's damp descending,
Nor sunshine, risen in glow, find darkened ending?

Thank God, thank God, the bright path grows but
brighter !
Thank God, pain's light yoke grows forever lighter !
The sunny course, which seemed at first so winning,
Confirms, a thousand fold, its fair beginning.

And thus the years, full five times five, so fleeting,
Told the sweet tale of strength and weakness meeting,
In summertide alike, and stormy weather,
Drawing the weak and strong closer together.

And one who came, full welcome, in life's entry,
Stands at our age's door, a loving sentry;
Fitly, with filial clasp in clasp maternal,
Binding the love-knot of our season vernal.

Hail, wedded pair, be yours no day of sorrows,
But only brilliant morns and glad to-morrows,
Till life at last, from earthly, grows supernal,
And joy, from earthly joy, becomes eternal.

TO SALLIE, ON HER EIGHTEENTH BIRTHDAY.

SPRING, with its bright and cheerful hours,
   Flies like the mist away;
But weaves around our fragrant bowers
   The light of summer's ray.

And summer, with its brilliant beams,
   Gives way to autumn's reign;
And every swelling garner teems
   With heaps of golden grain.

So childhood, like the spring, retires,
   That nobler youth may rise;
And youth to riper age aspires
   And yearns for Paradise.

So life rolls on ; each precious hour
  Swells with the life to be,
And ripening years prepare the dower
  Of immortality.

Leave the glad memories of the past,
  To holier calls respond;
Upward with joyful vigor haste,
  The goal is still beyond.

Passed is the limit that divides
  Childhood from ripening life ;
Go, see what work thy hand abides,
  And dare the noble strife.

God be thy guide, — His sheltering hand
  Direct and guard thy way ;
So shall life's promises expand
  In fair, immortal day.

OCTOBER 18, 1856.

TO FRANK, ON HIS TWENTY-FIRST BIRTHDAY.

SEPTEMBER 5, 1857.

SO! be a man and gird thy soul
    To life's exalted aims !
The world awaits thee; go and meet
  Its just and lofty claims.

Temptation round thy bark will roar ;
  Stem its o'erwhelming tide,
Breast all its waves with manly force,
  And in God's strength abide.

God calls the workman to his toil;
  Go with strong arm and free,
To do His bidding, and await
  Life's opening destiny.

As springs the oak, with budding hope,
  From the small acorn riven,
Spreads far and wide its sheltering boughs,
  And lifts its head to heaven, —

So from this starting point of life
  Pursue thy widening way,
Blessing and blest, till time shall bring
  The light of endless day.

EWING AT TWENTY-ONE.

LAUNCHED safely on life's sunny main,
  With morn's bright promise round thee spread,
Live nobly, that earth's waiting train
  May pour their blessings on thy head.

What e'er the voice of duty claims,
  Go forth, thy destiny to meet;
Let tireless hope and lofty aims
  Make darkness light and labor sweet.

Sow goodly seed in every field,
  From every field rich harvests bring;
None is too poor some fruit to yield,
  Let ripening glory crown life's spring.

So o'er thee — for love cannot tire —
  God's covenant grace shall still abide,
Like Israel's pillared cloud and fire, —
  By day, thy light; by night, thy guide.

And when, like autumn's withered leaves,
  The proud, the base, unnoticed, fall,
Thy deeds shall be like garnered sheaves,
  And God shall bind and keep them all.

TO MY WIFE AT FIFTY.

'TIS fifty years, — God bless her, —
    A little more, perhaps;
When the heart is good and loving,
  How fast the years elapse.
We count time, not by pulse-beats,
  Or wrinkles on the brow,
But by love's broad, lighted circle, —
  An ever-lingering Now.

I spoke of wrinkles — did I ?
  Oh, no, the loving lines
Drawn round the earth, like girdles,
  Have here impressed their signs;
And if white rose leaves sprinkle
  Their sheen upon her hair,
The once bright auburn tresses
  A silvery beauty wear.

I wrote it fifty, — did I?
  It might be thirty less, —
Her young heart has such power
  To care for and to bless;
As sunshine near the evening
  Smiles with a fairer ray,
And makes the hour of setting
  The sweetest in the day.

I might have written twenty, —
  But one that filled her nest
Boasts of her thirty summers,
  And a rosebud on her breast;
And one, grave years creep o'er him
  And graver scenes employ, —
Now, a young, doting father,
  But her once fair-haired boy;

And one, her babe caressing,
  With fond, maternal look;
And one, his life consuming
  O'er legal brief and book;
And two, intently watching
  The shadows cast before, —
I might have written twenty,
  But yet it must be more.

Yes, fifty years, — God bless her, —
  Perhaps a little more;
No matter what the number,
  'T is all a shining store, —
As summer wakes new blessings
  With every day that springs;
And every breeze comes wafting
  Fresh fragrance on its wings.

The days, in love and blessing,
    Like glancing sunbeams sped,
Since angels sang, responsive,
    Around her cradle-bed;
They chanted love and promise,
    Not time, or years, to be;
No matter what the number,
    Perhaps 't is fifty-three.

FEBRUARY 8, 1866.

OUR GOLDEN WEDDING.

1834–1884.

BEHOLD, dear wife, how things have changed,
    Through sunshine and through showers;
The spring has ripened into fall,
    The buds have turned to flowers.

What long, wide paths our feet have trod,
    Since the far days of old!
But love has changed each woe to good,
    The silver moon to gold.

These fifty years of wedded love,
    How brief and few they seem!
Swift as a summer-day of joy,
    Eventful as a dream!

The babes we fostered long ago,
    And called them "children" then;
The girls are into mothers grown,
    The boys to stalwart men.

We launched our bark in sunny youth, —
  The date seems far away ;
But years have shortened into months,
  Months into fleeting days.

Once, like new ships, that ride in port,
  With canvas all unfurled,
Successful voyagers, our keel
  Has sailed half round the world.

By day God's loving cloud has moved,
  A shelter o'er our head ;
And still by night our winding course
  The pillared fire has led.

Sail on, fair craft, so bravely kept
  Unharmed by wind or wave ;
The hand so skilful to direct,
  Is mighty, too, to save.

Sail on, sail on, till golden light
  Shines o'er the distant sea,
And guides the vessel to its port,
  Blest immortality.

September 16, 1884.

TO CARRIE ON HER FIFTIETH BIRTHDAY.

CHILD of my warm affection,
　　Hast thou so stately grown ?
And can thy years be fifty, —
　　My little one, my own ?
Thy love, thy sunny temper,
　　Thy sweet and blessed ways
Made thee a child of promise
　　In all thy early days.

The years have passed so swiftly,
　　I took no note of time ;
Art thou a wife, — a mother ?
　　While babes around thee climb ?
Art thou, in light and power,
　　One of the world's bright rays ?
Do thy companions bless thee ;
　　And are thy works thy praise ?

Ah, yes, the years advancing
　　Have brought thee joy and grief,
As thou to many a weak one
　　Hast ministered relief.
A blessing to the living,
　　A watcher o'er the dead,
Heaven weaves its crown of honor,
　　A halo round thy head.

And if thy darling left thee
  To find his home above,
Heaven has its many mansions,
  Heaven is the land of love;
Trial may prove a blessing.
  O heart, be still and brave,
Wait for the great revealing, —
  God takes but what He gave.

As from the eastern glory
  The morning sun ascends,
And in a fairer radiance
  His western journey ends, —
So from the sweet beginnings,
  A brighter noon shall grow,
And Heaven shall crown thy fifties
  With its immortal glow.

August 19, 1893.

MY WIFE, TO A FRIEND WHO WOULD GUESS HER AGE.

OH, no, my friend, you blunder there,
  Your guess is far from true;
She has grown dearer many a year,
  But not yet "sixty-two."

Time's careless fingers o'er her head
  Have dropped the crystal dew, —
The pearls flow down in silver gloss;
  But she 's not " sixty-two."

You think she 'd seen so much of life,
  Alike the old and new,
She must be quite advanced, perhaps,—
  Well, far from " sixty-two."

You might have guessed more wisely, friend,
  Had you a better clew;
You judge her by her wisdom?—Well,
  She is not " sixty-two."

Her cheerful face, her bonny curls,
  Her heart so warm and true, —
Tell tales of years of joy and love;
  But she 's not " sixty-two."

For years, home's sunny bowers more bright
  With clustering offshoots grew,
And other bowers have reared their young;
  But she 's not " sixty-two."

Diminish it by four, I pray;
  Her sky, still bright and blue,
Bends, loving, round her youthful head;
  Yet she 's not " sixty-two.'

The silvery brown that crowns her brow
  Suggests, " Serenely wait,
And sometime, on some pleasant morn,
  She 'll wake, just fifty-eight."

FEBRUARY, 1871.

OUR FIFTY-NINTH MARRIAGE ANNIVERSARY.

NOT gifts of gold or costly gems,
   But that which is all price above,
The festal marriage-day provides, —
   Mercies to cheer and hearts to love.

How many sunny years have passed !
   And each has left its radiant line ;
The fifty long ago were told,
   And now, behold, 't is fifty-nine.

God of the loving, God of love,
   Whose favor blessed the earlier days,
Shine on the years that yet remain,
   While silver hairs proclaim thy praise.

SEPTEMBER 16, 1893.

SIXTIETH ANNIVERSARY OF OUR WEDDING.

TO MY WIFE, SEPTEMBER 16, 1834-1894.

SIXTY benignant years,
   With all their joys and tears,
     Have rolled by,
Since we, made one for life,
Were wedded, man and wife,
     You and I.

The blest days we have seen,
The lands where we have been,
    You and I,
Will linger on the brain,
Like some sweet song's refrain,
    Till we die.

The friends our hearts have loved,
Whose love our hearts have proved,
    Yours and mine, —
Some are our solace yet ;
Some, like bright suns, now set,
    Still they shine.

The years and ages pass,
Like shadows o'er the grass, —
    Love endures ;
Plants of immortal root
Cluster immortal fruit,
    Ours-and-yours.

TO MARY REED (FRANK'S WIFE), AT FIFTY.

FEBRUARY 9, 1843–1893.

SO swiftly the years on their axles have rolled,
  The scenes they have brought us seem only a
    dream, —
Like shooting stars, crossing the ocean of blue,
  Or bubbles of air floating down on the stream.

When roused from our dreaming, we find 't is all real,
  The months, in their flight, have rolled up into years,
With shadows and brightness, with sorrows and joys,
  The glow of their hopes, and their faith, and their
    tears.

Our birthdays, like milestones, are stationed to tell
  How rapid the pace, and how far off the start;
We note them, we count them; but what are the
      years,
  If only young love lingers warm in the heart?

Methinks Father Time, in his hurry, forgot,
  And marked on his tally more years than have sped;
No blush of the red rose has paled from your cheek,
  No petal of white fluttered down on your head.

By sickness and weakness, bereavement and pain,
  Like flowers by the tempest your heart has been
    bowed;
But Love has provided more gladness than gloom,
  More mercy than judgment, more sunshine than
    cloud.

What mercy and goodness have gleamed through your
      years!
  How lovely, how swiftly the fifty have passed!
With glow of the sunset, and glory, and peace,
  May fifty be added, — the crown of the last.

TO MY BELOVED WIFE, AT SEVENTY.

THREESCORE and ten ! the blushing spring
   Has changed to autumn's brown ;
The glossy head, for auburn curls,
   Now wears a silver crown.

Fair day of life, so rich in good !
   So seldom tempest-tossed !
How joy and love have filled the space
   Between the bloom and frost !

And thou half round the globe hast trod ;
   Hast traced, from distant seas,
The northern crown and southern cross,
   And felt the tropic breeze.

Thy children, held in honor, stand,
   Known in the world's highways ;
Thy husband, too, — and he, with theirs,
   This loving tribute pays.

And all thy steps, divinely planned,
   God's loving care has led ;
And countless blessings has His hand,
   Like spring-flowers, round thee shed.

Threescore and ten ! the limit reached
   That human years may fill, —
God's covenant love, God's promised grace
   Will shield and guide thee still.

And life's long path, through sun and storm, —
Blest boon to mortals given, —
Or smooth, or rough, at last shall prove
One long, sweet path to heaven.

DAVENPORT, IOWA.

TO MY WIFE ON HER SEVENTY-FIFTH BIRTHDAY.

RETROSPECTIVE PICTURES.

A FAIRY girl, with wavy curls;
Her trade in books and pen,
Like one who scatters lovely pearls;
Her sunny years, — *just ten.*

Another figure, stately grown, —
What changes time has wrought!
How swift the sobering years have flown,
With noblest purpose fraught!

Twice ten, — the scene is changed; I hear
His, "Wilt thou?" her "I will;"
She pledged her faith without a fear,
Risking, or good, — or ill.

Again, *thrice ten,* — and clinging buds
In sweet affection twine,
Successive, with their tendrils fair
Around the clustering vine.

Four tens, — the happy summit reached,
  Life's harder conflicts done,
Her sunny curls with silver streaked,
  Life's golden prizes won.

Revered and loved, with honor crowned,
  Now with her *five times ten,*
In peace and hope she walks and lives,
  Lives, in her babes, again.

Sweet eminence, too fair to leave,
  And so she lingers still;
Her cup of good, at *six times ten,*
  What constant blessings fill!

The world is wide; like Israel's hosts,
  Sheltered and led of God,
At *seven times ten* her favored steps
  Remotest empires trod.

Five more are added, — years of joy;
  Walk on, with trusting feet,
Till years *full twenty-five* shall make
  Thy century complete.

February 8, 1888.

TO MY WIFE ON HER EIGHTIETH BIRTHDAY.

THIS poem divides fourscore years of life into four parts, of one score each. It proceeds on the idea that the first score of a life of eighty years is mainly a period of labor and promise, like spring; the second, of vigorous toil, activity, and growth, like summer; the third, harvest and fruit from the preceding period, like autumn; the fourth, rest and beauty, like winter, which is marked by the rest and crystalline beauty incident to that season.

First Score. — SPRING.

A SCORE of years! — as spring matures
    Its tender bud, and leaf, and bloom,
While Time's swift shuttle flies and weaves
The loveliest tints in nature's loom,
Day after day the picture grows
Beneath the weaver's skilful hand,
Till the sweet beauty stands complete,
Which love conceived and wisdom planned, —
So light and shade, and night and day,
Blessed the fair flower of human mould,
While frame and form, and heart and mind,
Hasted like petals to unfold;
What tint and tone of grace they bore,
What richest fruits! 't was just a score.

Second Score. — SUMMER.

A second score! — as summer calls
The fervent heart and toiling hand
To wield the scythe, to bind the sheaf,
To answer labor's high demand,

No hour is left for aimless play;
All the long day, till evening lowers,
Life bids to work, its stern behest
Demands the workman's grandest powers,—
So in the summer tide of hope
With ceaseless pains the matron wrought,
By noble deeds and nobler aims
Enriching life, inspiring thought.
What summer growth those labors bore!
What ripening fruits!—life's second score.

Third Score. — AUTUMN.

Threescore!—how richly autumn bends
Beneath her weight of fruit and flowers!
Beauty and plenty glow and meet,
Like garlands twined around her bowers;
The heat and drought, the dew and rain,
And wearing toil which months record.
God notes them all,—no work is lost,
And each at last brings large reward.
So harvests from thy heart and hand
Are heaped along the world's highways;
Children and children's children blend
Their voices in thy worthy praise.
Thy works, the third, the fruitful score,
Are like the autumn's garnered store.

Fourth Score. — WINTER.

Fourscore!—how sweet, how fair the scene,
When winter spreads, o'er all the earth,
Her bridal robe of purest white,
Her crystal gems, of heavenly birth!
Peace reigns where all was life and care;
Nature keeps jubilee of rest;

Of all the seasons, each admired,
This is the loveliest, the best.
So when the vessel nears its port,
Its anchor in smooth water cast,
With its rich cargo safe at home,
It rides the gentle wave at last ;
Yet sail along this peaceful shore,
I pray, dear wife, another score.

TO MY WIFE, AT EIGHTY-ONE.

I'VE known and loved her many a year
    Since first I called her mine.
"How many years?" I 'll tell you, friend, —
    Why, fifty years and nine;
So many years we talked of " ours,"
    And never " mine " and " thine."

She must be quite advanced, I think, —
    A queen with silver hair.
Oh, never mind the months and days;
    The things that people wear
Are all outside; there 's something else,
    That 's ever young and fair.

'T is love that makes the joy of life, —
    Love, the best gift of heaven ;
A clasp that holds when meaner ties
    Grow feeble, or are riven;
It keeps its circle perfect, like
    The Hebrew number " seven."

And so the years have trundled on,
   Alike in calm and storm ;
Our birdies, in bright plumage dressed,
   Of comely growth and form,
Have fled the nest, — the dear old nest, —
   And still the nest is warm.

The world is better for the songs
   Thy fairy lips have sung ;
And sweeter for the fragrant flowers
   Around thy pathway flung, —
God's gift, as true in silvery age
   As when they called thee "young."

Queen of my heart, queen of my house,
   Its gladness and its sun,
Dear for the thousand things thou art,
   For thousands thou hast done,
Blest are the years thy life has spanned,
   Thy fourscore years and one.

February 8, 1894.

TO MY WIFE ON HER EIGHTY-SECOND BIRTHDAY.

'TIS well to celebrate the days
    That mark the flight of years,
And, thoughtful, take account of stock, —
    The joys, the hopes, the fears,
That crowd the life, or broad or brief,
    Along the curious maze,
A precious tribute, each, in turn,
    On Memory's altar lays.

Thou canst not e'er forget the eve,
    In thy young brilliant life,
When, without change of soul or name,
    Thou wast a wedded wife.
Forget? Oh, no; nor, nobler still,
    The blessings of that other,
When infant beauty on thee smiled,
    Saluting thee as mother.

Refreshing as, in summer's heat,
    Comes to the rose the dew,
And gladdening as the perfumed breeze,
    Thy heart so warm and true ;
Knitting fresh links of love and bliss,
    An ever-lengthening chain,
Thine is the honored sum, to-day,
    Of fourscore years and twain.

FEBRUARY 8, 1895.

III. TENDER PARTINGS.

ELIZABETH, THE INFANT ANGEL.

ASCENDED, dearly loved, in life's young bud;
    Too fair, too sweet, 'mid earth's rude blasts to stay,
Safe in the bosom of thy Father, God,
    Bright, beauteous infant, from thy cumbering clay
So soon escaped, its happy heavenward way
    Thy soul hath taken.   Like the light of morn,
Thou didst shed on us one fair passing ray,
    Then to thy glorious Source, thou, babe, wast borne.

Dear infant angel, safe in joy and God!
    Babe of fair promise, child of fondest prayer!
Hail, rescued spirit! painful is the rod;
    But never will we mourn that thou art there.
Bright gem, we would not tear thee from thy crown,
    Nor bid thy harp, sweet seraph, silent lie;
Stay in thy mansion, infant, still our own,
    Never to grieve again, or fear, or die.

Short was thy pilgrim path, a sunny hour;
    Life was to thee too sweet a boon to last.
What joy it gave thee, gentle morning flower!
    How soon the glorious pageant o'er thee passed!
Passed! Yes, from earth, — but fairer life is thine;
    The vale of death thy little foot hath trod;
And now in life immortal thou dost shine,
    Dear infant, in the paradise of God.

MARCH 24, 1842.

THE JEWEL AND ITS SETTING.

I HAD a jewel passing rich,
   Set in its lovely frame;
How on the prize my heart was fixed
   From the bright day it came!

The setting was of choicest skill,
   As fair as fair could be;
And art divine had done its best
   To make it sweet to me.
The purple haze of distant hills,
   The evening's golden light,
The bending rainbow's painted arch,
   Were, to my eye, less bright.

The gleaming of the silver sheen
   Across the summer sea;
The grace that winds the clinging vine
   Around the greenwood tree;
The weeping elm, the stately pine;
   The breath of fragrant flowers;
The broad, blue sky, the landscape green,
   The leafy, sheltering bowers;
The dark line of the circling hills
   Around the horizon's verge;
The blue rim of the far-off sea,
   Where billows toss and surge, —
All have their glory; all, their worth;
   On each the dazzled eye
Loves to look lingeringly, and gaze
   Raptured and dreamily;

From each the mantle of such grace
  Seems round its charms to fall, —
The setting of my beauteous gem
  To me surpassed them all.

So fair the setting; fairer yet
  The priceless, sparkling gem,
Fit honor for a princely hand,
  Or regal diadem.
The jewel made the setting bright,
  Within whose clasp it shone;
'T was for its sake the frame was carved;
  The chief charm was its own.

And happy seasons onward passed,
  And mornings went and came;
And still the precious jewel there
  Flashed in its precious frame.
At last, some sad, sad chance befell,
  Which dashed it to the ground:
The precious setting, ruined, fell;
  The gem was safe and sound.

My babe was like the jewel rare;
  The frame, his cherished form;
I pressed it to my throbbing heart,
  Dreading some wasting storm.
The storm has spoiled the setting fair,
  But for a season given;
The gem I prized, unharmed, still shines
  Forever safe in heaven.

CHICAGO, 1885.

IN MEMORY OF MARY WHITE SMITH.

RANGOON, BURMAH, FEBRUARY 5, 1888.

I SEE the blessed angels there;
  They beckon me away
From night and pain, from sin and death,
  To gladness, light, and day.

I see them on the shining stairs;
  What pure white robes they wear!
'T will be a heaven of untold bliss
  To dwell forever there.

I see, I see their shining wings!
  I hear, I hear them raise,
In sweetest tone, in words unknown,
  Their songs of joy and praise!

Come, little pilgrim, come away,
  To you such grace is given;
Come, for of children such as thou
  The kingdom is of heaven!

She listened; up the shining stairs
  With happy feet she trod,
And found, so young, that blessed home,
  The paradise of God.

FEBRUARY 6, 1878.

TWO GARDENS,

THE HEAVENLY AND THE EARTHLY.

TWO gardens, flourishing and bright,
   Kept by one gardener's care,
Smiled in the sweet and sunny light,
   And breathed with perfumed air.

One stood, all bathed in heavenly joy,
   As if in early spring
An angel, clad in rainbow dyes,
   Shook beauty from his wing.

No frost the unfolding petals knew,
   No blight on bud or bloom ;
No lowering cloud, no chilling dew,
   No emblem of the tomb.

And one, o'er every fragrant bed
   A chastened sadness lay,
As when the evening shadows close
   Around a summer's day.

Lily and rose and violet smiled,
   Fair as a glorious gem ;
But rose and lily, doomed to fade,
   Sat on a fragile stem.

In one, a plant of beauty blessed
   A sweet sequestered bower,
Breathed fragrance where its bloom was nursed,
   And grew, a matchless flower.

The gardener saw its peerless charms,
  And chose a flower so rare
To grace his other garden-bed
  And so removed it there.

And now where angels walk in white,
  A laud of cloudless skies,
The gathered lily fitly blooms, —
  A flower of Paradise.

IV. REUNIONS.

SALLIE'S HOME.

THIS is my home, — my fair, bright home,
    The home of peace, and hope and love;
The green fields wide expand below,
    And heaven's blue arch bends sweet above.

Light sifts among the quivering leaves,
    Like angels floating from the sky;
And twittering birds around the eaves
    Whisper of unseen homes on high.

Mine are the windows where the sun
    Pours his fair light in golden streams,
And morn and eve and glowing noon
    Are gladdened by his healing beams.

Mine are the rooms, for rest and love,
    For patience, work, and worldly care;
For books, and friends, and widening thought,
    For tranquil joy, and holy prayer.

Mine is the landscape, rich and rare, —
    Beyond the wealth of Sheba's queen;
The pleasant homes, the clustering vines,
    The long cathedral aisles of green.

Mine, through His love whose reverend head
    Is pillowed on the Saviour's breast;
Mine, through His grace whose promise bids
    The widowed heart on Him to rest.

Mine, — yet not mine ; for all is God's,
    Myself and all I call my own.
I bow, submissive to His will ;
    I kneel, a supplicant, at His throne.

Mine, — yet not mine ; and He is mine,
    On Him I lean, on Him I call,
Rejoiced, were all my comforts fled,
    To find in Him my all in all.

BRIDGEPORT, CONN., May 24, 1891.

AT THE OLD HEARTHSTONE AGAIN.

SEPTEMBER 16, 1876.

ONCE, on a bright and happy night,
    At the full moon in September,
A fair young girl, in brilliant curls, —
    Long ago, but we remember, —
She pledged her loving heart and hand,
    In the joy of opening life,
Thenceforth to be, or weal or woe,
    A fond and faithful wife.

And so two souls, like mingling drops,
    Began their course together,
Making one life, — like rainbow hues
    Blended in showery weather.
A day, a happy moon, a year,
    The tide of time rolled on ;
Days, weeks and moons, — oh, who can tell
    Where the glad year has gone ?

One day within the happy nest
  Another life was breathing:
Three souls — not two — in union new,
  Young buds of joy were wreathing;
Two Marys made the mansion bright, —
  Two Marys, great and small;
And one high shadowing arm of love
  Embraced and gladdened all.

Yet more, as sped the rolling years,
  Like dewdrops of the morning,
The unwarlike infantry advanced, —
  Married life's best adorning;
And joy and promise, hope and love,
  Illumed with shining ray,
As sunbeams glittering on the sea,
  Life's varied, cheerful day.

At last, when the young curling locks
  White rose-leaves came to sprinkle,
And near the corner of the eyes
  Appeared just one small wrinkle,
Six youths and maidens stood within
  Those loving arms, caressing,
These prizing what those joyed to give,
  The sire's and mother's blessing.

And who are these ?   How swift old Time
  Works the most wondrous changes !
How the arithmetic of youth
  That slippery elf deranges !
The six are twelve ; the twelve, — ah me ! —
  Eleven more, sweet mother.
To these add HIM and HER ; and, please,
  The NINETY makes one other.

'T was only two, in earliest years;
    Then Mary made it three;
One wore, long since, the shining robes
    Of immortality.
My head is puzzled o'er the count;
    My brain is in a fix!
'T was two, 't was three, 't was four — and now
    They say it 's twenty-six.

One Mary once, — now Mary 's five;
    One Anna, — now two more;
One S. F. S., — now three; two Sa.'s,
    And babies, half a score.
Of lawyers, two; of preachers, four;
    Of presidents, a pair.
What wonders, in the land of dreams!
    On earth, what wonders rare!

So here, to-day, in grateful love,
    One precious band, we mingle;
Each for the others bound to live,
    No heart, no interest, single.
Some keep and bless the early home;
    Some watch where day beams wake;
And some where gorgeous evening dies, —
    All for each other's sake.

God keep the little circle whole
    For years, the jewels brightening:
Each joy, through Him, made richer joy,
    Each grief, He, for all, lightening;
Till, in some happy clime rejoined, —
    Rejoined, no more to sever,
We meet, and weep, and sing, and praise,
    And love, — love on, forever.

SOCIAL AMENITIES.

KIND GREETINGS.

THE FRIENDSHIPS WE FORMED.

HARVARD CLASS OF '29.

THE friendships we formed when life was still
    young;
The sports that we joined in, the songs we then
    sung, —
How oft from the chambers of memory they well,
Like the echo of waves in the beautiful shell.
The griefs we have met on the pathway of life,
The conquests won bravely amid the stern strife,
The light and the shadow, the joy and the woe, —
Form, like sunshine and raindrop, the radiant bow
That rests on the brow of the storms that are o'er,
That lights up the wave where it breaks on the
    shore,
That fades like the fair hues of hopes that are riven,
But sails, as it fades, thro' the blue arch of heaven.
The garlands we wove on the foretop of Time,
Tho' robbed of the freshness they wore in our prime;
The castles we built, so lofty and fair,
Tho' crumbled to dust, or vanished in air;
The barks we once freighted, with hearts beating
    high,
And launched on the sea without tremor or sigh,

Tho' sunk in the ocean or dashed on the reef,
The more grand their career, the more sad and more
      brief ;
Tho' the plants we have loved to angels are given,
Having climbed o'er the wall, and are blooming in
      heaven, —
Still this chain of our love does not weaken with
      years,
Nor wear with the friction of toil and of tears ;
Nor crumble in dust, nor vanish like breath ;
Nor chill with the darkness, and shadow of death ;
Nor perish in shipwreck, nor waste in the tomb, —
A thing to be lost in earth's gathering gloom.
Tho' Time's jealous fingers make all things decay,
We brighten its links as the years pass away ;
We fastened the lock in our youth and our glee,
Then wandered abroad and have lost the sole key.
But the heart-clasp unites so firmly the chain
That 't is welded by time, and must ever remain.

JANUARY 6, 1859.

TO A YOUNG FRIEND AT TWENTY-ONE.[1]

LIKE a swift racer, clear the lines
    That cross thy life's unfolding plan,
And leave the plays that please the child,
    For toils that dignify the man.

The world before thee waits thy choice ;
    The coming years to thee belong.
With stern ambition climb the heights ;
    Let hardships only make thee strong.

[1] Charles Foster Roby, of Chicago.   1893.

Cleave to the good, the pure, the just;
   Be thy whole life a life of love;
By noble thoughts and lofty aims,
   Thyself to men and God approve.

Love the dear land that gave thee birth, —
   The land thy fathers died to save;
They, the real nobles of the earth,
   The true, the loyal, and the brave.

Walk in the footsteps of the wise;
   Frown on the wrong, the right defend;
Spurn from thy soul all selfish aims;
   Do thy whole duty till the end.

So shalt thou leave a fragrant fame;
   Thy deeds thy monument shall raise;
The world shall bless thy honored name,
   And men unborn shall speak thy praise.

TO A YOUNG MAIDEN.

AS blushing tints still mantle o'er the shell
   Whose tiny owner dwells in it no more;
As fragrant rose-leaves to the traveller tell
   Where nodded in its pride the beauteous flower, —
So may thy path through this fair world be strewn
   With sweet remembrances, to rouse and cheer
The weary wanderer, gladly forced to own
   Where thou hast trod, a joy still lingers there.

SEPTEMBER 12, 1872.

REV. JAMES FREEMAN CLARKE'S 70TH BIRTHDAY CELEBRATION.

THREESCORE and ten! — the crimson sunlight, waning,
  Lights up the landscape with intenser glow;
The arch of days — some, bright; some, dull with raining —
  Is spanned and clasped with heaven's fair, radiant bow.

Threescore and ten! — the years consumed in toiling, —
  Honored and happy, how they fled away!
Earth of its woes, and time of stings despoiling,
  Day ever brightening into fairer day!

Threescore and ten! — how has the infant's prattle
  Changed to the eloquence of active men!
How many, fallen in life's stern storm and battle,
  Passed on, and crowned, will come no more again!

Threescore and ten! — how fondly memory lingers
  With friends and voices known and loved so well!
And deft with inspiration, Fancy's fingers
  Weave the old histories with their magic spell.

Threescore and ten! — yet marked by no decaying,
  The juicy vine festoons the sunny hill, —
Its summer foliage, fresh and full, displaying,
  And clusters ripening on the trellis still.

Threescore and ten ! — Oh, is it fact, or dreaming ?
  How strangely wrong our judgment is, of men ;
In form and feature, strong and youthful seeming,
  We lose the date, and think age young again.

Threescore and ten ! — the evening shadows lengthen,
  And whispering winds their fragrant incense breathe ;
Faith, hope, and love the pilgrim spirit strengthen,
  And hands unseen their benedictions wreathe.

O Life mysterious, whose slow unfolding
  Evades the prying of our human ken !
We trust the future to His wise upholding
  Whose love has watched the threescore years and
    ten !

DEACON GEORGE W. CHIPMAN, AT SEVENTY.

'TIS fitting thus to honor the man of threescore
    years and ten,
Who has fulfilled his mission nobly among the sons
    of men, —
Like a warrior, safe returning from a hundred well-
    fought fields,
Like a reaper, with his arms full of the sheaves good
    tillage yields.

Some silver hairs are creeping, one by one, among the
    brown ;
'T is always so when the angels set to weaving glory's
    crown,

Like the great sun in heaven, when it nears the horizon's rim;
Nor is his natural force abridged, nor his peerless sight
grown dim.

So a tall cathedral pillar, planted firm by ancient
hands,
So a tree amid the forest, braving storm and tempest,
stands;
So the lighthouse, sending forth its rays across the
billowy foam,
Unmoved while the generations pass, guides many
a pilgrim home.

Where are the children he once knew? Methinks
the birds are flown, —
The lisping girls are matrons; the boys, gray-beard
men are grown;
The old nests, or others like them, on the old branches
hang,
And the younger broods still warble as the birds of old
time sang;
And the eye that saw, the voice that led, the heart
that loved their trill,
Though fifty springs have vanished, sees them, leads
them, loves them, still.
How the many earlier reapers from the field of toil
have passed,
And memory round their absent forms has its mantle
of glory cast!
They passed as the twilight passes into the noontide
ray,
As the morning star is melted in the light of glowing
day.

The pastors whom he loved and helped, — some still
    reap earth's harvests white;
Some, glorified, walk with the Lamb on high, in raiment
    of dazzling light.
Thank God, as suns at setting shed their glow on each
    purple hill,
One orb, that shone at morn and noon, in its bright-
    ness lingers still.
A Nestor, in the field he tilled, we cannot think him old!
No ice has chilled his tropic heart, no rust forms on
    the gold.

His step is yet firm; his hand is strong; his mellow
    voice still rings.
He speaks, — men listen to his word; he moves, as if
    with wings.
Erect his form, and on his face not a channel left to
    show
How the glaciers of olden time slid down into the
    valleys below.
His bright meridian sun, perchance, down towards the
    horizon dips,
But sinks behind no shadowing cloud, is hid by no
    eclipse;
As new year follows new year, and day wakens after
    day,
Onward, and upward, upward still, it holds its shining
    way;
And setting, like the orbs of night behind the darken-
    ing west,
When the hours of noble toil have earned the fitting
    hours of rest,
It will set, alone to this lower sphere, but, by a law
    sublime,
Set only to rise in glorious light in a far brighter
    clime.

LYMAN JEWETT, D.D., ON HIS SEVENTY-FIFTH BIRTHDAY.

HONORED by all, where'er thy name is heard,
Beloved apostle of thy loving Lord,
We greet thee gladly on thy festal day,
And gladly at thy feet our tribute lay.

Honored, to sow the seed with toil and tears;
Honored, to reap for God the joyful ears;
Honored, to pray the prayer of faith and love;
Honored, to hear the answer from above;
Honored, when wavering faith, advised to yield,
Bravely to fight in front, and hold the field,
With valiant heart and never-flinching eye,
Foreseeing Christ enthroned, and victory, —
Like soldiers, ere the battle's rage is done,
Sending reports of richest trophies won,
Of armies slain, and hostile banners furled,
Prophetic emblems of a conquered world;
Honored, to bring thy own despatches home,
"The battle gained! The hour of triumph come!"
Honored, to see the idol-temples fall,
And ransomed thousands crown the Lord of all;
Honored, in lonely trust, with wearing toils,
To heap, at Jesus' feet, uncounted spoils
Till "the Lone Star," on heaven's immortal blue,
At last, a brilliant constellation grew.

O meek apostle, what rare bliss is thine!
What toils, what triumphs, in thy lot combine!

Wise, to discern the task thy Lord had given;
Faithful, to point the weeping eye to heaven;
Grand, a whole world in arms of love to embrace;
Patient, to fill, and grace, the humblest place;
Waiting, from youth to age, life's mystery,
And prompt, unquestioning, Lord, to follow Thee.

E'en now the light, that fills the world of bliss,
Shines o'er the battlements to illumine this;
The crowns, the crowns, almost thy eyes can see,
Bought by atoning blood, faith's mystery!
Songs of the ransomed thou canst almost hear, —
Their lofty melodies awake thine ear;
And earth, redeemed, the glorious pæan sings,
In mighty measures, to the King of kings.

Should thy dear life a rounded century see,
Thy feet three-fourths have trod towards immor-
    tality.

MARCH 8, 1888.

TO DEACON J. W. CONVERSE, ON HIS EIGHTIETH BIRTHDAY.

HAIL! friend and brother, on this bright birth-
    day!
  Bright in its thoughts, its memories, hopes, and
    feeling;
The years have scarcely tinged thy locks with gray,
  Thy honored age revealing, yet concealing.

O'er what long, winding ways thy steps have trod !
  What varied cares and trusts, successive pressing,
Have taught thee, leaning on the arm of God,
  The rugged path becomes the path of blessing !

What changes to thy wondering eyes have come !
  A scroll of miracles, slowly unfolding, —
Some, grandly understood ; mysterious, some, —
  But one dear Hand above, thy own hand holding.

And yet, so quick thy step, so lithe thy frame,
  The tell-tale years seeming so little weighty,
Thy buoyant, youthful vigor still the same, —
  It might be but eighteen, instead of eighty.

Sheltered and guided by that Power above
  To reverend age, up from the infant's prattle ;
Living for Christ's dear cause a life of love ;
  Honored to dare and do in life's great battle.

'T is thine to bring forth fruit still, even in age, —
  Thou to whom fruitful years have long been granted,
Like trees, still verdant 'mid the winter's rage,
  Like the rich palms in God's own garden planted.

The years roll on ; so from the mountain-thread
  Swells and expands the deepening, widening river ;
So life grows onward from its infant seed,
  Broadening, prophetic of the grand forever.

Long may thy well-strung bow in strength abide ;
  And far the day, thou to whom much is given,
Ere the celestial gates shall open wide
  To add to all the crown of life in heaven.

Jancary 11, 1888.

A GOLDEN WEDDING SONG.

REV. AND MRS. W. C. RICHARDS, 1841.

BLEST are these years of wedded love, —
  Gifts which attest God's loving hand,
Bright years in all their varied course,
  Like streams that glide o'er golden sand.

These fifty years, — so long, so short,
  Ten thousand blessings in their train,
Fraught with unnumbered passing joys, —
  Well might we live them o'er again !

The wedding song of love we sung, —
  To-day revives the sweet refrain ;
Love is undying in its source ;
  Bridegroom and bride, we live again.

And who are these in stalwart frame ;
  And these arrayed in sunny curls ?
"Our children, and their children fair, —
  Pledges of love, our boys and girls."

How blest the way thy feet have trod,
  Brother, to whom the trust was given ;
To feed the happy flock of God,
  And guide the wanderer's steps to heaven.

Nor this alone ; the world to thee,
  Has opened all its secret heart,
And taught her wonders to explore, —
  A miracle in every part.

Happy the pair whose gracious lives
  In long enduring love combine;
His, the firm trellis for support,
  And hers, the sweet and clustering vine.

The fire by night, the cloud by day,
  Guided and kept the loving twain;
And storms that swept the desert path
  Fell round their tent like gentle rain.

Long may the bow abide in strength!
  Oh, linger long thy peaceful days;
Let life be one long wedding feast,
  And its whole course, a psalm of praise!

Sing on, sweet singer, while the years
  Add to thy honors and thy fame;
Till heaven, on some far distant day,
  Bids to the wedding of the Lamb.

A GOLDEN WEDDING.

DR. AND MRS. J. W. PARKER.

FIFTY full years!— how fair and grand the record!
  Fifty full years! with every virtue rife;
Sweetly and sacredly bound to each other,
  A faithful husband and a faithful wife!

Bound to each other in devout affection,
  Witnessed by loving lives and loving word;
Made nobly one by heaven's divine selection,—
  One in each other, one in Christ their Lord!

Bound to each other, whether joy or sorrow,
  Sickness or health, prevailed, sunshine or shade;
Skilful from good or ill some boon to borrow,
  Each on the other's arm, both on God stayed.

Dear herald of the everlasting gospel!
  Filled with the grateful memories of the past,
Thanks that thy other self, like God's fair angel,
  Is spared to hover round thee to the last.

The last! Oh, no, earth's last is heaven's beginning!
  Earth's ties, dissevered, are but joined above;
Earth's service changed to service without sinning,
  And earth's imperfect, to heaven's perfect love.

Ye have walked nobly through these earthly shadows,
  As years to years were added, sun by sun,
Weaving the threads of life, or dark or shining,
  Still one in heart, — in love and purpose one.

God's choicest blessings o'er your heads will hover,
  Till the brave warrior wears the conqueror's crown,
Till the tired reaper in the gathering evening,
  Released from toil, shall lay the sickle down.

Then shall earth's fifty years, at heaven's bright portal,
  No more a symbol, marred by life's dull fever,
Expanding, change into the joy immortal,
  And souls, now one on earth, be one forever.

MRS. JOSEPH W. PARKER, LOS ANGELES, CAL.,
ON HER EIGHTY-THIRD BIRTHDAY.

DID I hear you say, " 'T is eighty " ?
　　Methinks it cannot be ;
I see no frosts nor snowflakes
　　Gathered on the sunny tree ;
There are only white-browed pansies,
　　Not a snowdrift to be found.
Oh, the snows are all white rose-leaves
　　Which flutter o'er the ground !

Did you tell me, " Eighty spring-tides,
　　With their tender buds, have passed,"
And how you watch expectant,
　　The fading of the last ?
I only see the blossoms,
　　And hear the sweet birds sing,
Prophetic of the beauty
　　Of the immortal spring.

Do you whisper, " Eighty summers
　　With their grace and glow have fled " ?
Do you mourn the early blossoms,
　　Now sleeping with the dead ?
'T is but a mortal counting,
　　That dotes on tide and clime ;
Your youthful heart is weaving
　　Summer garlands all the time.

Do you tell me, " Eighty autumns
  Have heaped their harvests in,
And the wintry winds come, blowing,
  Where the waving crops have been " ?
You are reaping, gentle lady,
  Richest harvests, day by day ;
The fruits of your bright seed-time
  Ever press your pilgrim way.

As the glad sun approaches,
  And all the stars grow dim,
The fringe of coming glory
  Lights up the horizon's rim ;
And the dear Hand that guided,
  Till the tale became fourscore,
Never weary, never fainting,
  Will be sure forevermore.

Yes, 't is eighty, — truly, eighty !
  How swiftly the seasons glide !
'T is eighty, — more than eighty, —
  And three happy years beside !
Why should we wish them fewer, —
  The years that God has given ?
The more the finished years of earth,
  The nearer, rest and heaven.

JANUARY, 1893.

GEORGE C. LORIMER.[1]

BROTHER and friend, with joy we meet
  Thy welcome form at home again ;
With joy thy honored face we greet,
  Like the glad rainbow after rain.

Not as a stranger in the fold,
  Not as a hireling for the flock,
Thy well known call sounds as of old ;
  The ancient key just fits the lock.

Come as a soldier from the field,
  From battles fought and victories won, —
Thy old commission newly sealed,
  A fresh and grand campaign begun.

Come 'neath the banner of the Cross ;
  The Prince of life shall lead the way,
Marshal the troops, or gain or loss,
  His Arm, resistless, wins the day.

So, in the tide of ripening life,
  The warrior yearns to tread again,
And bless, the fields of mortal strife, —
  The peaceful bivouac of the slain.

We know thee well ; our throbbing hearts
  In ardent love respond to thine, —
The new love, like the former, starts
  From the one Root of Life Divine.

[1] At Reception on his return to Tremont Temple, May 28, 1891.

Thy star will suffer no eclipse,
   If God thy burning words inspire ;
We trust in Him to touch thy lips,
   Dear prophet, with His hallowed fire.

March on, march on, triumphant band,
   Obedient to your Leader's call !
Wave the red banner o'er the land,
   And crown the Saviour Lord of all !

ADONIRAM JUDSON GORDON.[1]

ON THE TWENTY-FIFTH ANNIVERSARY OF HIS PASTORATE AT CLARENDON ST., BOSTON, DECEMBER, 26 1894.

SHEPHERD and Heavenly Friend,
   Almighty to defend
     Thy little flock,
In verdant pastures fed,
To living waters led,
We cling to Thee our Head.
     Our sheltering Rock.

Our shepherd heeds Thy voice, —
The shepherd of our choice,
     The proved, the tried ;
Strong to obey Thy will,
Thy service to fulfil,
Our loving shepherd still,
     Our friend, our guide.

[1] Dr. Gordon died on Saturday, February 2, 1895 (after a brief illness), universally esteemed and honored, representatives of other church organizations, and many religious and benevolent associations, joining in a tribute to his memory and character.

Kept near Thy gracious side,
Long may his arm abide,
   Strong in Thy might;
Speak through his lips that word
Which listening chaos heard,
And all its depths were stirred,
   "Let there be light."

Head of the Church, to Thee
Immortal glory be, —
   We wait Thy word!
Thy glorious kingdom bring,
Bid heaven's great anthem ring ;
Christ, Thou of kings art King,
   Of lords art Lord!

December 12, 1894.

IN MEMORY AND CONDOLENCE.

WILLIAM HAGUE, D. D.

WE emulate the path thy feet have trod,
    Brother, beloved of men, approved of God;
Thou of the brilliant speech and silver tongue,
On thy dear lips have wondering thousands hung.
Preacher and pastor, — faithful, polished, mild,
A man in stature, and in love, a child,
Whose look was eloquence, his words, a power,
His life a magic force, his faith, a tower,
His memory vast, an unexhausted store,
His soul, a volume of historic lore;
Man of the people, whom he swayed at will,
Man of the study and the polished quill, —
All good he praised; he pitied where he scorned,
And wise, as just, whate'er he touched, adorned.
Skilful expounder of the sacred word,
Quick to discern, prompt to reveal his Lord,
Profound in thought, wise to observe the times,
His mind, capacious, could embrace all climes,
Lived in all ages, took in land and sea,
The past, the present, and the yet-to-be;
His fervent heart no years could make grow cold,
And age, advancing, never made him old.
To the old standards of the Gospel true,
Nor spurned the old, nor pined for doctrines new;
Maintained the ancient truth with courage bold, —
That truth, forever new, forever old;
And as he died, — heeding the Master's call, —
Pronounced that truth enough for him, for all.

How nobly fitting was the parting hour:
One pulse, the bud, — the next, the full-blown flower;
One instant, here, — the next, beyond the skies;
Now, earth's high noon,— now, noon in Paradise.
This moment, bound by human woes and bars,
The next, in peerless light, beyond the stars;
From earth's high summer snatched, and blooming
　　　　bowers,
To heaven's immortal glow and fadeless flowers;
Now, on the threshold of the temple here,
Now, bowed before its inmost altar there;
With what strange joy the conqueror upward rode,
To worship, reverent, at the throne of God!

Ascended brother, may the mantle blest,
That fell from thee, on many a prophet rest;
Thy trumpet voice still sound the loud alarm,
Thy magic notes linger, to rouse and charm,
And, Heaven's high heralds, Heaven's high service done,
Achieve the honors, brother, thou hast won.

SEPTEMBER 26, 1887.

GARDNER COLBY.

The Legislature of Maine changed the title of Waterville College to that of Colby University, January 23d, 1867, in honor of Gardner Colby, of Newton, Massachusetts, who contributed $50,000 towards its endowment, and afterwards increased the amount by a bequest of $120,000.

PASSED from our sight, but grandly living still, —
   As glows the light behind the western hill
When towering summits hide the vanished sun,
And the long course of weary day is run ;
The disk concealed, the brightness backward turns, —
For other lands the same full radiance burns.
A noble life, cut off, still journeys on, —
A trail of light behind it, — when 't is gone, —
And life before, — a faithful life's reward, —
A joy to earth, — and ever with the Lord !

We hail thee, brother, favored now to see,
Unveiled at last, life's doubt and mystery :
What fields thy works have blessed ; what conquests,
     won,
Attest the worthy deeds thy hands have done ;
What hungry mouths thy willing love has fed ;
What souls enjoyed, through thee, the living Bread;
To what rich seeds thy life has given wings, —
Sheaves for the garner of the King of kings ;
What halls of learning, fostered by thy care,
Have nurtured men whose lips are trained to bear
To nations born, and nations yet to be,
Tidings of life and immortality.

Dost thou, from heaven, the honest praise disclaim,
Caring no more for earth or earthly fame?
Not for thyself we weave these honored bays,
Yet for thyself, and for the Saviour's praise.
All that was great in thee, we cherish still,
All that accorded with the Master's will;
Thousands the lessons of thy life shall read, —
The kind in word; the generous in deed;
The ready, helpful hand; the open heart;
The soul to feel; the tender tear to start;
The wealth of hand and brain to yield supply
To every worthy work, or low, or high,
Accounting nothing small which God deems great,
So prompt to act, so patient, too, to wait,
Holding of right with men an honored seat,
But laying all things at the Master's feet.

Long will his memory live in many a land,
Long the foundations which he planted stand;
And grateful thousands shall with glad acclaim
Breathe from full hearts their blessings on his name.

We leave thee, brother, and our way pursue,
Patient to bear, and prompt, like thee, to do;
Be ours, like thine, through grace the victory won,
And ours, like thine, the Master's glad "Well done!"

REV. ISAAC BACKUS,

ON UNVEILING A MONUMENT TO HIS MEMORY.

SACRED the ground we tread,—
　　Where sleep the pious dead,
　　　Supremely blest;
Their honored course is run,
The crown of victory won,
Bright as the glorious sun,
　　In Christ they rest.

Blest be the man of God
Who once these pathways trod
　　In Christ's own way;
His faith as noontide clear,
He sought in holy fear
The Master's voice to hear,
　　And, glad, obey.

Here in this solemn shade
(Tribute too long delayed),
　　This shrine we rear;
And carve his reverend name,
Worthy immortal fame;—
His holy labors claim
　　Such record here.

Mark well each lowly grave
Where rest the true and brave,
　　Till morn shall break;
Peaceful in Christ they sleep,
Heaven will their memory keep,
Till from their slumbers deep,
　　Joyful, they wake.

March 10, 1893.

A LOVING BEQUEST.

On the unveiling of a portrait of a lady who devised funds for building a church at Mattapan, Massachusetts.

L IVING, she loved the house of prayer;
　　Loving, she lived to plant it here,
And left what love could well afford,
A noble offering to her Lord.

No better monument could tell
What her heart loved, and loved so well, —
Such holy love breathed in her breath,
Lived in her life, survived her death.

Though marble piles in dust decay,
And human glory melts away,
Her gift abides in sins forgiven,
In souls redeemed, and heirs of heaven.

Blessings be on this favored spot, —
No act of love shall be forgot;
And Christ's approving word shall be,
She, what she could, has done for me.

May 8, 1889.

MARY POND.

On a tomb at Dresden, I read these words : " Fell asleep, September 18, 1874."

YES, " fell asleep," — but sleep implies two wakings
  One in the weary past, one, yet to be ;
One in this life of labor and heart-breakings,
  One in the bliss of immortality.

Yes, " fell asleep," — tired watch no longer keeping,
  With ever restless hands and busy brain ;
All sorrow past, — no grief, no sigh, no weeping,
  Like a sweet summer evening, after rain.

Yes, " fell asleep," — no more with dim surmising,
  Questioning what may be the life to come ;
She feels, in the freed spirit's glad uprising,
  Joy, peace, rest, grandeur, glory, heaven, home.

Yes, " fell asleep," — we watch for her low breathing,
  Like fragrant night-winds floating gently by ;
Like noiseless clouds of incense, upward wreathing,
  Her spirit, silent, points us to the sky.

Yes, " fell asleep," — the touch of those dear fingers
  Created life and beauty where it fell ;
Around her cherished works her spirit lingers,
  Like strains of music o'er the quivering shell.

Yes, " fell asleep," — so early quenched life's fever,
  So brilliant promise clouded o'er so soon ;
Faith, be thou strong ; God's purpose faileth never ;
  Earth had the radiant morning ; heaven, the noon.

Man gathers heaps of ore, a grasping miner,
  Toiling and burdened through the scorching day,
But sleeps at last ; and God, the great Refiner,
  Saves all the gold, and melts the dross away.

Yes, " fell asleep," — just as the curious kernel
  Of flower-life hides within the rigid grain ;
But, with the warm breath of the season vernal,
  It waves luxuriant o'er the fields again.

Yes, " fell asleep," — resting in God's safe keeping.
  So hides the worm within his narrow cell,
But bursts his chrysalis, and, heavenward leaping,
  Shining, proclaims that God does all things well.

Yes, " fell asleep," — O rest divine, immortal !
  Knowing nor pain, nor grief, nor death, nor sin ;
Rest that conveys the soul to heaven's high portal,
  And bids the weary wanderer enter in.

Yes, " fell asleep," — O mystery past our knowing !
  Beyond thick clouds we cannot see the sun ;
But patient, trustingly, we wait Heaven's showing,
  'T is God's own hand, — thy will, O Lord, be done.

DRESDEN, October 7, 1875.

"BLIND ANNA."

WE are all like blind men groping in the dark, —
    we cannot see ;
The lives we here are living are full of mystery.
How the plans of God are working, we strive in vain to
    tell ;
But faith can safely trust Him, for He doeth all things
    well.

His Providence leads wisely, like the pillared cloud and
    flame ;
And so on every milestone we record His blessed
    name.
All the happy Ebenezers His love and praises tell :
His arm has never failed us ; He doeth all things
    well.

If the keen, sharp eye can see Him, as sees the soaring
    lark ;
If, blinded, through His wisdom, we only trace Him in
    the dark,
In the glowing, glorious noontide, or in the deepest
    cell, —
We will trust Him, we will love Him, for He doeth all
    things well.

If the blessed light is darkened, if the eye is dull and
    blind, —
'T is ordered by a Father who is ever good and
    kind.

His purpose is in mercy, though His plan He does not
tell,
Wait till the seal is broken; He doeth all things
well.

There 's a world where all that tries us shall be made
divinely clear,
The eye no more be sightless, no longer deaf the ear;
The day shall rise in glory, — why should the heart
rebel?
God sees, and we shall see Him, for He doeth all
things well.

CHICAGO, January, 1893.

BLOSSOMING ON THE OTHER SIDE.

OH, weep not, ye whose child hath won
    A dwelling in yon glorious sphere,
Where sin is past, and labor done;
    'T is better than to linger here!

Oh, weep not, ye whose offspring wears
    A heavenly crown upon her brow,
Whose hand a harp of worship bears,
    Who sings the angelic anthem now!

Oh, weep not, ye whose child hath passed
    Thus early from earth's tempting scene;
In heaven, temptation's furious blast
    Can never reach the soul again!

Oh, weep not, ye whose child hath soared,
   A seraph, to the world above,
Where endless day is round her poured,
   And happy spirits dwell in love !

Oh, weep not, ye whom God hath left
   To mourn a tie so early riven;
She lives, — while ye are thus bereft, —
   First of your household, safe in heaven !

TO A SORROWING MOTHER.

OH, mourn not, fond mother, the joys that depart ;
   There is comfort and peace for the stricken in
      heart !
God has taken the spirit that basked in thy love ;
The beautiful angels have borne it above.

The plant thou hast reared to brighten earth's gloom,
Had fastened its roots in the soil of the tomb.
It smiled in thy garden, so gentle and fair ;
It has climbed o'er the wall, and is blossoming there.

The jewel once worn with pride on thy breast,
Now flashes its light in the land of the blest;
The rose is still fragrant, though torn from the stem,—
The setting is ruined, but safe is the gem.

Then gird thee to labor, to trial, to love ;
The treasure, still thine, awaits thee above.
Be faithful, be earnest, night soon will be riven,
And the lost one of earth, be thy jewel in heaven.

AGATHA E. CLAFLIN.

IS thy final rest more peaceful, —
    Is thy sleep more sweet, dear child,
Brought from Rome's gorgeous sepulchres,
    Back to thy native wild?
Or breathes the wind more gently,
    Where the chestnut and the pine
Above the tomb that holds thy dust
    Their clustering branches twine?

What was wanting in the shadows
    Of old imperial Rome,
That thou sighedst, midst its grandeur,
    For thy dearer western home?
Those fragrant airs and sunny bowers, —
    Could they not weave a spell,
With power to win, above the spot
    Thy young heart loved so well?

'T was there the proud Jugurtha,
    Subdued by famine, died;
But there, with bread immortal,
    Was thy spirit satisfied?
He, in his lonely prison chained,
    Perished in heathen gloom;
Thou soaredst upward, free of wing,
    And angels bade thee come.

And there a mightier warrior
    Waited his heavenly crown,

Found a martyr's wreath around his brow,
  And laid his armor down.
Brave Christian souls in Roman soil
  Repose in holy rest,
As sinks the gorgeous, crimson sun
  In glory in the west.

Thy footsteps trod the pathways
  Of grand, historic Rome;
Thy gaze, admiring, rested
  On picture, church, and dome.
Why, yearning with a tender love,
  Did thine eyes look back to see
The landscape round that cherished home,
  Where thy young soul longed to be?

Thy weary wanderings ended
  In a city grander far
Than home, or Rome, — in heaven, —
  As the sun outshines a star;
Earth on thy young eyes faded,
  As fades a glittering toy,
Bright opened on thy vision
  Heaven's home of love and joy.

Welcome again, fair sleeper!
  Peace to thy precious dust!
Rest calmly with thy kindred
  Till the rising of the just.
The winds shall sing above thee,
  Where the chestnut and the pine,
In thy own dear native forests,
  Their clustering branches twine.

Thy life, too early smitten,
  Lingers around us still,
As day-beams, after sunset,
  Shine, radiant, o'er the hill;
Thy loving voice, still sounding,
  Forbids us to rebel, —
God gave, and God hath taken, —
  God, who does all things well.

May, 1874.

------ ∞⚬⚬ ------

HARRIET J. WARDWELL.

BROUGHT home, where the dust of her kindred
      reposes,
To sleep 'mid the dew, and the breath of the roses,
In June, — of all seasons the sweetest and fairest,
Herself, of its blossoms the purest and rarest.

She sleeps her last sleep, while all nature rejoices,
And melody breaks from earth's thousands of voices;
Like distant sweet chimes on evening winds singing,
The music she breathed is in echoes still ringing.

Life's silver cord loosed, and the golden bowl broken, —
We bow to the mandate Jehovah has spoken;
God's promise proclaims, o'er the loved and lamented,
The silver cord, loosed, shall again be cemented.

We lay her in love 'neath the rose and the willow;
Peace sits by her ashes, — Peace breathes round her
      pillow.

How well that such graces and gifts should be given,
Like precious first fruits, an offering to Heaven!

God gave, and we bless Him; God took, and though
        parted,
Still trusting, still loving, we yield, broken-hearted.
Again, in the home of the blest, we shall greet her,
And youth bloom immortal, when, joyful, we meet her.

EPITAPHS.

SHORT was thy pilgrimage, dear child;
    Sweet is thy dreamless rest.
God on thy homeward spirit smiled,
    And made thee early blest.

Her ardent love, her spotless worth,
    Her humble faith were given,
Like buds of promise, plucked on earth,
    To bloom, transferred to heaven.

Her life to toil, her gains to God were given;
Sweet is her rest, and bright her crown, in heaven.

IN MEMORY OF A YOUNG MAIDEN.

SISTER, thou wast mild and lovely,
  Gentle as the summer breeze,
Pleasant as the air of evening,
  When it floats among the trees.

Peaceful be thy silent slumber, —
  Peaceful in the grave so low.
Thou no more wilt join our number;
  Thou no more our songs shalt know.

Dearest sister, thou hast left us;
  Here thy loss we deeply feel.
But 't is God that hath bereft us;
  He can all our sorrows heal.

Yet again we hope to meet thee,
  When the day of life is fled;
Then in heaven with joy to greet thee,
  Where no farewell tear is shed.

PART II.

POEMS OF COUNTRY.

AMERICA.

Written February, A.D. 1832, and first sung at a Fourth of July Celebration at Boston, the same year.

MY country, 't is of thee,
　　Sweet land of liberty,
　Of thee I sing ;
Land where my fathers died,
Land of the pilgrims' pride,
From every mountain side
　　Let freedom ring.

My native country, thee,
Land of the noble free,
　　Thy name I love ;
I love thy rocks and rills,
Thy woods and templed hills;
My heart with rapture thrills
　　Like that above.

Let music swell the breeze,
And ring from all the trees
　　Sweet Freedom's song ;
Let mortal tongues awake,
Let all that breathe partake,
Let rocks their silence break,
　　The sound prolong.

Our fathers' God, to Thee,
Author of liberty,
    To Thee we sing;
Long may our land be bright
With Freedom's holy light;
Protect us by Thy might,
    Great God, our King.

SCHOOLS AND SCHOLARS.

SENTIMENTAL.

THE SEAL ONCE LAID ON PLIANT WAX.

ADDRESSED TO A TEACHER.

THE seal, once laid on pliant wax,
    Stamps its own image, cancelled never;
The teacher's lineaments on the soul
Their vivid impress leave forever.
Lay careful hand on head and heart
While waits the youth at life's fair portal;
So shall your work, in beauty wrought,
Be beauty, stamped with life immortal.

NOTHING WITHOUT EFFORT.

SOME nice things, you think, can be done without
    toil,
As weeds grow, untilled, from the generous soil;
You guess men in black, with the cheerfullest air,
Eat bread without work, and live without care;
So happy they float, like clouds in the blue,
You think, very likely, they 've nothing to do

But to read pleasant books and court life with the
    Muses,
While the hand of the workman is sore from his
    bruises.
But no farmer grows rich who sets up for a shirk,
Nor merchant, whose aim is to live without work;
There is labor more wearing than digging a drain, —
Oh, that some men would try it, — 't is work with the
    brain !

I 'll tell you a secret, — the song of the poet
Springs not with a gush before one can know it,
As breaks from the fountain the tinkling rill
And flows from the side to the foot of the hill.
The thought, born to shine in his beautiful strain,
Lies, like gems to be cut, in the depth of his brain ;
But to clothe it with beauty, to point it with wit,
To fit to each line a shaft that will hit, —
To gather the glories, his lay to enfold,
From earth, air, and sea, from the crimson and gold,
That glow in the path of the opening day,
Or burnish the sky as the light fades away, —
Is never the work of a glance and a dash,
As the fluid-electric shoots out with a flash ; —
The search for a jingle, the chase for a rhyme,
Is a toil to the brain, and the labor of time.
As a steamer, — the monster, — caught fast in the
    narrows,
Or striving, in summer, to pass over shallows,
Drives fierce on her pathway, ascending the stream,
But is forced to fall back with a shock and a scream,
To try a fresh channel, to make a new tack,
Still foiled in her efforts, still doomed to push back,
Till at last, as if borne by a freak of good chance,
She floats o'er the shoal, and shoots, with a glance,

To the sea of deep water, and glides through the tide,
Where balmy winds kiss her, and navies might ride, —
So, often, the poet, intent on his chime,
Seeks, earnest, to match some choice word with a
    rhyme;
But bootless his efforts, — his search all in vain, —
He backs off from the shallow and tries a new strain,
Gives up the dear word on which swung his fine
    thought,
Abandons the rhyme, long chased, but ne'er caught,
Creeps back through the shallows, — recasts his whole
    plan,
And, foiled where he wishes, he sails where he can,
Then floats, proud in success, o'er the glorious main,
Till the rhyme-search shall ground him in shallows
    again.
O wisdom of Virgil! — the bard of the ages, —
A wisdom well worthy of prophets and sages,
No genius, untoiling, to glory is whirled;
"A line in a day" brings the praise of the world.

———•◦⦿◦•———

WHERE ARE THE BOYS OF EARLIER YEARS?

" THE BOYS." [1]

WHERE are the boys of earlier years,
    Once known and loved so well?
Where childhood's hopes and childhood's fears,
    O Muse of history, tell?

[1] Written for the "Old School Boys," of Boston.

Where are the noisy shouts that spoke
   In wild joy on the air ?
Where are the lips, in love which spoke —
   The echoes answer, Where ?

Where are the ready eye and hand
   That made our greetings sweet ?
Parted long since, — the choice old band, —
   Where will they ever meet ?

Where are they ?   Ask the manly face,
   White hairs, and furrowed brow ;
The veterans, with their antique grace —
   The boys are elders now.

Roll back, roll back Life's hastening tide,
   Nor count each passing year ;
Behold, their bows in strength abide,
   The ancient boys are here !

THE LADY AND THE POET.

I HAVE read of a poet whose minstrelsy woke
   The spirit of music in beautiful Spain ;
He was urged by a lady, not quite to his taste,
   To write her a sonnet, — nor urged she in vain.

In the noble Castilian 't were easy to write,
   From a madrigal down to a funeral knell ;
So this son of the Muses proceeded to draw
   The sonnet she claimed from his murmuring shell.

She deemed he would glory her beauty to praise,
  Her form, and her hair, and her dark Spanish eyes;
And her fancy was filled with the glow of his lays,
  Lighted up like the rainbow with heavenly dyes.

But her guess was at fault; not a word of her charms
  Was allowed by the minstrel to smile on his page,
Not a breath of true gallantry breathed from his lip,
  Not a soft note of grace warbled forth from his cage.

But he set for his quill the ingenious task
  Of making the sonnet, in measure and time,
As smooth as an eclogue, as bald as a stone,
  And as empty of meaning as faultless in rhyme.

The words were consummate in number and time,
  The lines were as faultless as eye ever read;
The sonnet was perfect, excepting alone, —
  'T was just what he purposed, — that nothing was
    said.

———◦◦❀◦◦———

HOW BLEST THE ART THAT LINKS IN SACRED BONDS.

PRESERVED THOUGHTS.[1]

HOW blest the art that links in sacred bonds
  The living present with the living past !
The life of other years to ours responds,
  Pulse-beat to pulse-beat thrills, and first to last.

The thoughts once breathed in prose, or rolled in song,
  Treasured in faithful records, sound again ;
Genius and love their harmonies prolong,
  And vanished souls converse again with men.

[1] Written for the Dedication of the Malden Library.

And books are thoughts; these alcoves fair shall
    hold,
Like rare and priceless gems, the sacred trust,
When monumental piles and shrine of gold,
    Battered and worn, shall crumble into dust.

Whose shall the honor be, O history, say, —
    When, passed from earth, the glorious thinkers
        sleep, —
Their thoughts, like jewels rescued from decay,
    In fitting chambers to arrange and keep?

Thank God! such trusts to human hands are given;
    Thank God! such trusts shall not be given in vain;
Earth's clustered blooms will show fair fruit in heaven,
    Thoughts, saved on earth, will shine in heaven again.

How blest the task, in this short life of ours,
    Life's loving work and influence to extend,
Clothing the mortal with immortal powers,
    Making all ages with all ages blend!

THE GENTLE MUSE OF TO-DAY.

Read at a Reception at the South Chicago Study Club, at Mrs.
Edward Roby's, May 10, 1893.

THE Muses, in the olden days, —
    They numbered barely nine, —
'T was theirs to wake the sweetest lays,
    To charm and to refine;

To teach the bliss of life and love,
  To make the whole world bright,
Ten thousand rills of joy to start,
  To shine, as shines the light.

But we, in later times, have found
  A hundred Muses more;
And on each gentle Muse we meet,
  Our love and praise we pour;
Each makes earth happier, life more blest,
  Brings to our homes a heaven, —
Dear charmers of our secret hearts,
  The best gift God has given !

Ardent, they study to expand
  The fields already won ;
And in their noble deeds surpass
  All that the past has done ;
By pinnacles of honor gained,
  By summits grandly trod,
They prove what woman can attain,
  Inspired and helped of God.

We honor all whose hearts are true,
  And gladly, proudly, raise
The noblest trophy art can bring
  Their glorious course to praise ;
A thousand blessings on them rest, —
  Blessings from heart and hand, —
The Muses we delight to own,
  They are *this* fairy band.

ANNIVERSARIES AND DEDICATIONS.

COME TO THE FESTAL DAY.

A HYMN FOR A SCHOOL ANNIVERSARY.

COME to the festal day,
　　Cheerfully welcomed, come!
Come join our songs; come share the joy
　　That crowns our school and home!

Here have our hearts received
　　Treasures of holy truth, —
God's living words, — the helps of age,
　　The loving guides of youth.

Come, for the rolling year,
　　With bursting buds and flowers,
Summons the sower to his toils,
　　And gladdens us in ours!

God's blessing cheers each task:
　　No work for God is vain:
His is alike the beaming sun,
　　And His the gentle rain.

Then to our festal day
　　And cheerful greetings, come!
Come join our songs; come share the joy
　　That crowns our school and home!

IN LOVING FAITH THIS STONE WE PLACE.

LAYING THE CORNER-STONE, NORUMBEGA, WELLESLEY COLLEGE.

IN loving faith this stone we place ;
   God is our trust, — in Him we build ;
All noble works through Him are wrought,
   All life is with His pulse-beat thrilled.

O Life of life! O Light of light !
   Our breath, our joy, our hope, our aim, —
We plant our corner-stone, we rear
   Our home, in honor of Thy name !

In love o'er all the work preside
   As wall, and tower, and peak ascend ;
And be its crown of glory, Thou, —
   Earth's noblest hope, life's highest end,

The broad, sweet landscape at our feet, —
   Forest and vale, and hill and sea, —
Reveal Thy wondrous skill and power;
   All space, all time, are full of Thee.

So let the building we prepare,
   The house we to Thy honor raise,
Be a new temple built for God, —
   Forever vocal with His praise.

JUNE 22, 1885.

IN FAITH THIS CORNER-STONE WE LAY.

FOR THE CORNER-STONE LAYING, WORCESTER ACADEMY, 1889.

IN faith this corner-stone we lay, —
  A tribute to fair Learning's shrine;
God is our wisdom, God our stay,
  And His the work our thoughts design.

We build in faith for nobler years,
  For generations yet to be;
As every soul its structure rears
  And builds for immortality.

Let children's children here be trained
  To love the paths their fathers trod,
To keep the boon their fathers gained,
  To love and trust their fathers' God.

And day by day the walls shall grow,
  And arch, and dome, and towers shall rise,
As, slowly, works of love below
  Tend to bright mansions in the skies.

NOT YET COMPLETE, — THE HALL WE REAR.

AN UNFINISHED MAIN BUILDING.[1]

NOT yet complete, — the hall we rear,
    O Learning, to thy shrine;
Not yet complete, — our character,
    To match the mould divine.

But wall, and architrave, and dome, —
    As stone on stone we raise, —
A finished temple shall become,
    Built for Jehovah's praise.

And year by year shall many a soul,
    Like marble from the mine,
Polished, and set, — a perfect whole, —
    In holy beauty shine.

As arch, and pinnacle, and spire
    Point upward to the skies,
O living souls, grandly aspire
    To shine in Paradise !

[1] Written for the Tenth Commencement of Vermont Academy,
Saxton's River, Vt., June 21, 1888.

HYMN FOR THE DEDICATION OF A SCHOOL-HOUSE.[1]

[TUNE: " *The Morning Light is Breaking.*"]

SOW ye beside all waters
  The seeds of love and light,
And train your sons and daughters
  To wisdom, truth, and right ;
Open fresh founts of beauty
  Along life's devious road ;
Fashion the soul to duty,
  And lead it up to God.

Prepare the peaceful bowers
  Where opening minds shall wake,
As rosebuds into flowers
  In blushing fragrance break ;
Water with skilful teaching
  The springing germs of thought,
Onward and heavenward reaching,
  With coming glory fraught.

As priests of God anointed
  To keep this high behest,
We take the charge appointed,
  To do such bidding blest ;
Here shall new gems be fitted
  With mild, fair light to shine,
The toil to us committed,
  The help, O God, is Thine.

[1] Used at the dedication of a new building at Hebron Academy,
Maine, June, 1891.

FAIR SEAT OF LEARNING! WHO SHALL TELL.

JUBILEE HYMN FOR MOUNT HOLYOKE SEMINARY,
JUNE 23, 1887.

FAIR seat of learning! who shall tell
    The joy we feel in greeting thee
On this glad day, thy festal day,
    Thy blessed day of jubilee!

O born of faith! O nursed in prayer!
    What grateful throngs repeat thy name!
What memories, lingering round the globe,
    With fervent blessing crown thy fame!

O loyal hearts! bring hymns of praise
    To Him to whom all praise is due;
With loyal homage pay your vows,
    In loyal faith your vows renew.

Glory to Him who planned, who guides,
    The years elapsed, the years to be;
For His dear sake, in His great name,
    We keep our hallowed Jubilee.

FAIR WORCESTER.

[Tune: *“Fair Harvard.”*]

FAIR Worcester, enthroned on the hills in thy pride,
　　With the city-domes gleaming below,
A gem on the robe of a beautiful bride,
　　Or a crown on a beautiful brow,
Thy children return to thy favorite halls,
　　With more joy than the home-flying dove ;
Their hearts burn with gladness to answer thy calls,
　　As they bring thee their tribute of love.

Dear Muse of our childhood, dear guide of our youth,
　　To our hearts what fond memories throng;
From thy chalice we drank the rich draughts of truth,
　　And our souls through thy strength were made
　　　strong.
No landscape was ever so fair to be seen ;
　　No such sunsets crowned day’s busy hours ;
No friends like the friends of our boyhood have been,
　　And no teachers so gracious as ours.

O favored of Heaven, thy sons have engraved
　　Their bright names on the wreath of thy fame ;
To guard thee and guide thee, around thee has waved
　　God’s broad pillar of cloud and of flame.
Still onward and upward pursue thy fair march,
　　Like an army with banners unfurled ;
While God bends above thee His covenant arch,
　　And before thee lies waiting the world.

November 13, 1891.

FAIR SUFFIELD, THY CHILDREN RETURN TO THY HALLS.[1]

FAIR SUFFIELD.

FAIR Suffield, thy children return to thy halls,
  As the birdlings fly back to their nest,
Delighted to welcome thy motherly calls,
  And to lean as of old on thy breast;
Whatever our lot in the future may be,
  And wherever our footsteps may roam,
Our hearts shall still turn with affection to thee,
  And shall find in thy bosom a home.

What lessons of wisdom we learned from thy lips!
  What ambitions thy teachings have fired!
The light of those teachings no years can eclipse,
  Nor imperil the love they inspired;
Thy light has shone far o'er the darkness of earth,
  Like the sunbeams that break from the sky;
Thy prophets and heroes have honored their birth,
  And their record stands written on high.

Oh, long from thy seat on the hills, in thy pride,
  Be thy glorious banner unfurled;
There draw every eye like a beautiful bride,
  And bring blessing and joy to the world!
The God of our fathers establish thy state,
  And His pillar of cloud and of flame
Defend thee and guide thee while thousands shall wait
  To be honored and called by thy name!

[1] A school song for Suffield Literary Institution, Conn., Jan. 25, 1892.

RE-UNIONS.

HYMN

FOR THE REUNION OF ALUMNI OF NEWTON THEOLOGICAL
INSTITUTION AT SARATOGA SPRINGS, MAY, 1885.

TOILERS from many a distant field,
Alike in shade or sun,
Each throbbing heart and beating pulse
Beats as the pulse of one.

A thousand memories of the past
Bind us in trust and love;
They make us one, — one band on earth, —
One here, and one above.

One work, one Christly work, inspires
The thoughts of every soul;
One aim, one Christly aim, makes one
The labors of the whole.

One hope, one glorious hope, relieves
And cheers our pilgrim way;
We see afar our crown, to grace
Christ's coronation day.

And so the men that toiled and loved
In trial, zeal, and pain,
Redeemed, shall find one home, at last,
In Christ be one again.

HYMN FOR NEWTON THEOLOGICAL INSTITUTION.

[TUNE: *Italian Hymn.*]

DRAWN to this blest retreat,
    What hosts, in converse sweet,
    These paths have trod;
What hosts have loved and prayed,
And on Heaven's altar laid
Their all, amid thy shades,
    O mount of God!

One bond unites the whole, —
Breathes, moves, one kindred soul,
    Our life, the same.
Our hopes, our aims, are one;
Christ is our central sun,
And all our works are done
    In His dear name.

Our ears the call have heard,
"Go, preach my saving word,"
    Here, Lord, are we;
Each in his chosen sphere,
Ready the cross to rear,
Answers, in accents clear,
    "Here, Lord, send me."

Behold, the nations wake!
Saviour, Thy sceptre take,
    Assume Thy throne;
Armed with the prophet's rod,
Thy servants wait thy nod,
God over all, our God,
    Come, reign, alone!

DAVENPORT, IOWA, April 5, 1893.

A SONG OF "LANG SYNE."

FOR THE CLASS OF 1829.

WHEN autumn blasts sweep o'er the fields,
    And slanting suns decline,
How bright the hour that gathers here
    The Class of '29!

How fair the day when round the heart
    Old friendships, hallowed, twine;
Blest be the ties that join in love
    The Class of '29!

Now college days come back afresh, —
    Secant, and curve, and sine,
Logic and Latin, that imbued
    The Class of '29.

Homer and Hesiod, Paley, Brown,
    Anacreon's love and wine,
And modern lore, that came t' adorn
    The Class of '29.

Around our brows, once bright with youth,
    Now age hangs out its sign;
But nobler grows the fame which wreathes
    The Class of '29.

Then hand to hand, and heart to heart,
    Like brothers, still combine,
Till not a name, unstarred, shall mark
    The Class of '29.

NOT YET THE FROST OF AGE.

HARVARD CLASS OF '29.

NOT yet the frost of age,
    Nor ardent summer's rage,
Nor history's burdened page
Has chilled or scorched the friendships of our youth ;
    Nor with a " finis " ended,
    Life's stories, vaguely blended,
    Which years have comprehended,
Are closed and bound and sealed with changeless truth !

    Like seamen, when they tack,
    Our eyes look gravely back
    Along the lengthening track,
Far to our sunny morn and booming spring ;
    When with our sails inflated,
    Time's mingled cup untasted,
    On the fair verge we waited,
And gazed intent, to see what life would bring.

    From old companions parted,
    The dear and noble-hearted,
    With whom the race we started, —
Like weary steeds, we watch the setting sun ;
    Climbed are the heights we sought,
    Our manhood's deeds are wrought,
    Our battles sternly fought,
Favored by God's good grace, and victory won.

Yet that old fervor burns,
Still the young blood returns,
Just as the summer ferns
Are green and strong till falls the autumn blast;
So to the clouds of even,
Grouped in the glittering heaven,
Ever new glow is given,
And never are they brighter than at last.

The dropping sands still fall;
From heaven new voices call;
We claim them each and all, —
The starred that shone, the unstarred names that shine.
Oh, fewer still, and fewer,
But never, never truer,
Just as when life was newer, —
God keep the unstarred names of " twenty-nine!"

At Parker's, Boston, January 10, 1884.

'MID THE TEMPEST AND THE STRIFE.[1]

HARVARD CLASS OF '29.

'MID the tempest and the strife,
　　With stern heart and ready hand,
As when amid the conflict dire
　　Embattled legions stand,
In a world where bounding joy
　　Comes alternately with tears,
As night dews follow noontide heat, —
　　We have finished fifty years.

Oh, blissful were the hours
　　When, with brilliant hopes and young,
We launched our bark on life's bright sea,
　　And wooed the siren's tongue,
And the future, calm and fair,
　　Stood undimmed by rising fears ;
Alas, our hearts had yet to learn
　　The scenes of fifty years !

But with steadfast eye and heart,
　　Ever up and onward led,
The joy of freedom round us cast,
　　Its light above our head,
As shouts the pilgrim from the height
　　The towering mountain rears, —
So on the summit gained, we stand ;
　　We have finished fifty years.

---

[1] Founded on the fact that the members of the Class of 1829, with
two or three exceptions only, are understood to be just fifty years
of age.

Now back we turn to view
  The path our steps have trod,
And, yearning, seek to press again
  With loving feet the sod,
And busy memory to our souls
  The fragrant past endears;
Yet comes that benison no more, —
  We have finished fifty years.

As the gray old ruin stands,
  And verdure o'er it creeps,
And clings in every nook and seam,
  And in silent beauty sleeps, —
So round our manhood's heart
  The bloom of youth appears;
Age nurtures these sweet-trailing flowers, —
  We have finished fifty years.

We have finished fifty years;
  But our friendship, warm and true,
Unchanging, mocks the lapse of time,
  Like heaven's immortal blue.
The radiant arch still smiles;
  And while faith the portal nears,
Our love outrides the storms of life, —
  The gales of fifty years.

So clasp each brother's hand,
  With a firm heart and a brave,
Strong to endure each adverse shock,
  To breast each beating wave,
And light the crested foam with joy,
  Howe'er the tempest veers,
Till storm and conflict, lulled, repose
  Beyond these mortal years.

TRIBUTES.

TO MR. SETH DAVIS, SCHOOL-MASTER.

ON HIS ONE HUNDREDTH BIRTHDAY.

HAIL, honored master! Hail, thrice-honored friend!
Before thy hundred years, we, reverent, bend;
Distinguished praises for thy well-earned fame
Our lips would speak, our grateful thought would
    frame.
Distinguished man, whose deeds, so bravely done,
Have charmed and blessed, in turn, both sire and son;
Lone pillar, thou, amid the wastes of years,
The sole survivor of their joys and tears;
Whose like our eyes will ne'er behold again,
Grand and alone, — a monument of men.

Distinguished, thou, dear man, above thy peers,
Rich in the circle of thy hundred years,
Whose eye, undimmed, has seen the months decay,
While generations thrice have passed away;
Skilful to teach, kind and discreet to guide,
Keen to discern, and honest to decide,
Acute to plan, and earnest to defend;
If e'er a foe in seeming, still a friend,
Training thy pupils to be good and wise.
Goodness lives ever; wisdom never dies.
Thy teaching made them men, both good and great,
Fitted to hold and grace the chair of state;

Great for the platform, pulpit, field, or mart,
But greatest in the goodness of the heart;
As fruits that ripen 'neath the genial sun,
Beauty and richness yield, combined in one.

Friend of our early youth and riper age,
The citizen, the patriot, and the sage;
Blessed with an eye to see, a hand to do,
A heart to throb, a soul both large and true;
Man of the present, treasury of the past, —
How has thy life been honored to the last!
Of old traditions, thou, a matchless store,
A walking volume of historic lore;
Lover of Nature in its varied moods,
Its brooks and flowers, its fields and leafy woods,
A thousand trees, set by thy loving care,
Attest thy taste and toil, which placed them there.

So on the hill, where forests used to stand,
One tall old tree — the monarch of the band —
Towers upward, all alone, in lofty pride,
While generations, nourished at its side
In gentle summer and in winter drear,
Have grown and fallen with every passing year, —
Each season crowns it with luxuriant leaves,
Each autumn round it some fresh glory weaves,
And twittering birds and sunbeams o'er it play,
While the old monarch suffers no decay.

May thy late years decline, O honored friend,
As setting suns their glowing colors blend,
Peacefully fading towards the darkening west,
Sinking serenely to their destined rest,
Prophetic of a new and brighter day,
When years and centuries shall have passed away!

September 3, 1887.

THE DEPARTED TEACHER.

GONE, but not lost! the star of day,
   Merged in the morning radiance, dies,
But holds, unseen, its onward way,
   And walks in glory through the skies.

The brilliant orbs that guard the night,
   Like priests around their altar-fires,
Quenched, but not lost, a living light,
   Are watching still, though night retires.

Gone, but not lost! the glowing sun
   Sinks, weary, 'neath the darkening west,
But tho' his daily race is run,
   New worlds are by his presence blest.

Gone, but not lost! the summer's bloom
   Lies sleeping 'neath the wintry snow;
But richer fruits spring from the tomb,
   From dark decay fair harvests grow.

Gone, but not lost! who lives sublime
   Lives beyond life, he cannot die;
Born for all years, for every clime,
   His a true immortality.

We weep as, one by one, we lay
   Our brethren with the garnered host,
While gratefully the ages say,
   No saintly life is ever lost.

Farewell, the reverend teacher sleeps,
    Taken, alas ! yet doubly given ;
His life undimmed, its pathway keeps —
    One course alike in earth and heaven.

JANUARY, 1875.

REQUIEM.[1]

ANOTHER, — yes, another, —
    We are passing, one by one,
Like soldiers, fallen in battle,
    Be the conflict lost or won.
Another, — yes, another,
    Like an evening star, has set;
Behind the western mountains
    The light is lingering yet.

Another, — yes, another, —
    The friends of earlier days,
As melt the mists of morning
    Amid the noonday haze,
Life's golden harvests, gathered,
    Pass on to other spheres ;
Life's early promise kindled
    Light round their riper years.

Another, — yes, another, —
    As ever on the lake
Wave follows wave, and shoreward
    Successive billows break ;

[1] For the Class Meeting, Harvard, '29, 1870.

Grand in the storm, but fairest
  When, all the conflict o'er,
In gentle ripples moving,
  They lave the silent shore.

Another, — yes, another,
  Torn from the golden chain,
Crowned, after life's stern conflict,
  Another warrior slain ;
With closer ranks, his valor
  Shall help us dare and do ;
Shorter the chain, but stronger, —
  We 'll weld the parts anew.

Another, — yes, another, —
  We drop like forest leaves,
When the year's crown of glory
  The mellow autumn weaves ;
But lives of love and duty
  Sink to no vain repose ;
Sunsets shed lingering radiance,
  Fragrance, the dying rose.

Another, — yes, another, —
  The calls more frequent grow,
As whitens round our temples
  More thick the silver snow ;
God of the weak and weary,
  Light of our joyful past,
Guide us, support and keep us,
  Till falls in death the last !

N. P. WILLIS.[1]

COME back to be buried beneath the green willow,
　　Whose long weeping branches trail over the
　　　　tomb;
The soil of thy birthplace prepares thee a pillow, —
　　Where kindled thy morn, for thy eve there is room.

Come back to be buried, where patriarchs holy
　　In faith breathed thy name at the altar of prayer;
Come back, from thy greatness, to sleep with the lowly,
　　Where pride sounds no trumpet, and fame is but air.

Come back to be buried, where honor first found thee,
　　And o'er thee her mantle deliciously flung;
Come back with thy robe of renown wrapped around
　　　　thee,
　　To rest where thy garlands in youth o'er thee hung.

Come back to be buried, as blossomings vernal
　　Fall back to the soil whence their beauty was born;
As sunset clouds glitter in glory supernal,
　　Returned from the earth which they moistened at
　　　　morn.

Come back to be buried, — but still shall the crescent
　　Of fame, early won, the record illume;
As chaplets of love, made sempervirescent,
　　Are saved from the night and the damps of the
　　　　tomb.

[1] Mr. Willis was born in Portland, passed his early days in Boston, died at Idlewild, N. Y., Jan. 20, 1867, and *came back to be buried* in Mt. Auburn, Jan. 24.

Come back to be buried, — mowed down by the Reaper,
   Whose pitiless scythe spares nor manhood nor
      bloom ;
Come back to be buried, O lone, silent sleeper,
   Thy kindred await thee, — come, pilgrim, come
      home.

EDWARD EVERETT.

MUTE is his eloquence: that silver tongue
   On whose sweet accents crowds, admiring,
      hung, —
Whose fitting words in heavenly beauty fell
On ear and heart, that owned the witching spell ;
Whose graceful cadence tides of feeling woke,
As if on earth some loving angel spoke, —
Now rests in silence, like a harp unstrung.
Its notes, unrivalled, on the breezes flung,
Still breathe in living echoes in the air,
As though the master-spirit lingered there.
Who can do justice to so great a name ?
Who speak in worthy words his matchless fame ?
In varied learning brilliant and profound ;
In taste a model, and in judgment sound ;
Above ambition's mean and shuffling arts ;
Too great to purchase power at public marts ;
In life so pure, in motive so unstained, —
He trod with honor all the heights he gained ;
His aims so worthy, and his powers so rare,
If first he stood, the people placed him there.
As stands a shaft on some far-reaching plain,
Rising o'er cottage-roofs and waving grain,

Catching the earliest morning's crimson streams,
And latest splendor of the evening beams,
Towering o'er all, it meets the distant sight,
And bathes its summit in the peerless light, —
So, in his country, in his age, alone,
As in the earlier times great Washington;
When foemen trod the stage with haughty stride,
He for his country spoke with manly pride,
Consoled the timid, made the fainting strong,
Stood for the right, and frowned upon the wrong.
As some brave soldier waves his flag on high,
And points his comrades on, to do or die,
Then plants the banner on the topmost height,
Borne through the fiercest whirlwind of the fight,
Himself forgetting, eager but to see
His nation's struggle crowned by victory, —
So toiled in love, so stood, till evening set,
The ripe, the brave, immortal Everett.
    Well at his funeral-pomp did wreaths of green
Adorn the places where his life had been,
And garlands deck, with sweet and cheerful bloom,
The opening gateway to his honored tomb.
The full-blown flowers, of pure and spotless white,
Symbols of finished life, a life upright;
The bursting buds, of fresh and bright renown,
Wreathed o'er his name, like an immortal crown, —
Each fragrant blossom round the good and brave,
Telling how virtue lives beyond the grave.
The martial dirge, with deep and solemn strain,
Fell on the ear as falls the gentle rain,
Breathing o'er troubled hearts a healing balm;
While mingling organ-notes prolonged the psalm,
As if the twofold music had been given,
Symbol of closing earth and opening heaven.
Thus when the good man parts from earth and time,
Soaring from toil and pain to joys sublime,

The flickering light of such a world as this
Melts in the splendor of ecstatic bliss;
The mortal, like the setting sunlight, fades,
While glorious visions rise that know no shades;
And earthly music, as the soul ascends,
Dies on the ear, and with the angelic concert blends.

OLIVER WENDELL HOLMES.

IN MEMORIAM.

D EAR master of the tuneful lyre,
　　How shall we breathe the word, " Farewell " ?
How shall we touch the trembling wire,
　　Which vibrates with thy mystic spell ?

The world seems poor, of thee bereft;
　　The evening sky without the sun;
The setting, not the gem, is left;
　　The frame remains, the picture gone.

As birds that float on heavenward wing,
　　Unseen, the air with music fill, —
Singing, they soar, and, soaring, sing, —
　　Thy broken harp yields music still.

Life's golden bowl was dashed too soon,
　　But love still holds thy cherished name;
No sunset thine, but fadeless noon;
　　No shadow, but immortal fame.

So the dear chrysalis we hide,
　For God's safe-keeping, in the tomb ;
And, in firm faith and hope, we bide
　The dawn that breaks the silent gloom,

Wait the fair day, the glorious hour,
　The precious form, enshrined in clay,
Instinct with new-created power,
　Shall wake, and heaven-ward soar away.

NEWTON CENTRE, October 18, 1894.

CIVIC INTERESTS AND OCCASIONS.

THE WORLD'S NEED.

OH, labor in darkness and labor by day, —
    The world waits for workmen, the brave and the
        true.
Go, work in all fields, and toil while you may, —
  The world waits your coming; there 's something
      to do.

O men, for the times, in the mission of life,
Be strong in the conflict, be brave in the strife!
There 's a crown for the good and joy for the brave
Whom toil cannot conquer, nor pleasure enslave, —
That joy, may you taste; that crown, may it shine
On each glorified brow with a lustre divine.

TRUE GREATNESS.

WHAT is true greatness? — where and whence?
    Who knows its secret drifts?
  Bright and mysterious as the light,
    Shot from the cloudland rifts?
  Whose life, in splendid blazonry,
    Shall find immortal fame;
  Who, 'mid the wreck of quaking worlds,
    Shall wear a deathless name?

Not piles of masonry, or pomp,
 Statue, nor marble bust,
Arrest oblivion, and preserve
 The frame from kindred dust;
Yet how shall human spirits shine,
 As shines the sparkling gem,
And, fadeless, glow like glorious stars
 In night's fair diadem?

No spirit of the cultured East,
 No wealth of skill nor pen,
No grain-fields of the widening West,
 Avail to build true men;
No genius, born of earthly germs,
 No haughty, base desire,
But nobler breath, imbreathed of God,
 Wakes in the soul new fire.

O mystery of human life!
 O wondrous end of man!
O theme, with curious questions rife,
 With God's divinest plan, —
Plan which no human mind can reach,
 No human tongue can tell;
Too deep for angel's speech or thought,
 Boundless, ineffable.

How doth the acorn from the germ
 Become the mighty tree?
How grows the infant spark of thought,
 Broader than land and sea?
The mighty oak its crumbling boughs
 Back to earth's bosom gives;
But ages come, and ages pass, —
 Mind, still expanding, lives.

What wealth, of faithful work is born !
  What greatness, won by toil,
E'en as the farmer's golden corn
  Grows from the deep-worked soil !
Spoil not thy soul with nerveless aim,
  With idle, weak desire ;
Strive nobly for a noble name, —
  To all high deeds aspire.

As from the crucible the gold,
  Refined by fierce heat, flows ;
As from the sculptor's dust and grime
  The chiselled wonder grows, —
So, from earth's friction, toil and grief
  Bring beauty, love, and truth,
Garments of praise for ripened days,
  The light and crown of youth.

They waste, they spoil, their time and toil,
  Who pleasure's goblet drain,
And fondly hope by idle wish
  Life's high rewards to gain ;
Like some bright, beauteous bird whose wing
  Is torn, or clipped, or bound,
And his rich dyes he vainly trails
  Along the dusty ground.

On wealth intent, in fierce pursuit
  O'er distant climes and isles,
The merchant drives with eager haste,
  And heap on heap he piles ;
Like sand-hills on the wave-washed shore,
  Like clouds of drifting spray,
Like mole-hills in the ploughman's path,
  His treasures melt away.

Ambition mounts his fiery steeds,
  Plumed o'er new heights to soar,
And waves aloft his potent wand
  O'er subject sea and shore, —
Nurse thy fair bubble, man of pride,
  Thyself, thy mighty care,
Reach forth for other worlds to rule,
  And grasp, — but empty air.

The athlete struggles in the race, —
  The expected crown, his life ;
Muscle and bone, and blood and nerve,
  Tense with the eager strife ;
O bootless task, such wreath to win !
  Triumph, alas, how brief !
His valor, nought but force of limb ;
  His crown, a fading leaf.

Proud of the flag that o'er him waves,
  Of deeds his bravery wrought,
Of rights secured, of wrongs redrest,
  Of battles grandly fought, —
The warrior, with his sword unsheathed,
  Cries, " Victory — or — death ! "
How soon his vaunted glory pales, —
  Brief as a passing breath.

Scorched on the line, chilled at the pole,
  Tossed on the billowy foam, —
Hope vainly lures the explorer on,
  With tireless zeal to roam.
Perchance, he finds nor sea nor land ;
  The phantom onward leads :
The fame, the wealth, the rest he seeks,
  False to his hopes, recedes.

But gold, nor art, nor costly show,
  Nor birth, nor regal state,
Nor palace tall, nor acres wide
  Make him who holds them great;
But wisdom, grace, and knowledge broad,
  A great and noble soul,
And God's blest image, God's high thought,
  Stamped grandly on the whole.

Oh, winnow grains of truth and love
  From this world's useless straw!
Who rules his life, he rules the end, —
  'T is Nature's changeless law.
Oh, blest the man, supremely blest,
  Whose life sublimely flows,
And God's approving sentence sheds
  A halo round its close!

O man, in God's own image formed,
  Offspring of God's great thought;
O man, for lofty aims designed,
  For noble purpose wrought, —
Build not on Time's illusive sands
  The pillar of thy fame,
But high, on monuments unseen,
  Carve an immortal name.

What harvest fields of joy and hope
  Whiten the world's broad face!
A sickle waits each willing hand,
  Each heart God's helping grace;
No seed is lost, no precious grain
  To earth can, useless, fall.
God guards the reapers and the seed;
  His love shall garner all.

WOMEN'S RIGHTS.

'TIS the question of the day;
    They discuss it every May,
With all their wit and learning;
And renew it in October, —
Dames, strong-minded, and men, sober,
    Stupid souls, and souls discerning.

Oh, for wisdom to pronounce,
To the tittle of an ounce,
    For our wives, and for some prim men,
The number, weight, and measure
Of that rich and precious treasure, —
    The rights, to wit, of women.

'T is my creed, — perhaps I 'm wrong,
But I 'll say it for a song, —
    Their right is to promote us
From bachelors to men,
To excel us with the pen,
    But never to outvote us.

Should we let her vote at all, —
Woman great or woman small, —
    Such majorities might aid her,
That the lords of this creation
Would lose their right and station,
And their claim to run the nation,
    From zenith down to nadir.

'T is their right, throughout the strife
Of this weary, toiling life,
　　To be gentle, loving, sweet,
And receive from us, the strong, —
Be the struggle brief or long, —
　　Shelter 'mid the dust and heat.

'T is their right in days of pain,
To calm the fevered brain,
Kind as the gentle rain
　　Or summer dew ;
And to find in *us* relief
In days of toil and grief, —
　　Like them, patient, mild, and true.

We yield to them the right
To be witty, brave, and bright,
　　In repartee to shine ;
Better than sparkling toys,
To be mothers to our boys,
Famed for quiet or for noise,
　　Be the youngsters one or nine.

'T is their matchless right, — we claim, —
Their glory and their fame,
　　Not for foreign joys to roam ;
But to break the clouds of sadness,
To strew earth's paths with gladness,
　　To be the sunlight of the home.

'T is their right in love to stand,
With tender heart and hand,
　　And to watch beside the bed,

Till the spirit upward flies;
And down the opening skies,
Like gleams from Paradise,
　　Heaven's light is round them shed.

'T is their right, with holy feeling,
To be found, all meekly kneeling,
　　Before the throne of prayer.
'T is there they find their power, —
Grace is their richest dower;
　　Their dearest rights are there.

Oh, no, we would not take
One right, — for their dear sake, —
　　Nor pull their power down;
Theirs to strew the earth with good,
As earth's lords never could,
　　And then wear Heaven's crown.

Oh, no, we are not wrong,
Say we it in prose, or song!
　　'T is our pleasure to promote them
To the headship of our table,
To whatever good we 're able;
　　But we always *will* outvote them.

DEDICATION HYMN.

SO, the fair structure stands,
The work of human hands
And human will;
Here, where the rippling wave
The sea-sands used to lave,
Soar towers and architrave,
Beauty and skill.

Here shall fair Commerce sit,
With wisdom, grace, and wit,
The state to bless;
Here land shall speak to land,
And hand be clasped in hand,
And noblest deeds be planned,
In righteousness.

Peace her white wings shall spread
O'er all the paths we tread;
Truth guide our way:
While patriot sire and son
Bends to the work begun,
And new successes, won,
Shall crown the day.

To Thee, great God, to Thee,
God of the land and sea,
These towers we raise;
Establish here Thy throne;
Rule in all hearts alone;
Thy sovereign right we own,
Thy name we praise!

FOR THE DINNER OF THE FIRST CITY
GOVERNMENT OF NEWTON, MASS.

BOSTON, FRIDAY, JANUARY 1, 1886.

I SUPPOSE I 'm the aim of your eloquent battery,
  And you wish for my rhymes as the pay for your
    flattery;
I own it accords with the ways of society,
And humbly I yield to the laws of propriety.

You 'll pardon my verse, if 't is undiplomatical,
Not Republican, Mugwump, or pure Democratical;
My calling is not to discussions political,
Nor yours, at a banquet, to be sharply critical.

To raise to a city this place of our habitat,
With aldermen, mayor, common council, and all of
      that,
Was better than marring the town and dividing it,
Or trotting some hobby out boldly and riding it, —
Making twain what is one by right systematical,
And calling that two which is one, geographical.
For praising it, people may charge us with vanity;
Not praising it, people would call it — insanity.
Our city régime was not sour grapes, pendulous;
But clusters, the fairest, of these we were emulous.
The young city, launched, like a ship on the sea to
      sail,
Was manned by a crew whose lot never should be to
      fail;

But, as good men and true need no props and no
    garnishing,
'T were useless to take up the business of varnishing.
My verse is sincere and hearty in praising them ;
The people were wise to such office in raising them.
Fair city ! they struck for success in beginning it,
And with every new year their successors are winning
    it.
It is just to speak well of the people who merit it ;
Their praise, it is fair that their sons should inherit it.
They were temperate men, never charged with ebriety,
Whose walk, like a deacon's, was marked by sobriety ;
Not ruled by some party end, blindly and slavishly,
Not planning, and fencing, and junketing knavishly ;
Not famed, in debate, for their fluent loquacity,
Not noted, in contracts, for grasping rapacity ;
Not eager to seek entertainments aquatical ;
Not puffed, like balloons, with soarings ecstatical ;
Not privily chasing some shadow they 're driving at,
And blind to foresee the ends they 're arriving at ;
With their fame nibbled thin, by their secret chicanery,
Like fair ears of corn by a mouse in the granary ;
Above playing fast, playing loose with their politics,
Like lobbyists, zealously plying their jolly tricks :
The men for the times, — and the times were a rarity, —
The times and the men were a wonderful parity.
Expenses, 't is true, in the ledger are debited,
But good things unnumbered, per contra, are credited.
So the first city fathers, we 'll not rate them badly, sir,
But praise them, and toast them, and honor them
    gladly, sir.
Your power, good sirs, is a thing of the preterite,
If you did not rule well, 't is too late to better it ;
Still, government measures are often a mystery,
But, foolish, or wise, — one year makes them history.

Methinks as we sit here, now eating, now talking fast,
The shades of the fathers are seen grimly stalking
        past,
Peering here, peering there, with their ancient eyes
        critical,
Charging this, charging that, as new-fangled, or mysti-
        cal.
They list to the sound of our steam-engines, clattering;
They hear, in our fountains, the bright water pattering,
They see, in our grounds, fruits and flowers exotical,
And brand our new schemes as insane or quixotical;
Deem some things we do proofs of maddest audacity,
And some, — they must own, — showing highest
        capacity;
Accusing our speeches of bombast and platitude,
As if lack of depth could be made up in latitude.
O shades of the fathers, suspend your opinions, do,
Or hasten away to your silent dominions, do!
You judge Time's inventions amiss, from not knowing
        them,
Like men who judge fruits from the seeds, without
        sowing them;
We know these new things are too good to dispute on,
        sirs,
And we're proud of the first city fathers of Newton,
        sirs.

SACRED, O GOD, TO THEE.

DEDICATION HYMN FOR THE DEDHAM HOME FOR WAIF BOYS.

SACRED, O God, to Thee,
    This home of ours,
Its sunny slopes and fields,
    Its peaceful bowers;
Sacred, O God, to Thee,
Thine may it ever be, —
    Both Thine and ours.

Here may the children learn
    To lisp Thy praise;
Here infant hearts grow strong
    In wisdom's ways;
All that is evil spurn,
For all true goodness yearn, —
    All to Thy praise.

And let Thy favor rest
    On those whose love
Opened this rural home,
    Garden, and grove;
As all the good are blest,
Thy blessing on them rest,
    Heaven and love.

After the weeping May,
    Springs a bright June;
After a brief eclipse,
    Shines the full moon;
After earth's twilight ray,
Be ours a peaceful day, —
    Heaven's glorious noon.

JUNE 11, 1886.

THE CONSECRATION OF A CEMETERY.

WRITTEN June 6, 1857, for the dedication of Newton Cemetery; also sung at dedication of Rose Hill Cemetery, Chicago, Ill.

DEEP 'mid these dim and silent shades
    The slumbering dead shall lie,
Tranquil as summer evening fades
    Along the western sky.

The whispering winds shall linger here
    To lull their deep repose, —
Like music on the dewy air,
    Like nightfall on the rose.

Light through the twining boughs shall shed
    Its calm and cheerful ray,
As hope springs from the dying bed
    And points to perfect day.

Around each funeral urn shall cling
    The fairest, freshest flowers, —
Emblem of heaven's eternal spring,
    And brighter lands than ours.

Gathered from thousand homes, the dust
    In soft repose shall lie,
Like garnered seed in holy trust
    For immortality.

Room for the households ! till the morn
    Its glories shall restore,
And on the silent sleepers dawn
    The day that fades no more.

CHANGE AND WORK.

From a poem read before the Lasselle Female Seminary,
Auburndale, Mass.

PROEM.

AS I sat, on "the Fourth," in the land of the free,
  With the banner of freedom above my head
    waving,
And sang of the bliss which true liberty gives,
  And praised the brave men who our blessings are
    saving,

A vessel of war sailed down on my lee,
  And calmly invited my bark to surrender,
With broadsides of compliments, such as you hear,
  When the borrower comes to pay court to the
    lender.

I found it was useless to plead for release,
  Or in terms of excuse to beseech him for quarter;
What landsman would venture to parry with words,
  The shots of an iron-clad craft of the water?

For safety, steer clear of all naval rigs,
Or gun-boats or monitors, frigates or brigs.
My bark to his mercy, I chose to surrender, —
"Lady Muse" is her name; of course he'll defend her.

So, here, Mr. Briggs, is your poem on "work;"
I couldn't refuse it, you good-natured Turk;
You're a despot of learning, and in power to-day;
So be absolute monarch, and have your own way!

POEM.

In nursery, college, work, fashion, and art;
In country and city, in village and mart;
In trade and mechanics, on land and on sea;
In climes ruled by despots, or ruled by the free;
Where flashes the flame of war's lurid glare;
Where wave the sweet banners of peace on the air;
In tropical heat, in the teeth of the cold,
With the youthful and fair, the wrinkled and old;
In circles polite, with the rough honest seamen;
In London, Berlin, Caffreland, and Van Dieman, —
It reigns over all, with a merciless sceptre,
Since Eve took the fruit, — O, had Adam but kept her,
Through grace, this great tyrant one triumph had lost,
And Earth's first temptation no sorrow had cost.

I sing no new theme; everywhere you shall find it:
No force can resist, no fetters can bind it;
No genius of man can command it away;
No strength but must bow, its nod to obey;
No bribe, no condition, can limit the range
Of that power despotic, ubiquitous, — Change!

It comes in our troubles, our bondage to sever;
Without it would toothache be toothache forever.
It rouses, but calms, the wild billows at sea;
It gathers the storm, but compels it to flee;
Wakes daylight from gloom, and purples each ray
That beams in the west at the setting of day;
Spreads earth in the spring with a mantle of pride;
And whitens and jewels it o'er like a bride,
When the nuts have been cracked by the frosts of
　　　October,
And beauty autumnal, grown silent and sober,

Rests under the snow, — fair mantle, but strange,
Wrought to hide like a pall, the triumph of Change !

We hate it ; we love it, avoid it, or seek.
We praise what endures ; yet, with attitude meek,
A change of condition we anxiously woo, —
Convinced 't will be better, if only 't is new.

So begs the fair child, as he runs from his play,
And stands by the side of his grandmother gray,
To see the new volume of pictures just bought,
Of things never seen, and of battles ne'er fought,
To turn every leaf, with the hastiest kiss,
In love with the next, impatient of this ;
The glance of an instant, enough for his brain ;
The scenery must then be shifted again.
The child, like a mirror, reflects but the man, —
Two sizes worked out on the very same plan.

The farmer, uneasy, is weary of toil,
Despises the slow-growing wealth of the soil ;
Aspires to be rich in a day without work,
To eat like an alderman, smoke like a Turk.
Leaving turnips and hay, he sells buttons and braid.
He stocks a fine store, plays gymnastics in trade ;
Talks wisely of tariffs and duties and laces,
Of cases of goods, and of fraudulent cases ;
Drives a fine, fancy horse, buys a costly piano,
And frowns if they say his wealth smells of guano ;
Consumes in one year what he gathered in ten,
And must climb from the foot of the ladder again.

He thought he should see his broad acres extend ;
Have money in plenty, to use and to lend ;
Take his wife to the mountains, the sea or the springs ;
Wear broadcloth the finest, and costliest rings ;

In talk about politics take his full share;
And live, dainty soul, untroubled by care,
In fashion recherché, a life without labor,
Assured of success, like some fortunate neighbor;—
But no farmer grows rich who sets up for a shirk,
Or aims, when turned merchant, to live without work.

The land swarms with men of that gaseous body,
The self-styled élite, — the American shoddy,
Raised up from the shop or the loom, in a day,
By arts reckoned honest, because "it will pay;"
But all things good and great, of human pursuit,
Are of patience and time the slow-growing fruit.
The gourd that grows swiftly, as swiftly may die;
The wealth quickly won, as quickly may fly;
The coral, reared up from the depths of the waves,
Where sea-monsters sport in their dim-lighted caves,
The effort of ages, built, grain upon grain,
Is slowly constructed, but long shall remain.

So springs, with bright promise, the germ from the
     shell,
Where, hidden, it lay in its prison-like cell;
And, nurtured by sunlight, by heat, dew, and rain,
It waves on the hill, it smiles o'er the plain;
It drinks every morning the sweet-scented dew,
Still drinking, and growing, and drinking anew;
It bathes in the glory of noon-tide and even,
But slowly matures, — like mortals for heaven.

.   .   .   .

He whom pain cannot conquer, nor hardship can foil,
Grows great by endurance, grows nobler by toil;
And fragrant with good are the paths which he trod,
And grand is his rest in the bosom of God!

PATRIOTIC EXAMPLES AND INCENTIVES.

THE FATHERS AND THEIR STRUGGLES.

A TRIBUTE TO COLUMBUS.

WESTWARD, brave seaman, sail,
   Pressed on by every gale ;
     God is thy guide !
Westward, and nothing fear ;
Westward, thy pathway steer,
Till some new land appear
     Beyond the tide.

Day and night went and came ;
Led by God's pillared flame,
     All sails unfurled,
The seaman trod the deck,
Fearless of storm or wreck,
When rose a distant speck, —
     Lo ! the new world !

What found he on these shores ?
Fair isles and golden stores, —
     Riches unknown ;
But, fairer still, to be
A land of liberty,
Reaching from sea to sea, —
     Freedom's high throne.

God of the sea and land,
We trace Thy mighty hand;
We own Thy power.
Here set Thy rightful throne;
Make the new world Thine own;
Rule its expanse, alone,
Forevermore.

OCTOBER 21, 1892.

AMERICA, THE WESTERN FLOWER.

'TWAS planted while the wintry winds
Athwart the earth were sweeping,
And deep beneath the snowy crust
The summer flowers lay sleeping.
"Take," said the sower to the sod,
"The seed I love and cherish;
Though bleak December, I must trust
The grain — survive or perish!"

Stern winter round the struggling plant
Sent down, in furious rattle,
Its rain and sleet, its hail and snow,
Like shot and shell in battle.
Sharp was the air, and rough the soil,
The tender rootlets grew in;
And half sent up a verdant sprout,
And half was but a ruin.

Above the growing plant they stretched
A blue and crimson awning, —
Fair as the brilliant arch on high,
That canopies the dawning,

Relieved with silver stars the blue,
  With white, the crimson edging,
The sacred soil with wavy lines,
  Like ocean surges, hedging.

But round the plant, while burning skies
  With heat scorched all the garden,
The awning wet with tears like dew,
  Stretched by the faithful warden,
Sheltered the flower with stamens dark,
  Till, morning's redness breaking,
The foe that watched the flower with hate,
  Slept, and knew no awaking.

And in the fragrant, sunlit air,
  Around the nations breathing,
First in the circle of delights
  The world's fair Eden wreathing,
Smiles the bright blossom, sweeter far
  Than flowers of Eastern story,
Watered with tears and blood, and reared
  To be a people's glory.

The seed was sown when pilgrim feet
  On Plymouth Rock descended;
And watered, when the sires and sons
  Their tears and labors blended;
And scorched by drought when conflict drove
  Its plough of desolation;
And waved in glory, when, like flowers,
  Bloomed here, a new-born nation.

THE PILGRIM FATHERS.

IN MEMORY OF THEIR LANDING UPON PLYMOUTH ROCK
ON THE 21st DAY OF DECEMBER, 1620.

THEY left old England's cultured homes,
    Its broad green fields, its sunny skies,
Its tall cathedral-spires and domes,
    As the first pair left Paradise.

They found a forest, wild and bleak,
    Cold, threatening skies and frozen sod, —
Brave noble souls, resolved to seek
    Deliverance from the oppressor's rod.

They left the dear ancestral shrines,
    The altars where their fathers bowed,
Graves where their hallowed dust reclines,
    The fields they reaped, the hills they ploughed.

They found a stormy, cheerless coast,
    Swept by fierce winds and savage men ;
Nature's rude growth, the heathen's boast ;
    The rockbound shores, the wild beast's den.

Yet came they fearless, bold, and brave, —
    Not theirs to bow to men the knee,
Unfettered as the ocean wave, —
    God's freemen, whom the truth made free.

The wintry forests' dim defiles
    Woke, their triumphant psalms to hear,
And rocks, and hills, and distant isles
    Echoed their pilgrim-hymns of cheer.

O wise to plan, O justly famed!
O strong in patient faith to wait!
These are the noble sires who framed
And built New England's early state.

TEA-DRINKING.

AN AMERICAN BALLAD.

"GOOD-MORNING, Ma'am, I come to bring
From mother, Mrs. B.,
Her compliments, and ask you down,
To take a cup of tea.

"Do come!" *aside* " ('T is such a fuss
To have one's friends to tea,
Ma wants to have it over with.)
Come early, — say, by three."

Now Mrs. B. was bound to have
A little talk, you know;
And Mrs. A. was bound to tell
Her thoughts, — just so and so.

A tax, dear Mrs. B. resolved
O'er Mrs. A. to come, —
"Bring threepence with you, Mrs. A."
"Yes, but I won't be dumb."

"You shall!" "I won't," said Mrs. A.,
"I'll speak my mind, I will!"
"You sha'n't," said Mrs. B., "you sha'n't;
But bring the pennies still."

And so the gentle ladies talked,
  Full of rare pluck and ire,
Till words, condensed, were changed to deeds,
  And tea distilled in fire.

"You 're a side-issue, Mrs. A."
  "You 're ditto, Mrs B."
So Father Adam used to say,
  Petting with Mother Eve.

"Whether a side-issue or not,
  I think, at last, you 'll see
There 's something brewing, red as blood,
  Coiled in a cup of tea."

Then Mrs. A. a feast announced,
  Long since, we well remember,
In Boston, near a famous wharf,
  One still night in December.

She hired some red-skinned caterers,
  Who lived beside the sea,
To heat the water, and prepare
  A real strong cup of tea.

Now Mrs. B. stood near, and leaned
  On Mr. Gage's arm, —
"I hope this party may not lead,"
  She said, "to any harm."

"Why, Mrs. A.," at length, she said,
  "Tea only, and no cakes!"
"I have some cake in Concord, Ma'am,
  I 've stored it for your sakes."

"Then bring it on!"   "I won't."   "You shall!"
  "Go take it, if you can!
Lord Percy, at his peril, tries,
  Or any other man."

An old conundrum asks, I think,
  Pray tell me, do you see, —
"Why is it, sir, that living men
  Sometimes are just like tea?"

"I 'm poor at guessing; ask, I pray,
  Old England's honored daughter, — "
"Because their worth is best revealed
  When plunged into hot water."

And Mrs. B., a noble dame,
  At last grew proud to own
Dear Mrs. A., — who stoutly spurned
  To bow to Britain's throne.

And Mrs. B. sent up her boys,
  Who soon marched down again;
They hurried back to Boston town,
  Wiser, but fewer men.

A little quarrel then arose,
  Dear Mrs. A. and B. —
Such pulling caps! such burning words!
  "You shall!"   "I won't!"   "You 'll see!"

'T was fourth July, when Mrs. A.
  Her pretty foot set down,
And said, "Now mark me, Mrs. B.,
  I 'll brook nor kings, nor crown."

The bands were cut.   A. shouted, "Free!"
  B. said, "Amen!" but missed her;
Compelled to yield, she nobly cried,
  "Dear A., thou art my sister!"

With tears of love and clasping hands,
  One blue arch bending o'er us,
One bright, broad sea, that binds the land
  Behind, to land before us.

Alike in faith, alike in speech,
  Nursed on one parent knee,
We're hasting o'er this watery track,
  To drink that cup of tea.

And while the fragrant fumes ascend,
  Like mists above the sea,
Each land, to the same tune shall sing,
  "My country, 't is of thee."

Britain the music shall provide,
  The mother land which lures us;
And we will bring the hearty words, —
  One soul, one ringing chorus.

STEAMER "PARTHIA" ON THE ATLANTIC OCEAN,
July 4, 1875.

PAUL REVERE'S RIDE.

HANG out the lantern ! Let oppression quail !
The pen of history shall record the tale ;
A feeble taper, flashing o'er the sea,
But the first signal light of liberty.

Hang out the lantern ! Veiled by friendly night,
A watchful horseman waits, to catch the light,
Then warn the sleeping people, far and near;
Who is the patriot rider ? Paul Revere.

Ride on ! Ride on ! O valiant horseman ! Wake
Fathers and sons a stern defence to make,
Armed with brave hands and hearts, resolved to be,
Through Heaven's behest, a nation of the free.

The foemen started bravely on their way,
But found the freemen ready for the fray,
Waiting their coming, — men who knew no fear,
Prepared for battle ! — roused by Paul Revere.

High thoughts, strong souls, firm wills then showed
their power;
Then Independence struck the nation's hour.
The patriots won the day ! and Percy's men,
Conquered and broken, sought their camps again.

The feeble lantern in the belfry hung,
With flickering rays o'er the still water's flung, —
A central sun, that nevermore declines, —
Still round the world, a radiant signal, shines.

Strong men, great hearts, the stirring times required,
With matchless zeal and fervent purpose fired,
But none more grandly served the cause so dear,
Than the brave patriot rider, Paul Revere.

OLD NORTH CHURCH, BOSTON,
April 18, 1894.

PATRIOT'S DAY.

APRIL 19, 1775.

WRITTEN for the "Sons of the Revolution," of the State of Iowa.

PRAISE to the brave and true !
　　Men prompt to dare and do,—
　　　To do, or die ;
Blazoned on history's page,
Men for their stormy age,
Fearless the fight to wage,
　　　Scorning to fly.

They, with prophetic eye,
Saw, through the lurid sky,
　　　The goal they sought,—
A nation of the free,
A land of liberty,
Stretching from sea to sea,—
　　　O glorious thought !

They hailed the coming state,
Patient to toil and wait,
　　　Suffered and bled ;

Death strode o'er hill and plain ;
With hunger, cold, and pain;
Hope rose, to sink again,
　　Till years had fled.

But forward, onward still,
They of the iron will
　　Pressed, undismayed.
A nation's love they claim ;
Born to immortal fame,
What lustre lights each name,
　　Never to fade !

Hail, patriots ! whose brave hands
Over these fair, free lands
　　Their flag unfurled ;
Men, by all times admired,
To noble deeds inspired,
By whom " the shot " was fired,
　　" Heard round the world."

O sons of noble sires,
Who, amid war's dread fires,
　　To triumph rode !
Proud of the deeds they wrought,
With countless blessings fraught,
Cherish the land they bought, —
　　The gift of God.

A PRIL 19, 1894.

INDEPENDENCE DAY, JULY 4, 1776.

AUSPICIOUS morning, hail!
  Voices from hill and vale
    Thy welcome sing:
Joy on thy dawning breaks;
Each heart that joy partakes,
While cheerful music wakes,
    Its praise to bring.

When on the tyrant's rod
Our patriot fathers trod,
    And dared be free;
'T was not in burning zeal,
Firm nerves, and hearts of steel,
Our country's joy to seal,
    But, Lord, in Thee.

Thou, as a shield of power,
In battle's awful hour,
    Didst round us stand;
Our hopes were in Thy throne;
Strong in Thy might alone,
By Thee our banners shone,
    God of our land!

Long o'er our native hills,
Long by our shaded rills,
    May Freedom rest!
Long may our shores have peace,
Our flag grace every breeze,
Our ships, the distant seas,
    From east to west!

Peace on this day abide,
From morn till even-tide;
    Wake, tuneful song;
Melodious accents raise.
Let every heart, with praise,
Bring high and grateful lays,
    Rich, full, and strong.

Onward the echo floats;
Sublime and swelling notes
    On the air sail;
From fearless hearts and free,
The lofty minstrelsy
Rises, O God, to Thee
    Hail, Freedom, hail!

THE CHILDREN'S INDEPENDENCE DAY.

THE first poem written for Lowell Mason, and for July 4, 1830.

HARK! Music wakes
        Among the mountains,
And thunder breaks
        Along the fountains;
Each river bank is gay with flowers,
More bright than rainbows in the showers.

CHORUS.

Come, children, bring a cheerful lay,
To welcome Independence Day!

The banner floats
    In beauty shining;
And charming notes,
    So sweet combining,
Proclaim 'tis Freedom's holy light
That beams on every side so bright!

CHORUS.

The temple gates
    Ring loud with singing,
While infant mates
    Their songs are bringing,
The God of victory to praise,
And swelling notes of triumph raise!

CHORUS.

We are the young
    Of Freedom's nation;
Wake every tongue
    In adoration.
Let music float on every breeze;
And whisper praises, all ye trees!

CHORUS.

This joyful day,
    Of glad emotion,
Shall pass away
    In sweet devotion
To God who gave our fathers peace,
To joyous friends, and childish bliss.

CHORUS.

THE FOURTH OF JULY REMEMBERED.

SCHOOL CELEBRATION, JULY 24, 1832.

HOW brightly shone heaven's holy light,
　　Along the path our fathers trod !
They girded them to deeds of might,
　　Depending on the arm of God.

So in the guiding cloud by day,
　　So 'mid the night, in pillared flame,
Did Israel see the chosen way,
　　Marked by their God, where'er they came.

Loosed from a foreign monarch's yoke,
　　The children of the brave and free,
O God, Thy blessing we invoke,
　　And yield glad homage, Lord, to Thee.

Our Father, let our happy land
　　Still smile beneath Thy guardian care ;
Let peace be ours, by Thy command,
　　And health be wafted on the air.

We bless Thee for the joys we know ;
　　We praise Thee for this happy day ;
Still guide us, in the paths we go,
　　And lead us in Thy own right way.

HYMN FOR THE FOURTH OF JULY.[1]

[TUNE: *"Keller's American Hymn."*]

LAND of the freemen and home of the brave!
Soil which our fathers have bought with their
blood!
Dear is each mountain, rock, river, and grave,
Fields where their feet on Oppression have trod;
Heroes, whose feet on oppressors have trod,
Green are their laurels and honored each grave;
Blest be the soil they have wet with their blood,
Land of the freemen and home of the brave!

Peace o'er this land of the happy and free
Folds her fair pinions in loving repose;
Liberty reigns from the sea to the sea;
Freedom, triumphant, exults o'er her foes;
Freedom, triumphant, exults o'er her foes;
Tidings of hope echo far o'er the sea,
Bidding the nations oppressed to repose,
Sheltered by peace, in this land of the free.

God, our protector, our strength is in Thee,
Strong to deliver, and mighty to save;
Calm each wild tempest that sweeps o'er the sea,
Calm the fierce passions that swell like the wave;
Soothe the fierce tumult that swells like the wave,
Breathe with the whispers of love o'er the sea.
God, we rely on Thy mercy to save;
God, our protector, our strength is in Thee.

[1] Newton City Celebration, July 4, 1870.

THE FATHERS REMEMBERED.

H OW pure in zeal, how firm in faith,
  Sternly the early patriots stood !
Ready to buy, come life or death,
  Their freedom at the price of blood.

They scorned in craven fear to bend ;
  No tyrant power could make them quail ;
" Our rights, as freemen, we defend ;
  Our cause is God's — it cannot fail."

Slender in means, in numbers few,
  But high in aim and grand in thought ;
Nobly they spoke, brave men and true,
  And nobler deeds of valor wrought.

A century's march, through peace and blood,
  Has left their influence still impressed
On all the hills their footsteps trod,
  On fields their presence never blessed.

Our fathers' God, we own Thy power ;
  Thy mighty fiat made us free.
Our help in that decisive hour,
  Still may we put our trust in Thee.

Windermere, England, May 30, 1876.

ODE IN MEMORY OF FRANKLIN.[1]

[Tune : "*Auld Lang Syne.*"]

OLD Time rolls by, but gently breathes
　　On Franklin's glorious fame,
And all its freshest laurel wreathes
　　Around his honored name.
Bring summer's bloom his brow to adorn,
　　Bring spring's most gorgeous flowers ;
He, with celestial yearnings born,
　　Made Nature's secrets ours.

Bid the swift lightning write his name
　　In blue electric fire,
And roaring thunders loud proclaim
　　Him whom all lands admire.
Stand, patriot, sage, in lasting bronze,
　　By grateful art enshrined ;
Live in ten thousand gathering sons, —
　　Thy meed, the polished mind.

The sparkling gift each year revives
　　Thy high renown again,
Linked with the history of our lives, —
　　Thy trophies, living men.
So Time rolls by, but gently breathes
　　On Franklin's glorious fame,
And all its freshest laurels wreathes
　　Around his honored name.

---

[1] Written for the "Association of Franklin Medal Scholars,"
Boston, Edward Everett, orator.

THE POET IN HIS STUDY. FEB. 22, 1895.

THE BIRTHDAY OF WASHINGTON.

Read before the Nonantum Drill Club, Newton, Massachusetts,
February 22, 1864.

HONORED and loved, the patriot and the sage,
  Born for thy own and every coming age,
Thy country's champion, Freedom's chosen son, —
We hail thy birth-day, glorious Washington.

Nurtured in courage, industry, and truth,
Thy noble childhood, and thy generous youth,
Like spring's sweet blossoms on the sturdy tree, —
Gave early promise of the fruit to be;
And well it ripened, as the years rolled on,
And stood in manhood, glorious Washington.

Dark was the storm that gathered, far and wide,
When rose in threatening might the oppressor's pride,
And men, brave-hearted, stood in battle strong,
Resolved to avenge the right and smite the wrong.
Fierce was the fight, and many a hero fell;
Green are their laurels, and they earned them well.
Nursed in the lap of hardship, sternly taught
To value great ideas and high, free thought,
With noble sacrifice they staked their all,
To stand with Freedom, or with her to fall;
And many a patriot mother gave her son,
But one alone gave glorious Washington.

Keep ye his memory green; preserve his fame;
Live in his spirit; love his honored name;
Teach lisping childhood how the warrior stood,
A tower of strength 'mid scenes of strife and blood.

Let men and mothers to their infants tell,
How Freedom triumphed and Oppression fell,
When he, the chieftain of the brave and free,
Led on our troops to joy and victory.
No son was his to bear his cherished name, —
No son, thank God! to bring his father shame;
But every patriot is a worthy son,
To bear thy name and title, Washington!

They wear their honors well, these sons of ours,
Trained by fierce fight to show sublimer powers;
Taught like the eagle, when the storm beats high,
With stronger wing to cleave the threatening sky,
And reach through raging winds the cliffs above,
Where dwell serenely liberty and love,
Grow strong, through toil, to bear our banners on,
As he once bore them, glorious Washington!

The storms will pass.   The flag, in battle torn,
Will wear new honors, by our sons upborne;
Fast anchored on the Right, a glorious rock,
The cause of Freedom shall not feel the shock
That aims its force against the Ship of State.
Weak billows, vain your vengeance, vain your hate!
More patriot mothers have more sons to send;
More noble hearts have treasures still to spend;
More patriot sinews have more strength to give;
More loving hearts have loving lives to live, —
And Freedom shall not lack a faithful son
To track thy steps, O glorious Washington!

THE SONS AND THEIR STRUGGLES.

PATRIOT SONS OF PATRIOT SIRES.[1]

[TUNE: " *Young America.*"]

THE small life, coiled within the seed, —
  A promise hid away, —
But dimly heralds what shall be
  When comes the perfect day ;
But sun, and rain, and frost, and heat
  Enrich the fertile fields,
And the small life of earlier years
  A waving harvest yields.

The corn that slumbers in the hill, —
  A disk of golden grain, —
Stands up at last, a rustling host,
  And covers all the plain ;
Who knows to what the infant germ,
  In coming seasons, leads,
Or how the golden grain expands,
  And mighty armies feeds !

The acorn, in its little cup,
  High on the breezy hill,
Waits for the fulness of the times,
  Its mission to fulfil,

---

[1] This poem was written on the 22d day of February, 1894, as the
closing patriotic selection of " Beacon Lights of Patriotism."

And year by year grows grand and strong, —
  What shall the future be?
A noble forest on the land,
  Or navy on the sea.

The bright-eyed boys, who crowd our schools,
  The knights of book and pen,
Weary of childish games and moods,
  Will soon be stalwart men ;
The leaders in the race of life,
  The men to win applause,
The great minds, born to guide the State,
  The wise, to make the laws.

Teach them to guard with jealous care
  The land that gave them birth,
As patriot sons of patriot sires, —
  The dearest spot of earth ;
Teach them the sacred trust to keep,
  Like true men, pure and brave,
And o'er them, through the ages, bid
  Freedom's fair banner wave.

THE CINCINNATAE.

At a meeting of the " Woman's Relief Corps, G. A. R.," in Boston, August, 1890, the author of " America " suggested the organization of a Society similar to that which, under the name of " Cincinnati " represents the " Sons of the Revolution."   The suggestion was entertained, and the following responsive tribute was written upon the occasion.

ROUSE to defend the land ye love,
   Ye stalwart men and brave ;
O'er all its breadth, from sea to sea,
   Bid Freedom's banner wave.

They heard, they stood, in serried ranks
   They marched at Freedom's call ;
One hope beat high in every heart,
   One thought inspired them all.

Deep in the furrow where it sank,
   The plough, ungeared, stood still,
While broader plans and loftier aims,
   Waited the freemen's will.

So Cincinnatus bravely led
   His Roman soldiers, true ;
So, fearless, trod through fields of blood
   Our Cincinnati too.

And who are these, of finer mould,
   With loving heart and hand,
Alert to feel, and quick to help, —
   A noble female band ?

These loving hands have waved farewell
  To men to glory led;
These loving eyes, with bitter tears,
  Have wept o'er soldiers dead.

And when the storm of battle ceased,
  'T was theirs to weld the chain,
Whose broken links were scattered wide,
  In brotherhood again.

Their loving voices join to swell
  The anthem of the free;
Their loving lips, harmonious, sing,
  "My country, 't is of thee."

Hail, mothers, daughters, sisters, wives
  Of men to freedom true!
The land redeemed is proud to claim
  Our Cincinnatae, too.

THE DAUGHTERS OF THE AMERICAN REVOLUTION.

WRITTEN at the request of Mrs. Edward Roby, of Chicago, on the gift of an autograph copy of the hymn "America," to Miss Eugenie Washington, a grand-niece of General Washington, in connection with the First Congress of the Daughters of the American Revolution, held in the City of Washington, June, 1892.

THEY gathered from the south and north,
  The mountains and the sea,
In memory of the men who died,
  Martyrs of liberty, —
Men pledged to plant, in this fair land,
  A nation of the free;

Who gave their wealth, who gave their blood,
  And gave them not in vain ;
And history spreads its halo round
  Where rest the patriot slain.
Where Freedom's glorious spirit throbbed,
  That spirit throbs again.

The harvest sown in blood and tears
  A grateful nation reaps ;
A hallowed jubilee of love
  The land they rescued keeps,
And o'er the green fields where they died
  Its fragrant tribute heaps.

From east to west, from south to north,
  From tossing sea to sea,
They breathe, in tones that love inspires,
  " Sweet land of liberty,"
Singing, in joyful harmony,
  " My country, 't is of thee."

The daughters of the good and brave
  Shall keep their memory well ;
And age to youth, and sire to son,
  The grand old tale shall tell ;
And woman's tears shall consecrate
  The rich fields where they fell.

I see them where above them bends
  The one o'er-arching sky ;
I hear the tune from Northern throats,
  I hear the South reply :
One heart, one home, one pulse, one land ;
  And one, we live or die.

Sisters, accept this grateful pledge ;
  Our hopes, our hearts are one ;
Or south, or north, naught shall divide, —
  We live beneath one sun.
Peace breathes, in ecstasy of love ;
  The goal we seek is won.

DAVENPORT, IOWA, March 4, 1893.

FLING OUT THE BANNER.

FROM verses read at the dinner of the Phi Beta Kappa Society at
Cambridge, July 17, 1862.

FLING out the banner on the breeze,
  Shake out each starry fold ;
Summon the stalwart soldiers forth,
  The mighty and the bold, —
The bell of Freedom from its tower
  Its solemn call has tolled.

Marshal the legions for the fight,
  The youthful and the brave ;
Stand for the noble and the right,
  The glorious Union save ;
Stand for the cause for which their blood
  Our patriot fathers gave.

Above the clouds the brilliant sky
  Shines in immortal blue ;
And light, like Heaven's approving smile,
  Streams in its glory through.
Be patient, till the strife is o'er ;
  Have faith to dare and do.

Bear on our banner, let it tell
    The triumph of the brave ;
On every breeze that sweeps our hills,
    In glory let it wave,
O'er all the land, o'er all our streams,
    O'er every soldier's grave.

A year of battles ! not in vain
    This contest of the free ;
This rousing of the nation's heart,
    Like storms that rouse the sea, —
The fiery test has but refined
    The love of liberty.

Then fling the banner to the wind,
    The emblem of the free ;
Strike the sweet harp-tones that proclaim
    The reign of liberty,
And bid the melody rebound
    From every trembling key.

And count each star that studs the blue,
    Whate'er the past has been,
A wayward wanderer welcomed back
    To fill its place again, —
A loving band of sister-lights,
    Just like the old thirteen.

Strike not one jewel from the crest
    The loving mother wore ;
Reset the gems upon her breast,
    Each where it shone before ;
Clasp in the glorious cynosure
    The entire dear thirty-four.

WAVE THE FLAG ON HIGH.

Read at a Flag-raising in Chelsea, Mass., July 5, 1869.

WAVE the new flag, exultant, o'er the land;
　Spread out its folds of beauty toward the sea;
Bid softest winds its blood-bought charms expand;
　Hail it with shouts, — the banner of the free!

Bears it the brilliant stripes of gleaming white ? —
　Our cause is righteous, and our aim is pure.
Bears it the red ? — we battle for the right;
　Red blood may flow, but Freedom shall endure.

Bears it the blue ? — to Heaven, our high appeal
　In Christian gratitude and faith we raise;
And every star, a new-made State, shall seal
　Our fervent trust in God, — our joyful praise.

Count all the stars, the stripes, — both white and red, —
　Where'er on sea or land the flag is seen;
They tell how God our growing States has led, —
　Stars, thirty-seven, and stripes, the " old thirteen."

Wave then. fair banner! men may pass away, —
　No mind can guess the changes yet to be, —
But thou, in beauty, hold thy blessed way,
　Our flag of peace, our symbol of the free.

THE PINE AND THE PALM.

AN ALLEGORY OF 1861–65.

ON Northern hills where bleak winds blow,
   And crystalled branches twine,
Stood, in its never-fading green,
   A strong and stately pine.
The evening came with balmy breath,
   And gold and purple dyes ;
And glowing noon its heat diffused
   From summer's ardent skies ;
And tempests roared, with crashing might, —
   But little cared the tree,
Rocked by the storms, it sang for joy
   Its own sweet minstrelsy.

On sunnier slopes, in milder airs,
   In endless summer's calm,
In fragrant beauty towered on high
   A graceful, nodding palm ;
Proudly it tossed its emerald head,
   Wrapped in its haughty scorn,
Like roses in the lovelit bower,
   Girt by the bristling thorn.

At length the winds grew fierce and loud,
   As through the palm they sung,
And reddening clouds around its head
   A fiery lustre hung ;
An angry cadence on the air
   Seemed fitfully to float,
And pine and palm, as if in ire,
   With wild, discordant note,

Driven by the tempest, answered each,
  In sounds like rushing fire,
As if some demon in his wrath
  Had swept his breaking lyre.

The sound passed on. A wreath of light
  Came like a white-winged dove ;
Hovered like angels in their flight,
  A messenger of love ;
Waved its bright form o'er pine and palm,
  And touched them as it passed, —
The storm was laid, and notes of love
  Came singing on the blast.

The flaming cloud dissolved in air ;
  It lost its fiery hue,
And quenched the crimson of its cheek
  In heaven's immortal blue ;
Peace shed again along the hills
  Its breath of fragrant balm, —
The waving palm-tree blessed the pine,
  The waving pine, the palm.

THE MORNING COMETH.

These verses were written in 1862, under the never-faltering conviction that out of battle-struggle would come a crowning peace which would bind in closer bonds than ever a reconciled and prosperous people.

I T IS COMING, it is coming !
  As comes the blessed rain,
When the burning heat and dryness
  Have scorched the waving grain.

We hail the early promise, —
  'T is not in vain to wait;
If the help serves God's great purpose,
  It never comes too late.

It is coming, it is coming,
  As comes the blessed dew
On the weary, fainting flowers
  When the noon-tide heat is through;
It comes in silent sweetness,
  To comfort and to bless, —
We never hear its coming,
  But it blesses none the less.

It is coming, it is coming!
  As the giant, rested, wakes,
As o'er the distant hill-tops
  The morning redness breaks.
While the soldier on his picket,
  His solemn vigil keeps,
The light already glimmers
  On the highest rugged steeps.

It is coming, yes, 't is coming!
  But, O prophet, poet, when?
We have lavished forth like water,
  Our treasure and our men.
We watch the cloudy pillar
  That guides our devious way,
And, blinded in the darkness,
  God bids our faith delay.

IT IS COMING, it is coming!
　　Love can calm the maddened brain,
And the palm-tree, and the pine-tree,
　　Interlace their boughs again ;
The corn and cotton ripen
　　For the loyal and the brave,
And free men till the acres
　　Of a land without a slave.

IT IS COMING, it is coming,
　　Peace o'er all the land shall rest,
With a glory and a beauty
　　Like evening in the west ;
The noon-tide brightness lingers,
　　But God can give it glow ;
The forest sleeps in acorns,
　　But God can make it grow.

MEMORIAL HONORS.

GRATEFUL, the pious feast we keep
　　In memory of the dead ;
And, where the valiant soldiers sleep,
　　Strew honors o'er their bed.

As spring-flowers deck the silent earth,
　　As stars the skies illume,
These loving tributes, lo ! we bring
　　To grace each hallowed tomb.

The land they saved their honor keeps,
  While dark oppression cowers;
And every tear affection weeps
  Is crystalled into flowers.

The deeds they wrought; the truths they sealed;
  Their memory, dear in death,—
Are fragrant as the blooming field,
  Or summer's perfumed breath!

God of the living and the dead,
  Like amaranths on the tomb,
The trust for which their blood was shed
  Keep in immortal bloom.

THE EVE OF DECORATION DAY.

In the parlor of one of the Daughters of the American Revolution several young ladies sang as they made wreaths for the following day, and these stanzas record the incident.

S WEET in the innocence of youth,
    Born of the brave and free,
They wove fair garlands while they sang,
  "My country, 't is of thee;"
How every bosom swelled with joy,
  And thrilled with grateful pride,
As, fond, the whispering cadence breathed,
  "Land where my fathers died."

Fair flowers in sweet bouquets they tied,—
  Breaths from the vales and hills,—
While childish voices poured the strain,
  "I love thy rocks and rills;"

Each face grew radiant with the thought,
  " Land of the noble free;"
Each voice seemed reverent, as it trilled
  " Sweet land of liberty."

And bud, and bloom, and leaf they bound,
  And bade the living keep,
Unharmed and pure, the cherished graves
  Where brave men calmly sleep.
And thus while infant lips begin
  To lisp " sweet Freedom's song,"
Manhood's deep tones, from age to age,
  Shall still " the sound prolong."

I hailed the promise of the scene;
  Gladness was in the strain;
The glorious land is safe, while love
  Still swells the fond refrain.
And what shall be our sure defence,
  Who guards our liberty?
Not men, not arms alone, — we look,
  " Our fathers' God, to Thee."

DECORATION DAY.

[Tune: " *Keller's American Hymn.*"]

STREW the fair garlands where slumber the dead;
  Ring out the strains, like the swell of the sea, —
Heartfelt the tribute we lay on each bed.
  Sound o'er the brave the refrain of the free;
  Sound the refrain of the loyal and free;
Visit each sleeper and hallow each bed; —
  Waves the starred banner from sea-coast to sea, —
Grateful the living, and honored the dead.

Dear to each heart are the names of the brave;
   Resting in glory, how sweetly they sleep;
Dewdrops at evening fall soft on each grave,
   Kindred and strangers bend fondly to weep, —
   Kindred bend fondly and drooping eyes weep
Tears of affection o'er every green grave;
   Fresh are their laurels and peaceful their sleep;
Love still shall cherish the noble and brave.

Peace o'er this land, o'er these homes of the free,
   Brood evermore with her sheltering wing.
God of the nation, our trust is in Thee;
   God, our Protector, our Guide, and our King,
   God, our Protector, our Guide, and our King,
Thou art our refuge, our hope is in Thee;
   Strong in Thy blessing, and safe 'neath Thy wing,
Peace shall encircle these homes of the free.

—••❊••—

PRECIOUS LIVES.

BREATHE balmy airs, ye fragrant flowers,
   O'er every silent sleeper's head;
Ye crystal dews and summer showers,
   Dress in fresh green each lowly bed.

Strew loving offerings o'er the brave,
   Their country's joy, their country's pride;
For us their precious lives they gave;
   For Freedom's sacred cause they died.

Each cherished name its place shall hold,
   Like stars that gem the azure sky;
Their deeds, on history's page enrolled,
   Are sealed for immortality.

Long, where on Glory's field they fell,
　May Freedom's spotless banner wave;
And fragrant tributes, grateful, tell,
　Where live the free, — where sleep the brave.

Bridgeport, Conn., 1865.

CHERISHED NAMES.

WE wreathe with flowers the peaceful graves,
　Where low our fallen comrades sleep;
While sunbeams smile, and verdure waves,
　And dews of evening o'er them weep.

Honored and loved, each cherished name;
　In vain, ye have not lived nor died;
A grateful country keeps your fame, —
　A sacred trust, — her joy and pride.

God bless the land ye nobly saved, —
　Where'er your blood has left its stain,
Where'er your conquering banners waved,
　May peace prevail and Freedom reign.

OUR FALLEN COMRADES.

SOFTLY, their labors done, the patriots rest,
　Honored in life, and in their memory blest:
Living, they earned and won a glorious name;
Dying, they found at once immortal fame.
Spring o'er their relics strews its fragrant flowers,
Smiles in the sunshine, weeps in dews and showers;
And summer spreads its freshest, sweetest bloom,
Green as their memory, o'er their honored tomb.

And Nature wraps around them, where they rest,
The dear old flag, in dyes she loves the best:
Blue, in the starry arch that bends above,
Like mothers bowed to kiss the babes they love;
White, when the earth is mantled o'er with snow,
A bridal honor for the brave below;
And red, when round their couch sweet autumn weaves
A burnished beauty with her fiery leaves.
The glorious banner wraps the rolling year,
And spreads its folds around the sleepers here;
As thousands weep the heroes who have bled,
For each a tear, a blessing on each head.
From granite crypts kind Nature fondly rears
The pillar hewed by love, and wet with tears,
The fitting record of the men who stood
True to the right, 'mid fire and death and blood;
And history writes their names high on her scroll,
Heroes of granite will, but loving soul.

Stand, massive record, as the heroes stood,
A tower of strength, when blood cried out for blood.
The names engraven on the rock are thine;
The men who bore them, grateful hearts enshrine.
Dewdrop, and rain, and grateful tear may dry;
But noble deeds, once done, can never die.
Though marble, shattered, may betray its trust,
And pile and column crumble into dust,
Heroic deeds a deathless pile shall raise;
A land redeemed preserves their lasting praise.
Not here alone their monument is reared,
To memory sacred, and by love endeared;
Where'er the oppressed the bonds of sorrow wear,
Where'er the slave lifts up his humble prayer,
Their high memorial lives, in fetters riven, —
A pile whose base is earth, whose crown is heaven.

These were the men who firm in battle stood;
The men who shrunk not from the flame or flood;
Who gave to Freedom's cause their noblest powers, —
Born for the nation's need, they died for ours.
Weep for their memory! — would they had not died!
Sing for their memory! — 't is the nation's pride.
They bore the toil; they earned the grand eclat;
Proclaim their memory with the glad hurrah!

No hostile foot this sacred soil shall tread;
No hostile banner wave above the dead;
No warlike clarion break their sweet repose,
Calm as the dewdrops, resting on the rose, —
But grateful tears their relics shall bedew;
The loved, the brave, the trusted and the true,
Mothers and maidens, gathered round the tomb,
Shall sigh, and sing the soldier's welcome home;
Mourning the fallen, — to their country given, —
With sweet will yielding to the will of Heaven.
"O grief unspeakable!" — yet Faith can see
Rifts in the cloud; "Our country, 't is for thee,"
And thus resigned, with calm and holy trust,
Mother and maiden leave the hallowed dust,
With woman's faithful heart their grief refrain,
Willing to make fresh sacrifice again.

Breathe soft, O winds, around this treasured trust;
Keep, holy earth, this loved and honored dust;
Sing your sweet pæans, birds of varied wing, —
In heaven's free air, let warbled freedom ring.
Keep nightly watch, ye stars, above their bed,
Teaching the living, smiling o'er the dead;
Though hid by tempests, gently still ye shine,
Keeping in heaven's blue field your march divine.

Though clouds may darken, though the tempest lowers,
Heaven keeps its stars unharmed, as we shall ours;
Clouds cannot quench them; God's great word once
    given,
Their light shall flash again, full in mid-heaven;
And every star that keeps its shining way
Glimmers prophetic of the coming day.
Lift your tall crests, ye trees, in verdant pride,
A hundred storms your sturdy trunks have tried;
Tempests have beat in fury round your head,
But still ye cheer the living, shade the dead.
So when the raging blast has spent its power,
And clouds no more in angry blackness lower,
The nation, saved, shall bloom in peace anew;
Its genial shades the weary pilgrim woo;
Thousands repose beneath each sheltering bough,
Made stronger by the blasts that toss it now;
The anxious watcher mourn no kindred slain;
The soldier seek his home and babes again;
The sword be sheathed, and war's dread tumult cease;
And spotless banners wave in joy and peace.

CHICAGO. — DECORATION DAY.

BURIAL OF GENERAL GRANT.

TAKE from our hands, O faithful earth,
    And safely keep this treasured trust!
The land redeemed proclaims his worth,
    The nation weeps his honored dust.

Unnumbered tongues his deeds shall praise;
    Unnumbered hearts revere his name;
His crown, a wreath which ne'er decays,
    His fame is an immortal fame.

Love hovers round his funeral urn ;
　　A nation's banner o'er him waves, —
So slept the ancient heroes, borne
　　With regal pomp to honored graves.

Rest, patriot, soldier, calmly rest !
　　No sound thy deep repose shall break,
Till the day dawn in glory dressed,
　　Till the immortal morning wake.

August 18, 1885.

THE STUDENT SOLDIERS.

HARVARD'S DEAD.

THEY fought on many a crimsoned field ;
　　They sleep in many a glen ;
They marched to glory and to death,
　　And came not home again :
But Science claims them for her roll, —
　　Her roll of honored men.

Some in the sunny days of youth,
　　And some in ripening age,
Went forth, with valiant hearts and hopes,
　　To breast the conflict's rage ;
And history every name records
　　On her immortal page.

Weep at the shrines where once they knelt,
　　And where the heroes sleep ;
Weep where the funeral pomp proceeds ;
　　At vacant firesides, weep.
When did thy sickle, mighty Death,
　　So precious harvests reap ?

And sing a pæan o'er their dust,
   A requiem for the brave;
Sing hymns of cheerful melody
   Above each soldier's grave;
In solemn joy, with festal folds,
   Let the old banners wave.

Freedom on every bloody field,
   Through them, new triumphs won;
Her honored wreaths are on the brow
   Of every favorite son;
And age is reckoned, not by years,
   But deeds of valor done.

While Fame inscribes ten thousand names
   Along her pillared nave,
Of patriot-sons, and sires who sleep
   In Glory's star-gemmed grave,
Of all the list fair Science claims
   The bravest of the brave.

January 8, 1864.

AFTER THE SOLDIER'S FUNERAL.

AND so we hide our dead in silent shade,
   And hasten back to life, and life's parade;
Plunge into duty, grind in labor's mill,
Till the eye sees not, and the heart is still;
Weep each reverse and shout each victory,
And breathe our benisons, dear flag, on thee.
Living or dying, nation of the free,
Our hopes, our hearts, our lives, are all with thee.

"SLEEP, COMRADES, SLEEP!"

IN thousand shaded valleys,
  On thousand sunny hills,
In thousands of still alleys,
  Beside the rippling rills, —
Who, who can tell the numbers
  Of green graves where they sleep?
But peace breathes o'er their slumbers;
  Love shall their ashes keep.

Sleep, comrades, in your glory!
  Sweet be your honored rest;
Thousands shall tell the story
  How ye, your high behest,
Bravely in love fulfilling,
  Gave up your lives, to be
A sacrifice most willing, —
  The seal of liberty.

Oft as the spring-time, breathing
  Sweet odors from fair flowers,
With dewy pearls comes, wreathing
  Our bright and peaceful bowers,
We bring the first and fairest,
  In honor to the brave, —
The choicest and the rarest,
  To deck the soldier's grave.

God of our country, o'er us
  Thy shield of glory spread!
Go Thou in love before us;
  Direct the paths we tread.

Faithful in every duty,
To us Thy grace be given,
And then, the crowning beauty
Of fadeless wreaths in heaven.

⸺∞⦂❂⦂∞⸺

"LIVING STILL."

FOR THE CLASS OF 1829.

BROKEN and bruised, from fields of strife,
A remnant saved retires, —
Few, but still warm with their young life, —
To stir the old campfires ;
How many marched with banners gay,
Who now, among the slain,
Sleep their last sleep at setting day,
And come no more again !

We con the old familiar list
Of boys, grown gray-haired men ;
Names and old faces, long time missed,
We see them, — boys again.
The ancient roll, whose magic date
Falls pleasant on the ear,
Rich as an argosy, its freight
Grows richer every year.

Dear is the roll of fresh young hearts
Which started for the fray,
Eager and strong, their honored parts,
On life's broad field to play.
Fond memory wakes them, — each and all :
We call them, name by name ;
Or long to stand, or soon to fall,
They come as erst they came.

While spring-time lingered in our sky,
  Some early passed away ;
Some, when the sun of life rode high,
  And poured his noontide ray ;
And some — as autumn fruits, more late,
  In mellow ripeness fall —
Fell, — and like watchers at the gate,
  The rest await the call.

Unchanged on memory's scroll they live, —
  Each face and form we see ;
Time, which mars all things, does but give
  Our dreams intensity ;
Like paintings which old mouldings guard,
  Drawn with a master's skill,
Ranged in old catalogues, and starred,
  To us they 're living still.

ON THE ERECTION OF A SOLDIERS' MONUMENT.

TAKE these choice treasures, gentle earth,
  And shield them in thy faithful breast,
Gathered like gems of priceless worth,
  And brought among thy dead to rest.

Take this new honor reared in love,
  Where sleep the trusted and the brave,
Pointing the mourner's faith above,
  To Him who takes, to Him who gave.

Round this fair shaft let summer leave
Its fragrant airs, at morn and even,
And golden clouds in sunlight weave
Pathways of glory into heaven.

Again the flag of peace shall float
O'er all the land from sea to sea ;
O'er all the land shall swell the note
Of Freedom's final Jubilee.

We build the shrine, we sing the brave,
Yet own how vain are human boasts ;
In God alone is power to save, —
Our trust is in the Lord of hosts.

Newton, April, 1864.

MEMORIAL HYMN.[1]

[Tune : *Italian Hymn.*]

THE God of battles praise ;
Pæans of honor raise,
With heart and song.
God is our shield and tower,
Our strength in danger's hour ;
To Him all might and power
And praise belong.

[1] Dedication of the Monument of the 32d Massachusetts Regiment, at Gettysburg, September 8, 1894.

Here, O memorial, stand, —
Here, where the patriot band
　Battled so well;
Here, where the nation's pride
The rushing storm defied ;
Here, where the true and tried,
　Unconquered, fell.

Tears for the loved and lost;
Joy for the land which cost
　Such sacrifice.
Fond memory, grateful, weeps
Where each dead martyr sleeps,
And love her vigil keeps, —
　Love never dies.

Sound, glorious trump of fame,
Salute each honored name,
　Praise for the brave:
Tell what high deeds were done,
What triumphs Freedom won, —
God was their help alone,
　Mighty to save.

THE ILLINOIS NINETEENTH REGIMENT AND CAPTAIN BREMNER.

A SONG of the Highland Guards,
　　Souls brave and true,
Born for the times of bitter strife,
　When in the balance hung
　　The nation's life ;
And men inspired to dare and do
Resolved to press the conflict through.

A song of the Highland Guards,
    Prompt and prepared ;
First to espouse the righteous cause,
    First rising to defend
        The land, the laws,
With patriot hearts and bosoms bared,
What toils they bore !   What hardships shared !

A song of the brave Nineteenth,
    Noted and known,
With them the noble Highland Guard,
    Eager for honor's post,
        Kept watch and ward, —
Foremost for deeds of glory done,
For battles fought, for victories won.

A song for the brave Nineteenth
    And Bremner's Band ;
Huntsville and Mission Ridge their praise.
    How oft they saved the day
        In fierce affrays !
Victor and vanquished, hand to hand,
Mighty to fight, or firm to stand.

A song for the brave Nineteenth, —
    Calls, loud and long,
Summon the bravest to the front.
    " Where is the old Nineteenth ? "
        Listen ! their song !
They muster, prompt to do or die, —
They come ! they strike ! — The foemen fly !

A song for the brave Nineteenth ;
    The colors wave

Where shell and shot, — a cruel rain, —
    Smite down — once, twice, again —
    The true, the brave.
The men who bore the flag may die;
But Bremner waves its folds on high.

——∘o⋛o∘——

THE TWENTY-FIFTH G. A. R. ENCAMPMENT,
1893.

THEY came from many a happy home,
    Those brave and valiant men,
From palace, cottage, shop, and farm,
    From mountain, vale, and glen,
Ready to save the land, or die,
    And ne'er return again.

They learned, in their young life, to love
    The anthem of the free;
One theme their childish souls inspired, —
    The tale of liberty;
Joyful, their infant lips had sung
    "My country, 't is of thee."

They came by thousands, as the tides
    Into the harbor pour;
Each brow was set, each stalwart form
    The air of purpose wore.
They answered to the call, "We come,
    Three hundred thousand more."

Fearless, they faced the rushing storm, —
  Sons of the brave and free;
In summer's heat and winter's chill,
  Alike on land and sea,
Their souls were throbbing with the pulse
  Of love and liberty.

Firm on the fields of mortal strife
  In serried ranks they stood,
Patient to bear, patient to wait,
  Alike in fire and flood.
" The Union must, — it shall, — be saved
  Though it should cost our blood."

Some in the bloom of early youth,
  Slain in the battle, fell ;
Some found again their happy homes,
  Where peace and freedom dwell, —
But wreathed as conquerors, or dead,
  We love them still, — 't is well.

Some with their cherished kindred sleep,
  Some in an unmarked grave,
Enriching by their honored dust
  The land they died to save ;
And wild birds and the sighing wind
  Chant requiems o'er the brave.

O land, the best of all the lands
  On which the sun has shone,
The purest, noblest heritage
  The sons of men have known,
Still hold thy reign from sea to sea,
  In queenly grace, alone.

Blest be the men whose fervent faith,
   Unwavering, met the gale;
Who passed the storm of war, unscathed,
   And live to tell the tale,
Men of our love, our hearts, our hopes, —
   Hail, the Grand Army, hail!

Peace spreads her angel wings abroad
   From sea to distant sea;
O'er all the land one banner floats,
   The flag of liberty;
And all her millions swell one strain, —
   The chorus of the free.

THE VETERANS.

SAD, but yet glad, our thoughts recall
   The days of woe, and blood, and strife,
When thousands rushed, to stand, or fall,
   For Freedom and the nation's life,

Hunger and thirst, and leaden hail,
   And frost, and heat, and rain, and dew,
And hopes deferred, like springs that fail
   In summer's drought, our forces knew.

The hurried march, the lonely rest;
   The trenches where we laid our dead;
The tangled paths our footsteps pressed;
   The arms that ached, the feet that bled;

The picket, on his silent beat;
  The foeman's gun with stealthy flash;
The fields where men were mowed like wheat;
  The sweeping cannon's deadly crash, —

How vividly they all return, —
  Scenes which the soul can ne'er forget!
Like quenchless watch-fires still they burn, —
  'T was there that death and glory met.

O land we love, united land!
  O'er thee one flag of freedom waves;
Living, our hosts one people stand,
  And freemen sleep in freemen's graves.

In God we trust, — our fathers' God;
  Our people spread from sea to sea;
We hear Thy voice, we heed Thy nod;
  Keep us one people, brave and free.

Speak to our hearts in peace and love;
  Lead us as by the prophet's rod;
Our honor one, O, let us prove
  One land, one people, for one God!

May 24, 1891.

ABRAHAM LINCOLN.

THIS Memorial Poem was written for the Twentieth Anniversary of
the death of President Lincoln, Springfield, Illinois, April 15th, 1885.

HEROIC statesman, hail !
    Thy honored name,
With instrument and song, we laud,
    And poets lays ;
How every mountain top, and sheltered vale,
    And rock and stream,
And lisping tongue of infancy and age,
      And manhood's prime and woman's love,
      Combine thy honored name to praise !

    As to Anchises' tomb,
With reverent love, pious Æneas came,
    Intent, with festal rites
    To crown his father's fame, —
So we, with grateful reverence, come to pay
This loving tribute at the sacred shrine,
    The statesman wise, the martyr prince,
      The peerless man,
And on his tomb our fragrant garlands lay.

    Like the wild eagle's flight,
    When from his rocky height,
Down on the plain he swoops, free as the air, —
    Born with a soul of fire,
    Born to be free,
Patient in toil, and danger, and alarm,
    He ventured all for love of liberty,
    And helped the lowly in that bliss to share.

Grandly he loved and lived;
Not his own age alone
Bears the proud impress of his sovereign mind.
Down the long march of history,
Ages and men shall see
What one great soul can be,
What one great soul can do,
To make a nation true, —
To raise the weak,
The lost to seek,
To be a ruler and a father too;
No scheming tool,
No slave to godless rule,
Gracious, efficient, meek, sublime, refined.

Ambitious, — not of wealth,
Nor power, nor place;
His aim, a nobler race;
His title eminent, — An honest man.
His, to lift up the rude;
His, to be great as good,
And good as great;
His, to stem error's flood;
His, but to help and bless;
His, to work righteousness,
And save the state.

Brave, self-reliant, wise,
Calm in emergencies,
Steady, alike, to wait, and prompt to move;
In counsel, great and safe;
Prudent to plan;
Righteous to deal with sin;
Prone, less to force than win;

Strong in his own stern will, and strong in God;
    Conquering, alone, to bless, —
    A loving man.

    Firm, but yet merciful;
    In pity bountiful;
Calmly considerate, serenely just;
Nobly forgiving to the fallen foe, —
He, the meek sufferer from Oppression's blow,
    Repaying ill with good,
    E'en as the sandal-wood
Bathes with rare perfume the sharp axe that smites;
    Unflinching for the right,
      Whate'er might come,
    And, until death,
Fervent, decided, faithful to his trust.

    Great souls can never die:
    Death and decay's damp fingers
    Waste but the mortal;
A nobler life spreads its far vista wide,
      Beyond death's portal.
    Like an unfading light
    The life work lingers.
The hero dies; statesman and soldier fall;
    The nation finds new life,
And prosperous years, and wealth, and peace,
      And hearts at rest, and grander aims,
      And righteousness,
      And souls that dare to be,
      Just as God made them, — free;
And he who falls, crushed in the bitter strife,
Lives magnified, exalted, ever lives;
    His work bears fruit immortal.

So the great sun, majestic, ploughs his way
Through clouds, and storms, and dim eclipse,
    And winter's cold and summer's heat;
      And, nightly, dips
His flaming disc in the broad western sea,
But scatters light and blessing all the day.
      Setting, he leaves the world
Richer and better for his light and love;
    Warmer, more fertile, more benign;
Sets, but to rise, on other lands, and shine
      Forever, in the galaxy divine.

SPRINGFIELD, ILL.

A CENTURY HYMN. 1789–1889.

THIS Hymn was written to be sung at the Celebration of the 100th
Anniversary of the Inauguration of Washington as President of the
United States, — April 30, 1889.

STRENGTHENED and trained by toil and tears,
  Born of the bold, the brave and free,
A nation, with its hundred years,
  Its tribute brings, O God, to Thee.

What blessings, from Thy sovereign hand,
  What trials, has the century brought!
How has this free and glorious land
  Been loved, defended, led, and taught!

Our cautious feet, by night, by day,
  Slowly the upward path have trod;
God was our light, and God our stay,
  In flood and fire, in grief and blood.

So the brave oak, in calm and storm,
　Spreads its strong roots and boughs abroad,
Grows grand in grace, and stalwart form,
　Honored of men, and loved of God.

The century ends, — our hosts in peace
　Hold the broad land, from sea to sea ;
And every tongue, and every breeze
　Breathes the sweet anthem of the free.

Still may the banner of thy love
　O'er all our land in glory rest,
Our Heaven-appointed Ægis prove,
　And make the coming centuries blest.

And every star that gems the blue,
　And every field for Freedom won,
Shall tell of heroes, firm and true,
　And swell the fame of Washington.

For the same occasion the following stanza was added to the National Hymn, " America," by its author.

Our joyful hearts to-day,
Their grateful tribute pay, —
Happy and free,
After our toils and fears,
After our blood and tears,
Strong with our hundred years,
O God, to Thee.

MEMORIAL DAY, 1894.

NOT costly domes nor marble towers
    Shall mark where friendship comes to weep ;
Let clustering vines and fragrant flowers
    Tell where the nation's heroes sleep.

They rest in many a shaded vale,
    By, and beneath, the sounding sea ;
The forest-winds their requiem wail, —
    The glorious sons of liberty !

Some, in the stalwart years of life ;
    Some, in the prime of manhood's bloom, —
Unshrinking, joined the bitter strife,
    Unconquered, found a soldier's tomb.

They merit all our hearts can give;
    Our praises and our love they claim ;
Long shall their precious names survive,
    Held sacred by immortal fame.

Blest be the land for which they fought, —
    The land where Freedom's banners wave ;
The land by blood and treasure bought,
    Where dwell the free, where sleep the brave.

Great patriots of the elder time,
    Dear patriots of our later days,
Inspired alike by faith sublime,
    One trump of fame shall swell your praise.

The patriot sire to patriot son —
    O'er the broad land, from sea to sea —
Has left the glorious portion won,
    The dear bequest of liberty.

The picket from his weary tread
    Has passed; his silent watch is o'er;
The myriad troops, to battle led,
    Shall march o'er fields of blood no more.

They gained what their ambition craved,
    Freedom and love to all to bring;
And peace, o'er all the land they saved,
    Broods, like the dove, with sheltering wing.

Honor the memory of the dead,
    Where'er the sun of Freedom shines;
Wreathe with fair flowers each sleeper's bed,
    Cherished and loved, as holy shrines.

MY NATIVE LAND.

WRITTEN on returning, after more than two years' absence in
foreign countries.

WE wander far o'er land and sea;
    We seek the old and new;
We try the lowly and the great,
    The many and the few.
O'er States at hand and realms remote,
    With curious quest we roam,
But find the fairest spot on earth
    Just in our native home.

We hold communion, high and sweet,
  With men in ancient lore ;
By day, by night, with reverent eyes,
  O'er volumes old we pore, —
But Rome, and Greece, and Orient lands,
  And heroes far away,
Great in their times, still lack the charm
  That lights our own to-day.

We seek for landscapes, fair and grand,
  Seen through sweet summer haze ;
Helvetia's mountains, piled with snow,
  Italia's sunset rays,
And lake, and stream, and crag, and dell,
  And new and fairer flowers,
We own them rich, and fair, — but not
  More grand, more fair, than ours.

With solemn air we tread, where trod
  The feet of ancient men,
And fill old palaces and courts
  With echoing sounds again ;
Temple and forum, bath and arch,
  Un-earthed, in glory stand, —
These with admiring gaze we view,
  But crave our native land.

We hear with joy the golden speech
  Of men of high renown ;
We see with praise the jewelled wealth
  Of sceptre, mace, and crown, —
But dearer far the golden words
  That made a people free ;
And crown and sceptre pale before
  A nation's liberty.

O land, where saint and pilgrim came,
    With loftiest purpose fraught,
Nurtured in hardship, toil and faith,
    O land, divinely taught;
As streams the light from headland tower,
    Guide o'er the stormy sea,
So hope, to all the oppressed, beams forth,
    Dear native land, from thee.

Part III.

POEMS: SACRED AND RELIGIOUS.

INCENTIVES TO EARLY PIETY.

OF SUCH IS THE KINGDOM OF HEAVEN.

CHILDREN of Freedom's land,
   Who know the Saviour's word,
To strains of grateful harmony,
   Wake every joyful chord!

Not where the heathen cast
   Their infants to the wave;
Not where they know not of the name
   Of Him who came to save;

Not in some distant isle
   Of the unpeopled sea, —
But amid temples, we were born,
   And where the holy be.

" Suffer the babes to come,"
   Of such, the Saviour said,
They, of " my kingdom," shall be heirs;
   For them, the Saviour bled.

Hither, with sacred power,
  The words of love are sent,
The cords of blessed truth to bind,
  While those of sin are rent.

Children of Freedom's land,
  Who know the Saviour's word,
To strains of grateful harmony
  Wake every joyful chord !

WATERVILLE, July 4, 1835.

MORNING PRAYER.

FROM THE GERMAN.

NOW gloomy night is gone,
  And smiling day comes on;
The morning-dawn is breaking,
And we, from slumbers waking,
Look up to Thee, our Saviour,
And seek Thy daily favor.

  Grant us Thy watchful care,
    To save from every snare;
  Oh, make us good and holy,
  And teach us to be lowly,
  And kind in every feeling,
  And to each other yielding.

  If pain and want we bear,
    Be Thou, our Saviour, near,
  To shine upon us brighter,
  And make the sorrows lighter,
  That are to mortals given,
  To make them fit for heaven.

Lord, give our daily food,
And make us mild and good;
And when the clouds of evening,
Their glowing forms are weaving,
We 'll look to Thee, our Saviour,
And praise Thee for Thy favor.

THINGS SMALL AND GREAT.

WHO shall not love the weak and young?
The oak-tree, wide and tall,
A shade on land, a ship at sea,
Was once an acorn small.

Who shall not love the bloom of youth?
The buds of blushing spring
In summer beauty will expand,
And richest harvests bring.

Who shall not love the cloud that floats,
Slight as the human hand,
But in its fertile bosom bears,
Blessings for all the land?

Who shall not love the opening world?
The morning's first faint ray
Shines, a sweet harbinger of joy,
Earnest of perfect day.

Who would not teach the infant tongue
To lisp the Saviour's name?
The Saviour ransomed such as these,
For such as these He came.

Who would not deem the smallest gem
　　Worthy his utmost care,
To fit it for the radiant crown
　　The Saviour's brow shall wear?

September 7, 1893.

THE DEWDROP AND THE SOUL.[1]

A BRIGHT drop on the rose-leaf rests,
　　A little quivering one;
Yet in its tiny globe it holds
　　The mighty, shining sun.

The soul, a gem, of birth divine,
　　Sparkles on life's fair tree;
But in its little compass, God,
　　The Almighty, deigns to be.

Each mirrors in its sunny depths
　　A light that ever shines;
Cradled in thorns, beaming with joy,
　　Such are life's varied lines!

What is the drop? Mere dew — a tear;
　　Exhaled, — 't is quickly gone!
Fraught with immortal life, the soul,
　　Like God himself, lives on.

How blest the life whose steady light
　　To this dark world is given!
Winds breathe and pass; such life will last,
　　A life for God and heaven.

[1] Translated from the Swedish.

RELIGION.

THE joys of earth are fleeting,
  And, quick, their charms retreating,
  Give place to grief and woe !
There is no scene of gladness,
That is not dashed by sadness ;
  There is no perfect bliss below.

But there are fadeless pleasures,
And ever-during treasures,
  Joys which no tongue can tell,
Sweet streams of consolation,
And rivers of salvation, —
  From pure religion's fountain well !

When sorrows gather o'er us,
And troubles crowd before us,
  Religion gives us light ;
The chains are loosed that bound us,
The skies grow clear around us,
  And all is peaceful, fair, and bright.

When mortal life is fading,
Thro' Death's dark Jordan wading,
  There is no painful gloom :
Religion cheers the holy,
And points the meek and lowly
  To joys that live beyond the tomb.

REMEMBER THY CREATOR.

ECCLESIASTES XII.

R EMEMBER thy Creator
  While youth's fair spring is bright, —
Before thy cares are greater,
  Before comes age's night.
While yet the sun shines o'er thee,
  While stars the darkness cheer,
While life is all before thee,
  Thy great Creator fear.

Remember thy Creator
  Before the dust returns
To earth, — for 't is its nature, —
  And life's last ember burns !
Before with God who gave it
  Thy spirit shall appear,
He cries, who died to save it,
  "Thy great Creator fear."

THANKSGIVING.

W HILE all creation sings for joy,
  Let thoughts of praise our hearts employ
Amid the harmony around,
Let not our tongues be silent found, —
  Our music still !

Ten thousand songs of praise we owe,
To Him whose glories round us flow,
To Him who bids our sorrows cease,
And fills our souls with sacred peace, —
    So great His love!

He guides our steps to living streams;
He leads our thoughts to holy themes;
Our wandering feet His love redeems,
By day He cheers us with His light,
And gives us sweet repose at night, —
    So rich His grace!

Let all who dwell below the sky
Join in the angels' minstrelsy,
Till earth no more is dark with sin,
And heavenly joys their course begin,
    No more to cease!

MARTHA AND MARY.

CUMBERED with earthly care,
    Her lot, to do and bear,
      To watch and wait,
Martha, with tender thought,
Her loving service brought;
It was for Christ she wrought
      Early and late.

Mary (a place most sweet!),
Low at the Saviour's feet,
      Hung on His word;

Hers, but in love sincere,
Waiting His voice to hear,
With meek and holy fear,
    Beside her Lord.

Be ours the bliss to sit,
Waiting at Jesus' feet, —
    The twain in one, —
Whether we hear or do,
With patient hearts and true,
To toil, and listen, too,
    To Him alone.

PERFECT IN CHRIST.

PERFECT in Christ, our spirits yearn to be;
    Perfect in manhood, — perfect, Lord, in Thee;
Strong in Thy strength, to love, to do, to bear;
Strong through Thy mighty arm, Thy ceaseless care.

Perfect in Christ, — no pain, no grief, nor loss,
Nor wearing toil, nor weight of wearying cross
Shall check the fond desire that bliss to feel, —
To bear the impress of the Spirit's seal.

As some glad morning bird, on joyous wings,
Leaps from her nest, and, soaring heavenward, sings, —
So would our souls, from sin's dark thraldom free,
Bound upward, Lord, to find their rest in Thee.

Perfect in Christ, these natures, weak and frail,
O'er sin and weakness shall at last prevail;
In Him complete, before Him reverent fall, —
Our Priest, our King, our Saviour, and our All.

FLEETING BLESSINGS.

FROM THE GERMAN.

THERE stood upon a river's bank
  A tall and branching tree,
Beneath whose shade a shepherd lived,
  From care and tumult free.
The rustling breeze, so mild and cool,
  Watched o'er his nightly rest;
And all day long the rippling stream
  In flashing light was drest.

But, ah! a torrent from the hills
  Rushed fiercely to the shore,
Tore from its root the stalwart tree,
  And down the current bore;
The flood passed by, and all was still,
  The broad, bright stream flowed on;
But when the shepherd sought the place,
  The sheltering tree was gone.

So sickness sweeps along the land;
  So death is drawing nigh;
And we, with all our life and joy,
  May droop and faint and die!
When God shall call our spirits home,
  We may no longer stay;
Dear Saviour, make us meet to dwell
  With Thee in endless day!

EARLY CONSECRATION.

TO Him who dwells above, all grace possessing ;
　　To Him, who sheds upon us every blessing, —
Ourselves, our all, we consecrate to-day ;
Our souls we yield to His delightful sway.

No earthly joy shall part, no sorrow sever,
Our hearts from Thee, our God, our King, forever ;
Our steadfast spirits shall in Thee confide,
And ever near Thy sacred throne abide.

Where'er we go, Thy fear shall be before us ;
Where'er we stay, no sin shall triumph o'er us.
In every hour, to Thee, our souls shall fly ;
To Thee, we yield our spirits, till we die.

The vows, blest Saviour, which our lips have spoken,
Shall never by deceitful hearts be broken ;
Still let Thy grace upon our efforts shine,
And we will evermore be only Thine !

OUR BELOVED TEACHERS.

AS fades the light of closing day,
　　As earth's fair flowers shut at even, —
So pass they from our paths away
　　Who led our infant feet to heaven.

The seed of living truth they sowed
  Shall in a genial harvest rise,
And children gathered home to God
  Be their bright honor in the skies.

Oh, happy they whose weekly toil
  Prepares fresh gems in heaven to shine;
Such wealth no worldly ill can spoil,
  Nor make its priceless worth decline.

Oh, happy they who, early taught
  To give their hearts, O Lord, to Thee,
Bind budding life and opening thought
  To life's great end, — eternity.

When earth and years and life are passed,
  And Heaven shall yield its long reward,
Gather our little flock at last
  To be forever with the Lord.

THE WORD OF GOD.

BLEST word of God, our help, our stay!
  Our star by night, our sun by day!
Our compass o'er life's pathless sea!
Our guide, O God, to heaven and Thee!

Blest source of truth, thy voice we hear;
Thy precepts love, thy law revere!
God's hand on every leaf we trace;
In every page we see His face!

How free the pardon it reveals !
How rich the covenant love it seals !
How safe on its Amen to rest, —
The Word of God, forever blest !

Far as the homes of man are known,
Reign Thou, Jehovah, God alone !
Send forth Thy Spirit with Thy word,
Till all earth's millions own Thee, Lord !

THE CLOSING WEEK.

HOW sweet the evening shadows fall,
    Advancing from the west,
As ends the weary week of toil,
    And comes the day of rest !

Bright o'er the earth the star of eve
    Her radiant beauty sheds ;
And myriad sisters calmly weave
    Their halo round our heads.

Rest, man, from labor ; rest from sin !
    The world's hard contest close ;
The holy hours with God begin ;
    Yield thee to sweet repose.

Bright o'er the earth the morning ray
    Its sacred light will cast, —
Fair emblem of the glorious day
    That evermore shall last.

SATURDAY EVENING.

DAILY the hum of eve returns ;
　　The twilight onward speeds, —
As night to day, and day to night,
　　In changeless round succeeds.

But busier is the evening hum
　　That swells upon the air ;
And quicker footsteps seem to tell
　　Of more than common care.

It is the night-fall of the week ;
　　It brings the joyful close
To earthly scenes awhile, and bids
　　The spirit take repose.

No work shall break the Sabbath rest ;
　　No care with harsh control
Shall bind, in mortal grasp, the strength
　　Of the immortal soul.

The day shall be a day of love,
　　With holy converse blest,
And urge the lingering spirit on,
　　To seek the heavenly rest.

Then let the evening hum be loud ;
　　'T is but the note that tells
Of preparation for the peace
　　That in the Sabbath dwells !

SABBATH MORNING.

HOW blest the Sabbath morning breaks
  O'er island, continent, and deep!
How sweet the thrill of holy peace,
  Whose pulses through the spirit creep!

All Nature wears a fairer hue;
  The balmy wind more fragrant blows;
While the blue canopy above
  Reflects and shares the glad repose.

The summer clouds that skirt the west,
  Heaped on the far horizon's rim,
Seem like an angel choir at rest,
  Intent to join earth's grateful hymn.

And thousands crowd from thousand homes,
  In every land where man has trod;
The babe to lisp, and age to learn,
  The wondrous works and ways of God.

Gather them in with loving zeal,
  From South to North, from East to West, —
To Him whose loving arms embrace,
  Whose loving voice proclaims them blest.

THE LORD'S DAY.

PLEASANT is the day of rest,
   Of the happy week the best;
Care and sorrow leave the breast
    On the Sabbath day.

Brightest beams the sun afar,
Sweetest is the evening star,
Fairest Nature's glories are,
    On the Sabbath day!

With the good I love to go
Where Salvation's tidings flow,
Breathing heaven while here below,
    On the Sabbath day!

Precious is the Sabbath-school,
Kind and gentle every rule,
Every scene of mercy full,
    On the Sabbath day!

Saviour, may I learn of Thee,
Meek and mild and good to be,
While Thy teachings come to me
    Every Sabbath day!

Guide me to the world above,
By Thy Spirit and Thy love;
May I all the joys improve,
    Of the Sabbath day!

Holier scenes await the just,
When they leave this mortal dust;
Teach me, Lord, in Thee to trust,
    On the Sabbath day!

ANNIVERSARY HYMN.[1]

[TUNE: *Italian Hymn.*]

BLEST be the day of rest,
  Of all the week the best, —
    Queen of the seven !
Day given to praise and pray,
Soothing life's weary way,
Turning our night to day,
    Emblem of heaven !

We love the house of prayer,
Breathings of heaven are there;
    Its hymns of praise
And messages of love
Attract our hearts above,
Bidding us come and prove
    Jesus' rich grace.

Blest be our gracious Lord !
Blest be His loving word, —
    " Let children come
To me," — their Guide and Friend !
He will our steps defend,
And, when life's toils shall end,
    Welcome us home.

[1] Sung at the Clarendon Street Baptist Church, Boston, October 14, 1889.

The hour that calls us here,
Marks one more happy year,
    In mercy given ;
When fades life's twilight ray,
Be ours the perfect day, —
Life, that feels no decay,
    Sabbath in heaven !

A SABBATH-SCHOOL HYMN.

FROM THE GERMAN.

ALL the week we spend
    Full of childish bliss ;
Every changing scene
Brings its happiness ;
Yet our joys would not be full,
Had we not the Sabbath-school.

Lovely is the dawn
Of each rising day ;
Loveliest, the morn
Of the Sabbath day !
Then our infant thoughts are full
Of the precious Sabbath-school.

To our happy ears,
Blessed News are brought, —
Tidings of the work
Love divine has wrought.
Gracious news and merciful, —
How we love the Sabbath-school !

Teachers, you are kind,
Thus to point the road
Leading us from sin
To our Father, God.
May we all be dutiful,
In the precious Sabbath-school!

Sweetly fades the light
Of each passing day;
Fairest is the night
Of the Sabbath day;
Then our hearts with praise are full,
For the precious Sabbath-school.

SABBATH EVENING.

SOFTLY fades the twilight ray
　　Of the holy Sabbath day,
Gently as life's setting sun,
When the Christian's course is run.

Night her solemn mantle spreads
O'er the earth, as daylight fades;
Nature rests in sweet repose,
At the holy Sabbath's close.

Peace is on the world abroad;
'T is the holy peace of God, —
Symbol of the peace within,
When the spirit rests from sin.

Still the Spirit lingers near,
Where the evening worshipper
Seeks communion with the skies,
Pressing onward to the prize.

Saviour, may our Sabbaths be
Days of peace and joy in Thee,
Till in heaven our souls repose,
Where the Sabbath ne'er shall close.

——∘∘≻⊙≺∘∘——

GOD BE OUR STAFF AND FRIEND.[1]

[TUNE : "*Bethany.*"]

FAR from the dear delights
   Of friends and home,
Summoned by life's high call,
   Pilgrims, we roam ;
Waifs on the world's highway,
Cheerful in hope, we stay ;
God make our darkness, day,
   Our winter, bloom.

Of scenes and seasons past,
   Fond memory tells,
Sweet as the lulling sounds
   Of vesper bells ;
But more than pleasures gone,
Are deeds of duty done,
And life's grand conquest won,—
   Draughts from deep wells.

---

[1] Written for a Young Men's Association of Boston, to be sung at a Thanksgiving Dinner ; also used at a Christmas Dinner, at San Francisco, 1884, by two hundred young men, away from home.

They gather, far away,
  The loved, the fair,
To keep this festal day
  With praise and prayer.
We know they love us still;
God save them all from ill,
Their ardent prayers fulfil, —
  The loved ones, there.

We trust His generous arm
  Through all life's fever;
God be our Staff and Friend,
  Strong to deliver;
Then, 'neath heaven's gorgeous dome,
No more like drifting foam,
The households, all at home,
  Shall feast forever.

THE YOUNG FOR CHRIST.

WRITTEN for the Societies of Christian Endeavor and other Young
Peoples' Societies' Convention held in Chicago, Ill., July, 1891.

DRAWN from a thousand distant homes,
  In Christ's dear love we meet;
The hosts who labor in His cause,
  In Christ's dear name we greet.

We hold one Lord, one central light;
  Our hopes, our aims are one, —
As planets, in their devious flight,
  Revolve around one sun.

Humbly, in loyal faith, we bow
　At one Redeemer's feet;
Our prayers, like clouds of incense, rise
　Before one mercy-seat.

If blossoms of the early spring
　Are doubly sweet and fair;
Our budding youth to God we bring,
　And leave the offering there.

One kingdom to our conquering Prince,
　From sea to sea, be given;
His will be done o'er the wide earth,
　Just as 't is done in heaven!

⸺∘∘⟩⟨∘∘⸺

ONWARD! CHRISTIAN WARRIORS.[1]

[Tune: "Webb."]

ONWARD! O Christian warriors,
　Where'er the trumpet calls;
Onward! the Leader summons,
　Beyond the sheltering walls;
Onward! the work awaits you,
　Fear not the world's cold frown;
Arm for the glorious conflict,
　Then wear the victor's crown.

Onward! with loving purpose,
　Where crime and sorrow reign;
Onward! like men in earnest;
　Onward! with heart and brain;

---

[1] For the Young People's rally, Dudley Street, Boston, November 26, 1894.

Onward! to save the erring,
  To break the bonds of sin ;
Onward! the lost to rescue ;
  Gems for Christ's crown to win.

Onward! the battle thickens ;
  The Captain's signal see ;
Onward! to deeds of glory ;
  Onward! to victory ;
Onward! with God assisting,
  Like soldiers true and brave,
Till o'er each conquered fortress
  Salvation's banners wave.

THE GOSPEL MINISTRY.

HARVEST-TIME.

FAR o'er the land the precious grain
　　Waves 'neath the sunny sky,
And ripening harvests offer sheaves
　　For immortality.

But who will reap the golden fruit,
　　And who at last will stand,
A faithful servant, crowned with joy,
　　O Lord, at Thy right hand?

Be ours the work, be ours the joy,
　　To us the charge be given,
To gather souls to Christ, and find
　　Our garnered sheaves in heaven.

Strength to the reapers, mighty God, —
　　Strength to the reapers send,
To bear the burden of the day,
　　And labor till the end.

There songs of triumph shall arise;
　　Then shall Thy kingdom come,
And echoing anthems greet at last
　　The heavenly harvest home.

SOWING AND REAPING.

A S whitening fields of precious grain
  On sunny hills expand,
The world's wide harvest, fully ripe,
  Waits for the reaper's hand.

But who shall reap the joyful crop?
  And who with gladness sing,
When he that sowed with tears and hope
  His sheaves shall homeward bring?

Each lowly toiler o'er earth's waste,
  Through paths of sadness led,
Shall bring some crown at last to rest
  On our Immanuel's head.

Then be our path through sun or shade,
  Be dark or bright our way,
We toil in hope and love, till dawns
  Heaven's pure and perfect day.

Then he that sowed on distant hills,
  In humble faith and prayer,
And he that reaped in fields at home,
  Shall sing together there.

Sower and reaper, from their Lord,
  Shall hear the joyful " Come ! "
Sower and reaper meet and sing
  Heaven's glorious " Harvest-home."

WELCOME TO A PASTOR.

COME to our waiting hearts and homes,
    O teacher, sent from Heaven ;
To thee, to guide our souls to God,
    The highest behest is given.

Come with the prophet's stern rebuke,
    The warning trump to sound ;
Come, point us to the Rock, wherein
    Alone is safety found.

Come with the words of heavenly grace,
    To cheer the fainting soul ;
Come with the Spirit's saving power,
    To make the wounded whole.

Come with the Shepherd's loving heart,
    The tender flock to guide,
To feed in pastures green, and lead
    Where living waters glide.

Come, for the waving field is ripe,
    The sickle waits thy hand,
And bending harvests, far and near,
    Around the reaper stand.

And when the workman, worn with toil,
    His finished labor leaves,
He, with rejoicing heart, shall bring
    Homeward his glorious sheaves.

A BLESSING SOUGHT UPON A PASTOR.

AND now the solemn deed is done ;
   The vow is pledged, the toil begun, —
Seal Thou, O God, the oath above,
And ratify the pledge of love.

The shepherd of Thy people bless ;
Gird him with Thy own holiness ;
In duty may his pleasure be,
His glory in his zeal for Thee.

Here let the ardent prayer arise,
Faith fix its grasp beyond the skies,
The tear of penitence be shed,
And myriads to the Saviour led.

Come, Spirit, here consent to dwell ;
The mists of earth and sin dispel ;
Blest Saviour, Thy own rights maintain,
Supreme in every bosom reign.

Oh, let our humble worship be
A grateful tribute, Lord, to Thee ;
And may these hallowed scenes of love
Fit us for purer joys above.

THE DIVINE PRESENCE INVOKED.

O THOU whose glory fills the sky,
    Exalted be Thy praise!
Let all below, let all on high,
    To Thee hosannas raise.

Light of the world, and Joy of all
    The saints around the throne,
While they, in holy reverence, fall,
    And worship Thee alone, —

Accepted at the throne of grace,
    Oh, may our praise ascend;
And unto us reveal Thy face,
    While at Thy feet we bend.

Contrite and humble hearts, O God,
    We fain would bring to Thee,
And, like the saints in Thine abode,
    Serve Thee in purity.

Spirit of God! with gracious power
    In Zion's courts appear,
And make it known, this sacred hour,
    That Zion's God is here.

BENEFITS OF THE MINISTRY.

BLEST is the hour when cares depart,
    And earthly scenes are far,—
When tears of woe forget to start,
And gently dawns upon the heart
    Devotion's holy star.

Blest is the place where angels bend
    To hear our worship rise,
Where kindred thoughts their musings blend,
And all the soul's affections tend
    Beyond the veiling skies.

Blest are the hallowed vows that bind
    Man to his work of love,—
Bind him to cheer the humble mind,
Console the weeping, lead the blind,
    And guide to joys above.

Sweet shall the song of glory swell,
    Spirit divine, to Thee,
When they whose work is finished well,
In Thy own courts of rest shall dwell,
    Blest through eternity.

GREAT IS THE WORK, BUT THINE THE POWER.

ORDINATION HYMN.

GREAT is the work, but Thine, O God, the power,
Our Strength in weakness, and in fear, our Tower;
Seal with Thy Spirit what our hands have done,
And crown with joyful fruits the work begun.

Sustain Thy servant in his varied toil;
Enrich the sower, bless the fruitful soil.
To prayer and faith, let souls redeemed be given;
Graces made perfect, spirits trained for heaven.

The work, the gifts, the heart to do and bear,
To us intrusted, crave, O God, Thy care;
Cheerful, we wait Thy will, our field assign;
Grant us Thy help, and be the glory Thine.

THE CHOSEN OF GOD.

OH, blest are they to whom 't is given
To shine as radiant stars above, —
The sons of light, the heirs of heaven,
The tenants of a world of love.

No grief shall draw the swelling tear
Of anguish from the pilgrim's eye;
No wearying toil, no anxious fear, —
The conqueror never more shall die.

No fierce disease, no chilling blast,
  Shall e'er that better land invade;
Faith's vision there shall change to sight,
  And glory o'er the scene be shed.

And there the peace that Jesus gives,
  In every ransomed soul shall reign;
There parted friends shall meet in joy,
  There mothers clasp their babes again.

O glorious world, in vain we strive
  To catch a glimpse of joys so high;
Nor thought can reach, nor words describe
  The scenes that glow beyond the sky!

With ardent zeal our souls are fired
  To pass beyond affliction's rod,
The crown of endless life to win,
  And reach the paradise of God.

THE SICKLE AND THE SHEAF.

'TIS mine to wield the sickle,
    Thine, Lord, to give the sheaf;
Through Thee the buds of spring-time
    Burst into life and leaf.
Mine is the toil of seed-time,
    And Thine the sun and rain;
Mine is the sweat and patience,
    And Thine the ripened grain.

Though wan and weary reapers
  Amid their labors fall,
And workmen, few and scattered,
  In vain for helpers call;
Though noontide heat burns fiercely,
  Or threatening tempest lowers, —
The gathering and the gleaning
  Is by mightier strength than ours.

We can wait with calm endurance,
  Though the drought curls up the leaf;
We can trust Jehovah-jireh
  To fill the swelling sheaf.
'T is ours the sturdy muscle,
  The vigorous arm to bring;
'T is Thine with heavenly blessing
  To make the valleys sing.

We shall reach the outmost furrows,
  In their drooping tassels dressed;
Beyond the field of labor,
  We shall find a place of rest.
We shall meet again the reapers
  Who share our grief and joy;
In the harvest-song of glory,
  We shall find one blest employ.

The eagle from her eyrie
  Flies forth at dawn of day,
Poised on her fearless pinions,
  With God to guide her way,
Soars upward, as the morning
  Glows with God's glory bright,
On, till her form, receding,
  Loses itself in light.

So, when the work is ended, —
    The garnered crop secure, —
And God shall bid His reapers
    Toil in the heat no more ;
We from all care and sorrow
    Shall find divine relief,
And lay before our Master
    The sickle and the sheaf.

CHRIST, THE CORNER-STONE.

WE build on Christ, our Corner-stone,
    That Rock of Ages we adore ;
Glory shall crown His name alone,
    Rock of our faith, eternal, sure !

Each stone we lay shall speak His praise ;
    And spire and pinnacle shall rise
In solemn grandeur, holy grace, —
    A grateful tribute to the skies.

In faith, this corner-stone we lay ;
    In hope, the house of God we rear.
Here God will answer when we pray ;
    Jehovah shall be worshipped here.

And when in silent dust we sleep,
    This sacred stone shall still record
That we and ours the covenant keep,
    That we and ours confess the Lord.

Newton Centre, August 27, 1887.

THE REAPERS.

FAR o'er the distant mountain ridge
  Climbs up the morning ray,
Whose growing light and warmth foretell
  The reign of perfect day;
O'er the wide fields the springing grain
  Shoots up its verdant threads,
Prophetic of the waving crop,
  And the wheat's ripened heads.

Joy for the reapers, when they lay
  Their gleaming sickles by;
And countless heaps of precious sheaves
  In yellow bundles lie.
From field and home, from plain and hill,
  Hasting in joyous throngs,
They make the bright and fragrant air
  Echo with grateful songs.

So shall the seed of truth and grace,
  Scattered by loving hands,
Harvests of untold wealth produce
  In all the earth's broad lands.
The germ, once dropped in fertile soil,
  A wondrous yield shall see,
Divinely sown, divinely fraught
  With immortality.

THE AGED PASTOR.

TO REV. C. A. THOMAS, D.D., BRANDON, VT.

HAIL, pastor ! with thy honored brow
　　And age's silver head ;
What memories of the loved and lost,
　　The living and the dead,
Crowd on the thoughts, as time recalls
　　The scenes of earlier years,
Weaving, like flowers with autumn leaves,
　　Garlands of joy and tears !

How forty years of life have made
　　Familiar faces strange !
While history with her pen records
　　How men and landscapes change ;
And near twice forty years, thy steps,
　　The wreath of cloud and flame
Has led, alternate, proving still
　　Thy covenant, God, the same.

Hail, pastor ! though the years have sped,
　　Faithful and trusted still ;
Trusted, on life's ascending slope,
　　Faithful, as slants the hill
Declining westward, where the sun
　　Turns toward the light of even,
And rests among the pillared clouds,
　　The gateways into heaven.

We bring no formal incense here ;
  We speak no empty praise ;
We hang not on the grand old oak,
  A wreath of heartless bays, —
While thankful memory wanders back
  Through all the growing years,
And eyes the busy world has dazed,
  Are dimmed with grateful tears.

The wide career our feet have trod ;
  The tasks of duty done ;
The conquered fields, the harvests gained ;
  The laurels sought and won, —
Are but his life, whose lips have taught
  Lessons of love and truth,
Embodied in our riper days,
  Taught in our tender youth.

And he whose lips and life alike
  Inspired us to be men,
Enshrined in Time's slow-gathering years,
  Shall live and move again,
As sculptured bust or painted form,
  The boast of ancient days,
Transmitted through all ages, still
  Lives for a joy and praise.

STEWARDSHIP.

Sung at the opening of the Seaman's Bazaar at Faneuil Hall, Boston, December 22, 1865.

IN marts of wealth, in gilded halls,
　　At power's exalted shrine,
With solemn voice, Jehovah calls,
　　" This wealth, this power, is mine."

Grateful, whate'er you need, enjoy,
　　Of all the bounteous store ;
The rest, 't is God's command, employ
　　To bless His suffering poor.

Give freely, like the fruitful seed ;
　　Give, like the sun and rain, —
Claiming no merit for the deed,
　　Nor asking aught again.

Those words of love, a rich reward
　　For every gift shall be, —
" Ye gave it unto Christ the Lord,
　　Ye gave it unto me."

GOD OF THE STARRY WORLDS ABOVE.

INVOCATION BEFORE THE DEDICATION OF A CHURCH.

GOD of the starry worlds above !
 God of Creation's goodly frame !
Glory, Thy robe ; Thy nature, love, —
 We rear this temple to Thy name.

Come, O Divine Shekinah, come !
 God over all, here hold Thy state !
Dwell in this house, — Thy chosen home ;
 These earthly courts Thy presence wait.

Come, like the peaceful twilight hour ;
 Come, like the glowing noontide ray.
Come, blessing by Thy glorious power ;
 Thy light diffuse, Thy grace display.

Come, as the gentle rain distils
 On new-mown fields, with quickening power ;
Revive us, from the heavenly hills,
 As dews revive the fainting flower.

And while our new hosannas here,
 With grateful heart and voice, we raise,
Descend in glorious grace, and rear
 A living temple to Thy praise.

COME, O DIVINE SHEKINAH, COME!

DEDICATION HYMN.

COME, O Divine Shekinah, come !
  With glory fill this new abode :
Come, — in our waiting souls there's room, —
  Display Thy power, — a present God.

Come to our shrine, O God of love, —
  Come as a God of love and power ;
Refresh Thy people from above,
  As dews refresh the drooping flower.

Come as a spring and fount of grace,
  Our temple with Thy light adorn,
As crimson rays of glory trace
  The gorgeous rising of the morn.

Come as a dove, with wings of peace,
  The sad to cheer, the bruised to heal,
The wounds that sin has made, to ease,
  The covenant of our life to seal.

Display Thy power, a present God ;
  Come, in our waiting souls there's room ;
With glory fill this new abode, —
  Come, O Divine Shekinah, come !

DEDICATION OF CARYVILLE CHAPEL.

COME, God the Father, for our hands have reared
This sacred shrine to Thy almighty name;
Come, as, of old, the solemn cloud appeared,
When to the temple veil Thy presence came.

Come, God the Son, display Thy healing power;
Accept our gift, and here set up Thy throne;
Our refuge Thou, our hope, our only tower,
Thy blood our ransom, reign in us alone.

Come, God the Spirit, teach our hearts to bring
Words of true prayer; our human lips inspire;
Thine is the temple, Thine the psalms we sing;
Our hearts are Thine; Thou art our souls' desire.

Come, Father, Son, and Spirit, God alone;
With reverent homage at Thy feet we bow.
We yield to Thee the work our hands have done, —
Our temple stands, its crowning glory, Thou.

GOD OF THE MOUNTAINS AND THE SEA.

RE-DEDICATION OF SEAMEN'S BETHEL, NOVEMBER 8, 1893.

" The abundance of the sea shall be converted unto Thee."

GOD of the mountains and the sea,
    Thy grateful people come to Thee,
To offer humble praise and prayer,
Thy love to own, — Thy grace to share.

Come, enter, Lord, our Bethel gates,
The temple for Thy presence waits;
Display Thy power, Thy grace make known;
In every heart erect Thy throne.

We dedicate the house to Thee;
Here let Thy saints Thy glory see,
Thy name to waiting souls reveal,
The contrite soothe, the wounded heal.

Gather from every land and shore
Glad trophies of Thy saving power,
And own the abundance of the sea,
A rightful offering, Lord, to Thee.

THE FATHERS, WHERE ARE THEY ?

WHILE centuries pass with solemn tread,
  And kingdoms sink, the Church remains, —
From life's immortal fountain fed,
  A light whose glory never wanes.

Where are the fathers ?   Once they stood
  With fervent faith, with armor bright;
Now, gathered with the sons of God,
  As stars at morning melt in light.

Here have they worshipped ; here they died ;
  And here their fallen mantles rest ;
Though gone from earth, their works abide,
  Like sunset glory in the west.

The censers, from their hands we take,
  And wave with hallowed incense still ;
They sleep in death ; their children wake,
  The lamps with golden light to fill.

Head of the Church, our All, our Guide,
  We own Thy power, we sing Thy grace ;
Still to new conquests Thou shalt ride,
  And added centuries speak Thy praise.

SWEEP ON, O CAR OF LIGHT!

DEDICATION OF THE GOSPEL CAR "EMMANUEL," IN
DENVER, COLORADO, MAY, 1893.

SWEEP on, O car of light!
    God bless thy holy flight;
      On thy wheels bring
Peace to the troubled breast,
And, to the weary, rest;
Glad, for thy mission blest,
      The angels sing.

Roll o'er the mountain's height;
Roll to the waters bright,
      The distant sea;
Visit the lonely vale,
Outfly the wintry gale;
Thy errand will not fail,
      God moves with thee.

Ride on, triumphant Lord !
Thy Spirit and Thy word
      Shall speed Thy way.
Scatter the shades of night;
Command, "Let there be light !"
Gird on Thy sword of might,
      And win the day.

Salvation's chariot, roll
On, till from pole to pole
      Christ reigns alone;

Till darkness turns to day,
Till earth shall choose His sway,
And all its trophies lay
Before His throne.

Davenport, Iowa, March, 1893.

FAREWELL TO THE OLD CHURCH.

DEAR is each well-remembered face,
Preserved in memory's shrine;
No scene will drive them from their place,
Or dim one precious line.
We linger, chained by love, to-day,
Amid the hallowed past,
And weep, as mournfully we say, —
This hour must be the last.

Here were our early footsteps brought,
And here, in riper years,
Our hearts, with joy or sorrow fraught,
Burdened with doubts and fears,
Like rivers, swollen with floods in spring,
Gushed with repentant grief,
Or felt the power of grace to bring
The needed, sweet relief.

Here pilgrims came, with weary feet,
And sat in pious trust,
And left, their pilgrimage complete,
The memory of the just;

We linger in the places where
  Their honored footsteps trod,
And trace the path of faith and prayer,
  By which they passed to God.

Here we have pledged the solemn vow
  To Him who reigns above;
Here learned in humble faith to bow
  To Him whose name is Love.
Here have we stood, a grateful band,
  Nor sought such bonds to part,—
Dear every brother's faithful hand,
  Each sister's loving heart.

As pilgrims, doomed awhile to roam
  On some far distant shore,—
Returned to seek their early home,
  Their well known cottage-door,—
Mourn for the friends of earlier times,
  For many an honored head,—
Some passed, long since, to other climes,
  Some, sleeping with the dead,—

Some, rifled of their youthful bloom,
  White rose-leaves on their brow,
Some, shadowed o'er by clouds of gloom,—
  Alas, how altered now!—
We seek the friends to memory dear,—
  How many — but in vain;
Oh, who will bring our loved ones here,
  Just as they were, again?

Gone, but not lost,— in nobler spheres,
  Redeemed and saved, they shine;

Each hand a palm of glory bears,
   Each brow, a light divine;
And we on earth, and they above,
   Led by one Shepherd's hand,
Encircled by one wreath of love,
   Form still one blessed band.

T' is done, — we leave the hallowed ground,
   But keep what grace has done ;
The rushing tide of life has found
   New victories to be won ;
But, temple, where the saints have prayed,
   Where God has deigned to dwell,
How shall we let thy glory fade ?
   How shall we say " farewell " ?

How shall we leave the sacred shrine
   Where once our fathers trod ;
How darken here the light divine
   Of those who walked with God ?
With quivering lip, with tearful eye,
   With calm, but bleeding heart,
We sit in mournful sympathy,
   And breathe the word, — Depart.

But yonder, springs in joyous light,
   A temple high and pure ;
The tenants, clad in raiment bright,
   Shall leave its courts no more ;
No night shall darken o'er its wall ;
   No sigh with anthems blend ;
No mourners weep, no shadow fall, —
   Its worship never end.

Then they that sowed in faith and tears
    Shall reap in endless joy;
And saints from all the varied years,
    Shall find one glad employ.
Cemented by one bond of love,
    Striking one heavenly strain.
Our members all shall meet above,
    BALDWIN PLACE CHURCH again.

THE LIVING CHURCH.

THE ROCK OF AGES.[1]

BUILT on the Rock of Ages, Lord,
    Thy living Church abides secure;
Nations and men may fade away,
    Thy work of Grace shall still endure.

This temple, to Thine honor reared,
    Waits for Thy crowning presence now;
Accept the work our hands have wrought;
    We are but dust, — almighty, Thou.

Here men of God shall speak thy praise;
    Treasures of thought be gathered here;
And truth, from living lips dispensed,
    Fall, welcome, on the listening ear.

With humble faith, with holy joy,
    We lay our gift before Thy face:
'T is dark, but for Thy radiant light;
    'T is poor, but for Thy heavenly Grace.

Then let Thy glorious presence, Lord,
    O'er all the hallowed work appear;
And let the living record stand, —
    The place is holy; God is here.

[1] Sung at the dedication of a church edifice.

GOD ALL IN ALL.[1]

GOD of all grace, supreme, alone;
    Thy robe, the light; the heavens, Thy throne;
The winds, Thy voice; Thy path, the sea, —
Reverent, we bow, and worship Thee.

In all Thy works, Thy hand we trace;
Creation does but veil Thy face.
Thy life, our life; Thy warmth, our spring;
Our only rest, Thy sheltering wing.

Thy breath makes every pulse-beat thrill;
We feel the whispers of Thy will;
We come, we go, at Thy command;
We wait the moving of Thy hand.

Plant in our hearts Thy love and fear;
Teach us Thy precepts to revere;
And fashion us, through grace, to be
But living temples meet for Thee.

DIVINE PROVIDENCE.

DEDICATION HYMN.

OH, praise ye Jehovah; His glory proclaim!
    Bring joyful hosannas to honor His name;
With glad acclamations His altar draw near;
Bow low to His footstool; Jehovah is here.

[1] Sung at Tremont Temple, Boston, February 24, 1890.

He speaks in creation; He rules o'er the flood,
Through Nature's wide realm the Omnipotent God;
But chooses the temples we build to His praise,
As shrines for His name, and abodes of His grace.

Then come where we wait Thy blessing to prove,
Thou, strong to redeem, and Thou, matchless in love;
Like light breaking forth from the gates of the morn,
May rays from Thy glory this temple adorn!

THE REDEEMER'S TEARS.

'TWAS at the grave of Lazarus,
    The two fond sisters, in their sackcloth robes,
Drenched in affliction, and the godless Jews,
In that one scene made lovely, as they went
To weep with Mary at the sepulchre,
Stood there, a grieving circle. She came forth,
Obedient, e'en in sorrow, to the call
Of Him who called for her. There was no voice
Among the whited stones that pointed out
The home of dead men, and no scenery,
Or sweet, or gorgeous, in the hills or vales
Of loveliest form and hue that spread around them,
To call forth a moment's admiration;
There was one absorbing sense of sorrow,
That burned at the heart's core. The glorious voice
Of Him who raised, triumphant, the dead brother
Had not broke out in holy thanksgiving;
But there they stood, consumed by their deep grief,
And there — there, *Jesus wept.*

The evening sun slanted among the hills
Where Zion's temple shone.   Down the descent
Of Olivet a joyous crowd advanced,
Singing hosannas unto Him that came, —
The Son of David, and yet David's Lord,
The prophet of their nation ; not as when
Each heart beat sadly, and the silent tears
Stole down the cheeks of all the sorrowing band
At the dead brother's tomb.   Now all was gay
And bright.   But unto a devoted place,
Cursed as the dwelling of the crucifiers,
The crucifiers of the Lord of life
And glory, they were drawing near.   The crowd,
Rejoicing in their city, and the sheen
Of their own glorious temple, pressed their way,
Thoughtless of coming evil.   But, behold!
Amid the happy throng one stretched His gaze
Into eternity, soon to receive
The uncomforted inhabitants, whose towers
Were ready to their fall, — the inhabitants
Who knew not when their visitation came ;
One gazed in silent sadness as He thought
Upon their coming fate, and *Jesus wept.*

Wept twice on earth, — once at the tomb of him
Whose sorrowing sisters He had loved ; and once,
When He foresaw Jerusalem's dread fate.

THE LAST SUPPER.

JOHN XIII. 1; XIV. 14, 23, 27.

FROM the villages retiring,
  Burning with a holy flame,
Though His last days were expiring,
  Jesus to the city came :
Still His own disciples loving,
  He had words of peace to say ;
Anxious thoughts His breast were moving
  As drew near the farewell day.

Round the sacred table sitting,
  When the traitorous foe had gone,
Love their souls more closely knitting,
  As the dreadful scene drew on,
Pledges of His love He gave them,
  Sweet memorials of His name ;
Then declared how He, to save them,
  From the Father's bosom came.

Peace I leave — my dying token —
  'T is my peace I give to you ;
Let the words that I have spoken
  Be your trust and comfort too.
For a little while I leave you,
  To my Father I must go ;
Yet I will not — will not grieve you,
  But the Comforter bestow.

Mansions in yon world of glory,
  I am going to prepare ;
Though the path be dark and gory,
  Ye shall all be with Me there.
Father, let Thy mercy guide them,
  Sanctify them by Thy grace ;
And, whatever woes betide them,
  Let them see Thy smiling face.

GETHSEMANE.

BEYOND where Cedron's waters flow,
  Behold the suffering Saviour go,
    To sad Gethsemane.
His countenance is all divine ;
Yet grief appears in every line.

He bows beneath the sins of men ;
He cries to God, and cries again,
    In sad Gethsemane.
He lifts His mournful eyes above, —
" My Father, can this cup remove ? "

With gentle resignation still,
He yielded to His Father's will,
    In sad Gethsemane ;
" Behold Me here, Thine only Son ;
And, Father, let Thy will be done."

The Father heard; and angels, there,
Sustained the Son of God in prayer,
    In sad Gethsemane ;
He drank the dreadful cup of pain,
Then rose to life and joy again.

When storms of sorrow round us sweep,
And scenes of anguish make us weep,
    To sad Gethsemane
We 'll look, and see the Saviour there,
And humbly bow, like Him, in prayer.

THE LORD IS RISEN!

THE Lord is risen ! and angels wait
  Around the place where Jesus slept;
'Mid Roman swords and Jewish hate,
  Unseen, their loving watch they kept.

The Lord is risen ! The guard, the seal,
  Conspire to hold their trust, in vain.
He lives ! He lives ! Before Him kneel !
  The Conqueror now, though once the Slain.

The Lord is risen ! The timid few
  Heard with faint faith the wondrous word ;
"Can such deep mystery be true ?"
  "Where, gardener, hast thou laid my Lord ? "

He looked! He spoke!—His loving word
  Made the sad woman's heart rejoice;
"Mary,"—she knew her risen Lord;
  "Rabboni,"—'t is the Master's voice!

The Lord is risen!—Death's reign is o'er;
  The goal achieved, the victory won.
The Lord is risen! His name adore!
  The great atoning work is done!

THE LIVING CHURCH SWEEPS ON.[1]

CENTENNIAL HYMN.

BLEST be the ancient men whose feet
  Once sought these holy towers;
Blest be the saints whose voices sweet
  Hallowed the sacred hours.

Blest be the sires whose Christly speech
  In silvery accents flowed;
So skilled to pray, so skilled to preach,—
  Men grandly taught of God.

Numbered among the holy dead,
  Their forms from earth are gone;
Through all the century's silent tread,
  The Living Church sweeps on.

[1] Written for the Church of the Epiphany, New York City, May 10, 1891.

Have faith in God; His sceptred arm
  O'er time and tempest reigns;
His little flock, secure from harm,
  Safe on the Rock remains.

God of our fathers, in Thy name
  Our banners still we raise;
Thy changeless love, the years proclaim,
  And swell Thy sounding praise.

A RICH BEQUEST.

WHERE are the ancient men who reared
    In faith this honored shrine?
Where are the godly souls whose deeds
  On this fair record shine?

Joined to yon glorious host on high, —
  The heavenly Bridegroom's train;
Choice souls! — to them, to live was Christ,
  To them, to die was gain.

The Church, the world, their native land,
  They served with noble lives;
Loved and lamented! and their faith,
  A rich bequest, survives.

The long procession upward winds
  To the celestial shore;
The living, loving, keep the path
  The leaders trod before.

As beams the sun from age to age,
  With undiminished blaze,
Lord, may the light they kindled here
  Shine ever to Thy praise.

Head of the Church, while rolling years
  Their solemn course fulfil,
Smile on the work the fathers wrought,
  And bless their children still.

MAY 9, 1890.

CHRISTIAN EXPERIENCE.

THE PRESENT AND THE ETERNAL.

'TIS but a step to yon bright world,
  The home above the skies ;
As evening beauty scarcely pales,
  E'er morning's glories rise.

'T is but an hour, — and scenes of grief
  Shall change to joy again,
As rainbows crown the passing cloud
  With sunlight, after rain.

A tale of woe, a sad farewell,
  A shriek of pain or grief, —
'T is but a wave that stirs the air,
  A breeze that fans the leaf.

'T is but a shadow, when the sun
  Is hid in dim eclipse ;
'T is but a frozen dewdrop when
  The frost the rose-leaf nips.

The frost dissolves ; the dew exhales ;
  The rose-tree blooms anew ;
The shadow passes ; burns the sun,
  As erst, in heaven's bright blue.

'T is but a night when darkness rules,
  And mortals tread uncertain ;
Quick comes the dawn, and beaming morn
  Pours sunlight through the curtain.

Not time, nor space, nor work shall e'er
  Love's clasping tendrils sever ;
As clinging vines still upward climb,
  And, climbing, cling forever.

O blessed bond of loving hearts ;
  Blest union, never broken ;
Blest land, where tears are never shed,
  And farewells never spoken !

Through joy and grief, through pain and death,
  We tread towards heaven's high portal,
And yield, unmoved, the things that change,
  For flowers and fruits immortal.

November 7, 1866.

DESPONDENCY.

THE clouds of affliction and pain
    Have shrouded in mourning the sky ;
Thick darkness conceals all the plain,
    And tempests are hurrying by.
I cry out, with sorrow o'erwhelmed,
    While tears from my weeping eyes break ;
When shall I with sorrow be done ;
    Oh, when in Thy likeness awake ?

Yet 't is not my friends that I mourn, —
  I weep not that loved ones retire;
I grieve not that I am forlorn,
  And earthly enjoyments expire.
My Saviour! my Saviour! my God!
  Why dost Thou my spirit forsake?
Oh, when shall I throw off my load?
  Oh, when in Thy likeness awake?

The winds of temptation arise,
  And howl o'er my pathway of night;
The cloud never moves from the skies,
  To show the blest beaming of light.
With madness I rush into sin,
  Then grief comes, my poor heart to break;
When shall I be sinful no more?
  Oh, when in Thy likeness awake?

Oh, when shall my Sabbaths again
  Be sweet and delightful to me?
When shall I, my Saviour, obtain
  Communion of spirit with Thee?
This darkness and dulness I long,
  I long from my bosom to shake;
When shall I to gladness return?
  Oh, when in Thy likeness awake?

My Saviour! my Saviour! I wait,
  I wait till Thy glory arise;
I watch at Thy merciful gate,
  Till light bursts again from the skies.
Then gladness shall swell in my breast,
  No more these complaints shall I make;
But calmly my spirit shall rest,
  And I, in Thy likeness, awake.

CONSECRATION.

'TWAS God who heard when hope was dying;
    'T was God who made me look and live.
He saw me to His covenant flying,
    And condescended to forgive.

From long distress and thoughts of anguish,
    He gave my spirit sweet release ;
No more in sorrow left to languish,
    My bosom now has perfect peace.

Tell me, dear Saviour, what oblation
    To Heaven's high altar shall I bring ?
What sacrifice for such salvation,
    To Thee my life, my God, my King ?

My soul, myself, my all, I give Thee,
    Forever to be Thine alone ;
And let my praise — for Thou art worthy —
    Swell in rich numbers to Thy throne.

Accept my service, blessed Spirit,
    Till I my course on earth have sped ;
Then let me endless life inherit,
    Still onward by Thy guidance led.

IMPORTUNITY IN PRAYER.

"LET ME GO, FOR THE DAY BREAKETH."

GO? When the promise stands,
　　That a faithful God will hear !
Go? when the Intercessor's voice
　　Sounds in the Almighty's ear !
Go? When my inmost spirit breaks,
　　For the longing it hath for Thee !
Oh, no ! the Blessed shall not go,
　　Until He blesses me !

There is life in the gracious God, —
　　A fountain that cannot fail;
A gentle hand that can wipe the tear,
　　And soothe the contrite wail.
There is One who can speak the word,
　　And the blind shall rise and see;
Oh, then, the Blessed shall not go,
　　Until He blesseth me !

Yes, ashes and dust may plead
　　With the Holy One above;
And the earnest prayer ascend
　　To the God whose name is Love;
Angels may not be sent
　　In their heavenly ministry, —
But the Blessed shall never go,
　　Until He blesseth me.

My spirit glows in faith,
  My heart in strong desire ;
And God will come — will come
  Ere the lamp of life expire.
Thou wilt not desert, I know,
  The heart that clings to Thee ;
Oh, no ! the Blessed will not go,
  Until He blesseth me !

FAR FROM EARTH.

FAR from earth retreating,
  From its scenes so fleeting,
Lord, I come to Thee.
From Thy glorious dwelling,
Where heaven's joys are welling,
  Saviour, look on me !
    Let Thy light
    Dispel my night ;
Let Thy holy peace come o'er me,
While I bend before Thee.

Worldly hopes, I speak not,
Worldly good, I seek not,
  Here before Thy throne ;
Let Thy Spirit, shining,
Come, from sin refining ;
  Let Thy blood atone.
    From my heart
    Let earth depart,
Every idol object sever ;
In me reign forever.

Lord, behold me waiting,
Freely consecrating
  All I have to Thee;
Near Thy cross abiding,
In Thy love confiding,
  Longing Thine to be.
    Come, then, come,
    My heart illume;
Make my soul Thy Spirit's dwelling,
Rebel thoughts expelling.

Grace has made me willing, —
Grace, my spirit filling;
  Lord, the praise be Thine;
When, with free salvation,
Saved from condemnation,
  Near Thy throne I shine,
    Then the strain
    Shall swell again, —
Glory to Thy love, blest Saviour!
Reign, O reign, forever!

—————•o;o;oo—————

PASSING ON, PASSING UP.

PASSING on, passing up, to the platform of life,
  Its honors, its trials, its glory, its strife;
Passing on, passing up, as day follows on day, —
Passing on, passing up, and then, passing away.

The honored, the cherished, the good, have passed on,
Like morning stars, lost in the glow of the sun, —
The seal on their virtues, in safety their fame,
No stain on their record, no blot on their name.

The silver-tongued prophet sleeps silent, aside ;
The statesman lies low in his manhood's young pride ;
Our comrades in toil have passed on before, —
Passing on, passing up, to the heavenly shore.

Still the flag of distress, in our sight, is unfurled ;
Still waits for the sickle, the field of the world ;
Still high on the tower where the herald has been,
Is emblazoned the call, " Wanted, Christians, and men ! ''

O men for the times ! with heart and with hands,
Go, toil where the Master your labor demands ;
And, faithful, toil on, till the close of the day, —
Passing onward and upward, and passing away.

MAY, 1868.

THY WILL, O LORD, BE DONE.

THY way, O God, is best, —
   Thy way, not mine ;
Patient beneath Thy rod,
Quick to obey Thy nod,
Because Thou art my God, —
   Thy way, not mine.

I know Thy wise design ;
   Thy will is mine.
From earthly dross refine,
Shape to the mould divine,
My soul shall ne'er repine, —
   Thy will, not mine.

Clay in the potter's hand,
   Thy will is mine.

'T is Thine, the vase to make,
Or Thine, dear Lord, to break ;
Thine, or to give, or take, —
Thy will, not mine.

Sorrow, or joy, be sent, —
Thy will is mine ;
In all, Thy love I see ;
Whate'er my lot may be,
I trust my all to Thee, —
Thy will is mine.

March 30, 1892.

YE ARE NOT YOUR OWN.

OH, not my own these verdant hills,
And fruits and flowers, and stream and wood;
But His, who all with glory fills,
Who bought me with His precious blood !

Oh, not my own this wondrous frame,
Its curious work, its living soul;
But His, who for my ransom came,
Slain for my sake, — He claims the whole !

Oh, not my own, the grace that keeps
My feet from fierce temptations free !
Oh, not my own, the thought that leaps,
Adoring, blessed Lord, to Thee !

Oh, not my own ! I 'll soar and sing,
When life, and all its toils, are o'er ;
And Thou Thy trembling lamb shalt bring
Safe home, — to wander never more !

ALL THINGS ARE YOURS.

ALL that is pleasant to the eye, —
  The earth with all her stores,
The glowing sun, the rainbow's dye, —
  All present things are yours.

The throne where all the holy bow ;
  The mansions where they rest ;
The sweet, refreshing gales that blow ;
  The raptures of the blest ;

The harp, the robes, the diadem ;
  The never-fading flowers ;
Heaven's shaded walks and living stream, —
  All coming things are yours !

All things are yours, for Jesus dwells
  Within your glowing heart ;
And many a raptured feeling tells,
  He never will depart.

All things are yours, and Christ is God's !
  Tho' grief your day obscures,
Soon you shall see heaven's bright abode,
  And know that all is yours !

A PRESENT HELP IN TROUBLE.

WHEN God is near,
    O heart with sorrow swelling,
Pour out thy grief, thy tale of anguish telling;
    And love will wipe each flowing tear,
    When God is near.

When God comes nigh,
Peace quells the soul's commotion,
And sheds the sweet serene of calm devotion;
    And every cloud of grief must fly,
    When God comes nigh.

When God comes near,
Let every heart receive Him;
Slight not the Spirit's call, nor dare to grieve Him;
    " The still small voice," be wise to hear,
    When God is near.

When God is nigh,
Covet not earthly pleasure,
But seek in heaven an ever-during treasure;
    Each tear is seen, and heard each sigh,
    When God is nigh.

THERE'S REST FOR THEE.

THERE'S rest for thee,
　　Fond heart, who life art wasting.
　Remit thy eager search of earth-born bliss ;
　The Saviour seek — true fount of happiness.
Flee to that refuge while thy days are hasting !

　　There's peace for thee ;
Whose heart is all commotion,
　　The voice of Christ can calm the troubled sea.
　　Forsake thy sins, and to His covenant flee,
And sweet shall be thy course o'er life's rough ocean.

　　There's hope for thee,
Whose soul is rent with sadness.
　　With humble trust thy all to Jesus give ;
　Give Him thy heart, for Him resolve,
Then, on thy night, shall rise the star of gladness.

　　There's life for thee,
Who, weary with delaying,
　　Shalt haste to Jesus, while He waits to save,
　Who for thy life His life so freely gave, —
The sacred call of love at once obeying.

ALL ONE IN CHRIST.

ALL one in Christ, — though, plains and hills
    dividing,
Our earthly homes are far asunder placed ;
All one in Christ, — in Him our souls abiding,
    O'er the broad earth or on the ocean waste.

All one in Christ, — bound in divine communion,
    And He the cynosure, — the changeless Word.
One Sovereign rules ; the watchword of our union,
    One faith, one baptism, and one risen Lord.

All one in Christ, — should grief, or joy, betide us ;
    Or health, or sickness, life, or death, be ours, —
His word shall cheer, His loving hand shall guide us,
    His name revive, like incense-breathing flowers.

All one in Christ, — His voice the fiercest battle,
    Like Galilee's wild waves, can quell and calm ;
Assuage the tumult, still the tempest's rattle,
    For pain give ease, for waiting, victory's psalm.

All one in Christ, — man's passions, like the billow,
    May roar and dash around with frightful shock ;
Held in His leash, light as the air-swept willow,
    They lash in vain the Everlasting Rock.

All one in Christ, — our paths, in varied winding,
    May seem unheeding of Heaven's grand accord ;
The rills of life, new channels ever finding,
    Shall all converge in Him, our loving Lord.

All one in Christ, — life's discipline and rasping
  May fret, and grind, and wear the sufferer down;
But there's a gracious Hand, the faint form clasping, —
  The cross to-day; be patient, then the crown.

All one in Christ, — the fields must have their tilling;
  O'er earth, His heritage, for Him we roam;
With ready hands we toil, and spirit willing,
  Till the great Husbandman shall call us home.

All one in Christ, — soon will the great forever
  Yield to the weary workers needed rest;
Toil waste no more, and sorrow grieve, — no, never, —
  The loved disciple on the Master's breast.

FOLLOWING CHRIST.

WITH willing hearts we tread
    The path the Saviour trod;
We love the example of our Head,
    The glorious Lamb of God.

On Thee, on Thee alone,
    Our hope and faith rely, —
O Thou, who didst for sin atone,
    Who didst for sinners die!

We trust Thy sacrifice;
    To Thy dear cross we flee.
Oh, may we die to sin, and rise
    To life and bliss with Thee.

CHRISTIAN FELLOWSHIP.

PLANTED in Christ, the living vine,
This day with one accord,
Ourselves, with humble faith and joy,
We yield to Thee, O Lord!

Joined in one body may we be;
One inward life partake;
One be our heart; one heavenly hope
In every bosom wake!

In prayer, in effort, tears, and toils,
One wisdom be our guide;
Taught by one Spirit from above,
In Thee may we abide.

Complete in us, whom grace hath called,
Thy glorious work begun, —
O Thou, in whom the Church on earth,
And Church in heaven, are one!

Around this feeble, trusting band,
Thy sheltering pinions spread,
Nor let the storms of trial beat
Too fiercely on our head!

Then, when, among the saints in light,
Our joyful spirits shine,
Shall anthems of immortal praise,
O Lamb of God, be Thine!

JESUS IS PASSING BY.

"THE RESOLVE."

THE voice of joyful ones I hear,
    It warbles sweet and high;
Arise, my soul, the Lord is near, —
    Jesus is passing by!

Long have I waited at the pool;
    Why should I longer stay?
Come, Saviour, make my spirit whole;
    My Saviour, come away!

No longer will I, listless, wait;
    No more, excuses frame;
No more with earth and sin debate;
    No more Thy goodness blame.

The world no more shall have my heart;
    I will rebel no more;
From cherished sin, to-day, I part,
    And sparing Love adore.

The chief of sinners, Lord! I come,
    And cast myself on Thee;
Thou art the weary wanderer's home, —
    My home, dear Saviour, be!

The work is done; my God is mine, —
    Glory to God! I sing;
Jesus, the glory all be Thine;
    Let all creation ring!

A FORETASTE OF HEAVEN.

BLEST be the sacred tie that binds
  All Christian hearts in one;
Blest be the fellowships of earth, —
  The joy of heaven begun.

Blest be the scenes, the sacred scenes,
  When tears forget to start;
When soul, to happy soul, responds,
  And heart, to Christian heart.

Blest be the hours, the sacred hours,
  Foretaste of bliss above;
Each speaking eye, each throbbing pulse,
  Speaks, throbs, with Christian love.

Dear antepast of joys to come!
  Earth hails the radiant glow;
Light from that world illumines this,
  And heaven is felt below.

OCTOBER 12, 1886.

ABOUNDING MERCY.

AFTER TWO HUNDRED YEARS.

OH! sing to the praise of the Saviour above,
  Unchanging His wisdom, immortal His love;
Extolled be His mercy, and hallowed His name,
Who dwelt in the pillar of cloud and of flame.

His hand through the desert has guided our way,
Our shelter by night, and our glory by day;
The fathers are garnered at rest in the grave, —
But Jesus still triumphs, almighty to save.

The harvests are waving, as waves the ripe grain,
Fruit, once sown in tears, of the centuries twain;
The billows no more beat with furious shock;
The Church safely stands on its basis of rock.

More ages, still following, their circuit shall run;
More gems light the crown which our Saviour has
      won;
More trophies of grace to their Lord shall be given, —
Then echo the Jubilee anthem in heaven.

UP! YE SAINTS!

FROM THE GERMAN.

UP! ye saints, and raise
    Songs of grateful praise;
While your hearts are warm,
While, in calm or storm,
River, hill, and tree,
You, your God can see,
All the glories showing
Of His love o'erflowing!

    Once you trod the path
    Leading on to death;
    With the Spirit strove,
    Scorned His offered love,

And, with wicked hands,
Burst His sacred bands.
All this He forgave you;
How He longed to save you!

Light, He sweetly shed,—
Peace about you spread;
O'er the guilty soul
Bade salvation roll.
Cleansed your heart from sin,
Kindly entered in;—
Scattered all your sadness,
Filled your souls with gladness!

Tell your joys abroad!
Praise your Saviour, God!
Sinful wanderers bring
From their wandering,
Back to Him, who knows
All their wants and woes,—
Joyfully returning
While His love is yearning.

Then, what glories wait
Your celestial state!
Ever ye shall shine,
Clothed in light divine,
Where the ransomed sing,
And glad voices ring,—
While each spirit raises
Never-ending praises!

SALVATION.

WHAT peace is this that springs within my mind;
     What light and joy, where all was dark and
        blind?
How lovely all creation looks to me!
Tell me, my soul, can this Salvation be?

My weight of guilt has hasted all away;
I cannot make one thought of sadness stay;
From God, in terror, I no longer flee, —
Tell me, my soul, can this Salvation be?

All Nature seems to echo, "God is love!"
Sweet voice! it rings around me and above;
That glorious God, my spirit sighs to see, —
Tell me, my soul, can this Salvation be?

Ye men of God, I love your blest retreat;
I love your names; converse with you is sweet;
To dwell in God's dear house, is bliss to me, —
Tell me, my soul, can this Salvation be?

O blessed, gracious Saviour, well I know,
'T is from Thy love these fond emotions flow;
'T is from Salvation's fount, so full and free,
These joys, so pure and grateful, come to me.

While to the cross, my heart, dependent, clings,
"Glory to God!" my happy spirit sings.
No storms of earth my pleasure can impair;
Peace fills my bosom, — peace is rooted there.

THE TRUSTING SOUL.

PSALM XCI.

THE man who dwells
    Beneath Thy shade, Most High,
  Shall in Thy love abide;
    Thy grace dispels
His fears, when storms are nigh;
  Thou dost His footsteps guide.
The Lord from pestilence will guard Thee,
And no temptation shall retard thee;
    'T is God that heals.

    Beneath His wing
Thy steadfast soul shall trust;
  His truth shall be thy shield,
    Tho' death should bring
His thousands to the dust,
  And fainting hope should yield;
Tho' dark disease should hover by thee,
No hurtful damp shall e'er come nigh thee,
    Nor sorrow sting.

    Because thy heart
Hath made its refuge God,
  No woe shall thee befall;
    No poisoned dart,
No desolating rod,
  Shall mix thy life with gall;
But angels in their hands shall bear thee
Above the foes that would ensnare thee,
    And peace impart.

Because the soul
Hath set on Me his love,
I will from danger save ;
And peace shall roll
By him whom I approve,
Its soft and soothing wave,
His voice shall call, and I will hear him,
And in his trouble will be near him
Till joy be full.

BLEST BE THE HOLY BANDS.[1]

BLEST be the holy bands,
Uniting hearts and hands, —
One chain of love ;
One life, one hope, one aim ;
One faith in one blest Name ;
Our Rock, our God, the same,
Below, above.

Cleansed by atoning blood,
Washed in one healing flood,
One God we own ;
Ours, to accept His word,
Ours, to obey our Lord,
Making, with glad accord,
Our hearts His throne.

The whispering pine and palm
Shall blend in one sweet psalm,
Dear Lord, to Thee ;

[1] Reception at Richmond, Va., of 500 New England guests, May, 1886.

We seek the world to save ;
We form one army brave,
As thousand drops, one wave,
All streams, one sea.

Glory to God our King !
Saviour, Thy kingdom bring,
Thy will be done ;
Exert Thy glorious might,
Put all Thy foes to flight ;
Triumphant, claim Thy right,
And wear Thy crown.

BLEST BE THE BONDS OF CHRISTIAN LOVE.

BLEST be the bonds of Christian love
That bind our hearts in one ;
Blest foretaste of the bliss above, —
Our heaven on earth begun.

Kindred in Christ, our hopes we rest,
Alike on His dear name ;
One love inspires each throbbing breast, —
Our covenant-vows, the same.

Our prayers from many hearts ascend, —
One cloud before the throne ;
Our many grateful voices blend
In one harmonious tone.

So joy for joy, and tear for tear,
And grace for grace is given ;
So the glad harvest, ripened here,
Shall crown our love in heaven.

A CENTENARY HYMN.[1]

WE reap to-day the glorious fruit
    Of labor, prayers, and tears,
And, joyful, sing the precious root,
    Strong with its hundred years.

In cold and heat, in calm and storm,
    The thickening fibres spread, —
Modelled in heaven, its life and form
    With heavenly juices fed.

And far o'er all these sunny slopes,
    The outstretched boughs expand;
True to the fathers' early hopes,
    It shades and fills the land.

Honored and loved, where none molests, —
    His labor finished well, —
The noble planter calmly rests,
    Where first the fruitage fell.

And still the healing branches toss,
    And still its head it rears,
Feels no decay, and shows no loss,
    Strong with its hundred years.

Come from the weary toil and strife,
    And sit beneath the shade;
And hail it, like the tree of life,
    Whose leaf shall never fade.

[1] For the First Baptist Church, Haverhill, Mass., 1865.

MISSIONARY HYMNS AND ODES.

PRAYER FOR THE HEATHEN.

GOD of the ocean and the shore,
　　Thy law we love, Thy name adore !
Let the abundance of the sea,
Be, Lord, converted unto Thee !

Through every ship that cleaves the wave,
Proclaim Thy love, Thy power to save ;
From tropic seas to either pole,
Loudly let Heaven's sweet anthem roll!

Speak, Lord, and o'er the stormy flood,
Thy name shall swell, Thy peace shall brood,
Thy praise shall ring from every voice,
And distant climes in Thee rejoice!

Then land and sea, then flood and shore,
Through man redeemed, shall bless Thy power;
And earth and sea and heaven shall own
Salvation's glorious triumph won !

HERALDS OF SALVATION.

GO, heralds of Salvation, forth ;
　　Go, in your heavenly Master's name,
From east to west, from south to north,
　　The glorious Gospel, wide proclaim !

Go, bid the thirsty desert bloom ;
　　Go, bid the weary spirit rest ;
Go, seek the wanderers through the gloom,
　　And guide them to the Saviour's breast !

Go forth, to sow the living seed ;
　　Seek not earth's praise, nor dread its frown ;
Nor labors fear, nor trials heed ;
　　Win jewels for Immanuel's crown !

Lo ! I am with you, saith the Lord ;
　　My grace your spirit shall sustain ;
Strong is My arm, and sure My word ;
　　My servants shall not toil in vain.

Go forth in hope ; My burden take,
　　Till God's great reaping-day shall come ;
Then, they who sowed in tears shall wake,
　　And hail the joyful harvest home !

THE MISSIONARY ANGEL.

ONWARD speed thy conquering flight,
  Angel, onward speed!
Cast abroad thy radiant light,
  Bid the shades recede;
Tread the idols in the dust;
  Heathen fanes destroy;
Spread the Gospel's holy trust, —
  Spread the Gospel's joy!

Onward speed thy conquering flight;
  Angel, onward haste!
Quickly on each mountain's height
  Be thy standard placed;
Let thy blissful tidings float
  Far o'er vale and hill,
Till the sweetly echoing note
  Every bosom thrill!

Onward speed thy conquering flight,
  Angel, onward fly!
Long has been the reign of night,
  Bring the morning nigh;
'T is to thee the heathen lift
  Their imploring wail;
Bear them Heaven's holy gift,
  Ere their courage fail!

Onward speed thy conquering flight,
  Angel, onward speed!

Morning bursts upon our sight, —
  'T is the time decreed.
Jesus now His kingdom takes, —
  Thrones and empires fall ;
And the joyous song awakes,
  "God is all in all !"

GOD BE WITH THEE.

GO with Thy servant, mighty Lord !
  Attend his work with power divine ;
Gird him with strength to preach Thy word,
  And round him make Thy glory shine !

Before his face prepare the way,
  And put the idol gods to shame ;
Touch with Thy fire the lips of clay,
  And magnify Thy saving name !

Bid, where he treads, the desert bloom ;
  Guide with Thy hand his unknown way ;
Scatter the clouds of grief and gloom,
  And change the darkness into day !

Triumphant Prince, gird on Thy sword ;
  Tread all the powers of darkness down ;
Almighty, re-ascended Lord,
  Assert Thy power, and wear Thy crown !

CHRIST'S DISCIPLES DIVIDE THE FIELD.[1]

BEFORE each of the first three verses, the following recitative is rendered.

"And I heard the voice of the Lord saying, ' Whom shall I send, and who will go for us ? '"

Response by Some Destined to Foreign Lands.

FROM dear New England's happy shore,
　　Where all our kindred dwell,
We hasten, to return no more, —
　　Our native land, farewell!

Response by Others Destined to Domestic Missions.

And we, where seldom on the ear
　　Salvation's tidings swell,
Go forth, to dry the mourner's tear, —
　　Our pleasant home, farewell!

Response by Others Destined to Home-Service.

Where all our earthly friendships blend,
　　Bound by affection's spell,
We, in God's work, our lives will spend, —
　　Brothers, a short farewell!

All, in Unison.

From these dear cherished scenes we go,
　　The home of praise and prayer,
To meet earth's gladness, or earth's woe,
　　For Christ, to do and bear.

[1] Anniversary, Andover Theological Seminary, September, 1832.

Farewell, beloved, who shared our joy,
  In whose fond hearts we dwell;
A noble work shall now employ
  All that we are — farewell.

Brethren, we press the parting hand,
  Our songs of parting tell;
Then, till we reach Heaven's holy land,
  A sweet, but brief, farewell!

THE MISSIONARY'S FAREWELL.

YES, my native land, I love thee;
  All thy scenes, I love them well;
Friends, connections, happy country,
  Can I bid you all farewell?
    Can I leave you,
  Far in heathen lands to dwell?

Home, thy joys are passing lovely,
  Joys no stranger heart can tell;
Happy home, indeed I love thee,
  Can I, can I say, "Farewell"?
    Can I leave thee,
  Far in heathen lands to dwell?

Scenes of sacred peace and pleasure,
  Holy days, and Sabbath bell,
Richest, brightest, sweetest treasure,
  Can I say a last farewell?
    Can I leave you,
  Far in heathen lands to dwell?

Yes, I hasten from you gladly, —
  From the scenes I loved so well;
Far away, ye billows, bear me.
  Lovely, native land, farewell;
    Pleased I leave thee,
  Far in heathen lands to dwell.

In the deserts let me labor;
  On the mountains let me tell
How He died — the blessed Saviour —
  To redeem a world from hell;
    Let me hasten,
  Far in heathen lands to dwell.

Bear me on, thou restless ocean ;
  Let the winds my canvas swell;
Heaves my heart with warm emotion,
  While I go far hence to dwell.
    Glad, I bid thee,
  Native land, farewell ! farewell !

—oo¿ø¿oo—

LIGHT O'ER THE HILLS.

MISSIONARY HYMN.

LIGHT o'er the hills! Light o'er the hills
  The promised morning wakes ;
The day foretold by seers of old
  In wondrous glory breaks.

They come ! The Saviour's voice they hear,
  And, glad, His call obey,
Chosen in Christ, His name to wear,
  A nation in a day.

Ride on ! ride on, victorious Prince !
  Ride on, triumphant King !
From land and sea, from earth and heaven,
  Thy myriad trophies bring.

So, gather all the tribes of earth,
  To hear and heed Thy call,
Till man, submissive, at Thy feet,
  Shall crown Thee, Lord of all !

THY KINGDOM COME, IMMORTAL KING !

MISSIONARY HYMN.

THY kingdom come, immortal King !
  Thy right maintain, Thy power display ;
Earth's myriads to Thy footstool bring ;
  Make all the nations own Thy sway !

Come, with the eagle's daring flight,
  Conquer the hosts of death and sin ;
Flood the whole globe with holy light,
  O kingdom of our God, come in !

Come as the swelling tides that break
  In mighty waves on every strand ;
Kingdom of God, in triumph wake
  O'er every sea, o'er every land !

We wait Thy breath, immortal Dove !
  Speak to earth's woes Thy healing word ;
Come, wafted on the wings of love,
  Make all the nations own Thee, Lord !

Thy kingdom come! — rise, Saviour, rise!
    Assume Thy power, ascend Thy throne,
Till universal Nature cries,
    "Strike the glad hour, — the work is done!"

PRINCE OF PEACE, OH, COME!

EARTH waits Thy advent, Prince of Peace, —
    Oh, come, with power divine!
O'er every sea, o'er every land,
    Bid the blest Gospel shine!

Like myriad drops of morning dew —
    Each drop, a sparkling gem —
Transfuse with light unnumbered souls,
    To grace Thy diadem.

Before Thy throne, triumphant Lord,
    Let willing captives bend,
And men of every name and tongue,
    Their hallelujahs blend.

Then shall the Great High Priest, this globe,
    A fragrant censer, swing,
And praise, from every smoking pore,
    Like incense sweet shall spring.

From hill to echoing hill, the shout
    Of victory shall resound, —
While hosts to answering hosts proclaim
    The Lord, with glory crowned.

TO A DEPARTING MISSIONARY.

O. S. C.

THE ship floats bravely on the sea,
　　The perfumed breezes play,
And many a fervent prayer is breathed
　　To speed her on her way.

She bears the merchant's golden wealth
　　To Asia's burning shore;
She bears a dearer burden far,
　　That comes to us no more.

She bears the friends we long have loved,
　　The friends we long have known;
"Farewell," — perhaps no more to meet,
　　Till life's bright hours have flown.

Yet, ye will find, beyond the waves,
　　Some noble Christian bands, —
Heroes, with pure and loving hearts,
　　And wise and faithful hands.

We meet again, — no farewell tear,
　　In heaven, is ever shed;
We meet again, — no farewell prayer,
　　In heaven, is ever said.

We meet where all is joy and peace,
　　Where throbs no thrill of pain;
We meet in heaven, where all is bliss,
　　And never part again.

WELCOME TO A RETURNING MISSIONARY.

SUNG at the return of Mrs. Harriet Carpenter from her mission-field in Japan.

WHEN the scarred hero from the field
    Of mortal strife retires to rest,
Glad greetings from a grateful throng,
    With heart and voice, pronounce him blest.

So thee, O Christian warrior, now
    Our souls with a high welcome greet;
And thou shalt all thy trophies lay,
    Tribute of love, at Jesus's feet.

Welcome the Christian heart, which throbs
    With loving purpose, strong and brave,
Burning to see the Lord enthroned,
    The strayed to seek, the lost to save.

Triumphant Prince, Thy power display,
    Till all mankind shall heed Thy call,
And earth, redeemed, with glad accord,
    Shall crown Thee, King and Lord of all.

SEPTEMBER, 1893.

THE KING OF GLORY.

Written for Mrs. M. B. Ingalls, of Thongze, Burmah, and sung at her " Burmah Curio Exposition," held in Boston.

HASTE to the conquest of the world,
   O King with glory crowned !
Gather Thy trophies far and wide,
   Wherever man is found.

Ride in swift triumph o'er the earth ;
   Lift up Thy sceptred hand;
Thine is the kingdom, Thine the right, —
   Ride forth, o'er sea and land.

Then round the conquered world Thy praise
   In waves on waves shall ring,
And shore to shore, and sea to sea,
   In answering chorus sing.

Adoring thousands at Thy feet,
   In faith and love, shall fall;
And countless souls, redeemed from sin,
   Shall call Thee Lord of all.

Then he that sowed in patient hope,
   Through all the weary years,
Shall find, at last, abundant sheaves,
   And joy, for toil and tears.

THE LONE STAR.

AT the Anniversary of the Missionary Union in Albany, New York, in 1868, it was proposed by some to abandon what was called the " Lone Star " mission in Nellore, India. Dr. Smith, then the guest of Judge Harris, being asked his opinion, in the evening, quietly replied, " You have it here," handing him the following verses. The poem was read to the audience the next morning, without consulting the author, who happened not to be present. Some wept, some sobbed; and the mission was saved. That mission, soon afterwards developed into the largest band of communicants, under one charge, in the world. The poem entitled Faith's Victory records the fulfilment of the prophetic words of the " Lone Star " poem. At a subsequent visit of the poet and his wife to that mission they were hailed with a joyous welcome. Each planted a palm-tree still respectively called by the native Christians, " Dr. Smith " and " Mrs. Smith."

SHINE on, " Lone Star!" Thy radiance bright
   Shall spread o'er all the eastern sky;
Morn breaks apace from gloom and night,—
   Shine on, and bless the pilgrim's eye.

Shine on, " Lone Star!" I would not dim
   The light that gleams with dubious ray;
The lonely star of Bethlehem
   Led on a bright and glorious day.

Shine on, " Lone Star!" In grief and tears,
   And sad reverses, oft baptized;
Shine on amid thy sister spheres:
   Lone stars in heaven are not despised.

Shine on, " Lone Star!" Who lifts his hand
   To dash to earth so bright a gem,
A new lost " Pleiad " from the band
   That sparkles in night's diadem?

Shine on, " Lone Star!" The day draws near
　　When none shall shine more fair than thou;
Thou, born and nursed in doubt and fear,
　　Wilt glitter on Immanuel's brow.

Shine on, " Lone Star," till earth, redeemed,
　　In dust shall bid its idols fall,
And thousands, where thy radiance beamed,
　　Shall crown the Saviour Lord of all.

FAITH'S TRIUMPH.

WEARY and wan, his furrows long,
　　The patient ploughman trod,
Turning, with endless care and pains,
　　The sluggish, barren sod;
And morning came, and daylight went,
　　And strength and hope were gone,
The tearful eyes grew dim, — and still
　　The wearying toil went on.

Smitten beneath the burning sun,
　　The fainting workman cries,
" Master, how long this iron earth?
　　How long these brazen skies?"
" Ploughman, toil on in loving trust;
　　Yield thee to My sweet will.
Faith wins its victories; weary soul,
　　Believe, and labor still."

And tears and love and faith prepared
  The deeply furrowed field,
To hide and keep the precious grain, —
  Seed of a bounteous yield;
And dew and rain and sunny skies
  Enriched each seed that fell,
Lost to the eye of man, but God
  Knew how to guard it well.

Oh, long and sad the sower's care,
  As seasons went and came!
And God forgot the toiler's lot,
  And put his hope to shame.
"Vain work," a timid faith proclaimed;
  "Poor toilers, faint and few!
Bury and hide your useless seed;
  Bury the sowers, too."

But God's great mystery of grace
  Its mighty pathway holds,
And, like the budding rose of June,
  In beauteous life unfolds.
The bursting germ, the verdant leaf,
  Break forth from hidden graves;
And far o'er all the swelling hills,
  The joyful harvest waves.

Whence are these myriad forms that bow
  Before Messiah's throne?
Whence the grand chorus that uplifts
  Thy name, O Christ, alone?
Whence are the clustering clouds that seek
  The same celestial goal?
And one new song holds every lip,
  One pulse-beat, every soul.

These are the ploughman's garnered wealth,
  Born of his toil and pain ;
These are the sower's faith and tears,
  Transformed to golden grain.
God watched the toilers at their work ;
  And, when His wisdom willed,
The pledge His loving heart had made,
  His loving hand fulfilled.

Then hail, Lone Star ! of all the wreath,
  Thou art the brighest gem,
As once, o'er fair Judea's plains,
  The Star of Bethlehem.
Shine on ! We learn to pray and wait,
  To toil and trust, through thee, —
A star of triumph on Christ's brow,
  And faith's high victory.

THE WORD OF GOD GLORIFIED.

O BLESSED word of God, thy living ray
    Turns shade to sunshine, light to heavenly day ;
Dispels earth's sorrow, calms the troubled breast,
And guides the pilgrim to the endless rest ;
Explains life's mystery, and shines through woe,
As threatening clouds with sunset radiance glow ;
Breaks with its joy earth's wintry gloom and night,
And turns its sable robes to bridal white.
Go forth, great word of God, thy force display ;
Convert the world, — a nation in a day.
Teach China's millions, saved, on God to call,
And crown the living Saviour, Lord of all.

Light from God's truth gilds all thy isles, Japan,
Light, born in heaven, for universal man;
And flashing oars on all the crystal flood
Gleam with the radiance of the word of God.
Rise with thy light, and pour thy healing beam
On all the hills, by every winding stream,
Where the proud Burmans to their idols bow,
Hearing, with hardened neck, and lofty brow,
When men of holy heart and loving speech,
Man's only hope, in earnest accents, preach;
In India's myriad tongues let God's blest words
Proclaim the glory of the Lord of lords;
And all its tribes, in heaven's new song, proclaim
The love and power of Christ's own saving name.
In Afric's central heart new triumphs win;
And bid the Congo, found at last, begin
To seek new hope; to learn, on bended knee,
New lore of truth, and Heaven's blest mystery.
While haughty Moslem sees the crescent pale
Before the cross, whose empire ne'er shall fail,
But make its broad domains through love extend,
One reign o'er all the earth, one kingdom without end.

THE LIVING BREAD.

O THOU whose voice the tempest stilled,
   And made the wild waves calm,
Whose hand, with gentle touch, had power
   To heal, like Gilead's balm, —

Speak to the storm-tossed sons of earth,
   And draw their hearts to Thee;
And let Thy healing touch redeem
   The wanderers of the sea.

Renew Thy miracle of love, —
Thyself, " The living Bread ; "
Arise and let the fainting throngs,
On ship and shore, be fed.

Ride forth in glory, — land and wave
Thy mandate shall obey,
And all the peopled earth, redeemed,
Shall own Thy rightful sway.

JEHOVAH REIGNS.

SWIFTLY the years roll on ; so swiftly comes
The day when every nation unto God
Shall swell Salvation's song.   From the far South
The scented breezes bring a welcome voice
Upon their wings, — the voice of many tongues,
Asking of Christ and heaven.   The western fields,
Far stretching towards the setting sun, send back,
From all the busy hum of gathering tribes,
The call for men of God.   The frozen North,
With her sparse nations, and the swarming East,
Have heard that Christ for man was lifted up.
The story, simply told on some stray leaf,
That came, they know not whence, wakens a thrill
Of deep responsive feeling.   There 's a chord
That answers in the human breast to all
The word of God declares.   As for the light
The eye is formed, and for the eye the light, —
So for the heart of man the words of life ;
And for those words the human heart was made.

They send their soothing cry o'er ocean's waste;
The voice is heard above the roaring storm
Of earth's wild bustle.   Many a stolid ear
Erects itself to hear ; and many a heart
Cries in its fervor, — " I will go and tell
The dark idolater the way to God."
    O ye of little faith, 't is but a day,
And sin will vanish !   All earth's withering woes
Will pass away ; the Gospel's blessed words,
Borne by its ministers to every land,
Will heal them all.   God will be glorified
In human blessedness ; and, morn and eve,
The ransomed tribes shall send up to the throne,
From all earth's surface, hallelujahs, sweet,
And loud as many waters.   Heaven itself
Will seem descended ; earth will seem a heaven.
    Come, O Thou Lamb of God, hasten Thy work ;
Cut short the reign of sin ; and if not here,
Oh, soon from our bright thrones above the sky,
Let us but catch the strain from all who dwell
Upon the earth — JEHOVAH REIGNS !

"AROUSE YE, O SERVANTS OF GOD!"

[Music: " *The Cross and Victory.*"]

WRITTEN for the hymn, and dedicated to Societies of Christian
Endeavor.

AROUSE ye, arouse ye, O servants of God!
   His right arm, your strength, and your leader,
      His rod.
Oh, haste from the north, from the south, to His call;
His cause shall prevail, — He shall reign over all!
Farewell to your dreaming; no longer delay;
Go tell the glad tidings! God's hand points the way.
Go forward! go forward! to conquer or die;
      God will make sure the victory.

CHORUS.

   Haste and bear the banner forth,
   East and west, and south and north;
   Haste to lift the cross on high,
      The pledge of victory.
   Haste and bear the banner forth,
   East and west, and south and north;
   Haste to lift the cross on high,
      The pledge of victory, —
      The cross, and victory!

The morning has broken, the noonday is near;
Go forward with courage, nor doubt ye, nor fear.
Rely on His promise, His oath, and His word;
His Spirit your helper, His Gospel, your sword.
The Prince of Salvation is winning His way, —
Bring crowns for His brow, — joy, joy, for the day!
Go forward! go forward, to conquer or die;
      God will make sure the victory.
CHORUS.

FROM EARTH TO HEAVEN.

COME UNTO ME.

THOU whose heart with pain is broken,
  Long with grief and woe oppressed,
Hear what God, the Lord, hath spoken,
  Weary wanderer after rest.
    Come to Me, thy sins forsaking,
    God's great mercy gladly taking:
    With the world and folly part.
    Give Me, give Me now, thy heart.

Come to Me, the meek and lowly;
  Come, My easy burden bear;
Be thou one among the holy;
  Cast away thy dull despair;
    I will make thy burdens lighter;
    I will make thy pleasures brighter;
    Restless as the troubled sea,
    Come, forsaking all for Me.

Who that ever sought My favor,
  Though My grace was long abused,
Who that yielded to the Saviour,
  Asked My love and was refused?
    At the throne of mercy bending,
    On the arm of God depending,
    Come to Me, from labor cease;
    And in Me thou shalt have peace.

O LORD, REMEMBER ME!

WITH crowds around upbraiding,
  And curses on the blast,
While things of earth were fading,
  And life was ebbing fast, —
The malefactor, praying,
  To Christ upon the tree,
Breathed out his spirit, saying,
  " O Lord, remember me ! "

The Saviour looked in meekness,
  Though death was drawing nigh ;
He heeded not His weakness,
  When came the contrite sigh.
He said, while thoughts of pity
  Beamed from His dying eyes :
" To-day thou shalt be with Me,
  In yonder paradise."

If scenes of joy and gladness,
  In life my lot should be,
Or should my days bring sadness,
  O Lord, remember me !
Receive my parting spirit,
  Where joys unfading rise,
And take me to inherit
  A place in paradise.

THE ALL-SUFFICIENT REFUGE.

O ROCK of Ages! when the storm
   Of trial drives across my path,
And vainly struggles human power
   To stand against its sweeping wrath,
Then shield me by Thy towering head,
   Then in Thy clefts, O, let me hide, —
No ill can reach the soul that leans,
   Trusting, on Christ the Crucified.

O Rock of Ages! when my tears
   In streams of contrite anguish flow,
And, penitent, my lips confess
   How just the hand that strikes the blow,
Then to Thy massive, shelving cliffs,
   Then to Thy shadow let me flee;
The dying Christ sustained the shock,
   And, Lord, the soul is safe in Thee.

O Rock of Ages! when my heart,
   Struck by some sore bereavement, bleeds,
And earthly props and comforters
   Have proved themselves but broken reeds,
Then to Thy shelter let me press,
   Which stands from age to age the same;
Christ changes not, — the stricken soul
   Finds comfort in His healing name.

O Rock of Ages! if the cross
   Of shame for Christ's dear name I bear,
Or suffer loss, because I choose
   His seal upon my brow to wear,

Then, calm and fearless, let my soul,
  Safe in Thy great protection, rest ;
Christ is a refuge, — troubled hearts
  Find shelter in the Saviour's breast.

O Rock of Ages ! when in death
  My strength grows weak, my spirits fail,
And earthly helpers leave my feet
  To tread alone the solemn vale,
Then from each cliff and slope and crag,
  Let light, from heaven reflected, shine ;
Christ is earth's sun, and Christ alone
  Can gild the tomb with rays divine.

As clings the seaman, when his bark
  Is shattered by the raging wave,
To fragments of the broken wreck,
  And vainly hopes his life to save, —
So, in all times of risk or need,
  My spirit to Thy shade shall flee ;
Secure, in life or death, to find
  O Rock of Ages ! all in Thee.

THE EVERLASTING SHELTER.

NO sorrow, like a sweeping storm,
  Around the soul fierce conflict wages,
But Christ has power its force to quell, —
  No storm can move the Rock of Ages.

O yearning thirst of human hearts !
  Thirst which no earthly good assuages, —
Seek water from the Smitten Rock ;
  That Rock is Christ, — the Rock of Ages.

O hearts and hands consumed by toil,
  Confined to earth, as birds in cages !
Rest for the weary — endless rest —
  Lies in Thy shelter, Rock of Ages.

Search all the wisdom earth can boast ;
  Bring all the light from saints and sages, —
Vain is the quest for peace and rest,
  Till sought within the Rock of Ages.

What thought, what hope, what love, what joy,
  The heart — the curious heart — engages ;
Joy, love, and hope surpassing thought, —
  All centre in the Rock of Ages.

There is a land serene and fair,
  Where falls no blight, no passion rages,
Sheltered and safe from grief and sin,
  O'ershadowed by the Rock of Ages.

Grateful, our heavenward path we tread,
  Mount by successive steps and stages,
And wait secure the day of God, —
  Hid in Thy clefts, O Rock of Ages !

LIFE'S RAPID RIVER.

A S flows the rapid river,
    With channel broad and free,
Its waters rippling ever,
    And rushing to the sea, —
So swift our days are ending,
    Short is each joy and grief, —
Summer with winter blending,
    The longest life, how brief.

As moons are ever waning,
    As hastes the sun away,
As stormy winds, complaining,
    Bring on the wintry day, —
So fast the night comes o'er us,
    The darkness of the grave, —
Death ever just before us,
    God takes the life He gave.

Be then thy choicest treasure
    Laid up in worlds above;
Be thine the highest pleasure,
    Thy God, to serve and love;
And use, with wise endeavor,
    The talent Heaven has lent,
Lest thou lament forever,
    A precious life, misspent.

AS SUMMER CLOUDS.

AS summer clouds in richness sleeping,
  Are scattered by the winds away;
As flowers, awhile their beauty keeping,
  Are withered at the close of day, —
    So life is ever, ever flying,
    And bringing on the hour of dying;
    The cloud departs; the blossom fades;
    And death draws on its silent shades.

How brief the rainbow's peaceful brightness!
  Its glowing colors melt away;
How vain the busy insect's lightness!
  Its life is sweet, but will not stay.
    Earth's dearest joys are tinged by sorrow;
    The soul may wade in grief to-morrow.
    The rainbow melts; the insect dies, —
    But man to endless life may rise.

The noonday hours are bright, but fleeting;
  The time for labor soon is gone;
The gentle twilight, fast retreating,
  Forsakes the world, and day is done.
    So fast the day of life is spending;
    So fast the time of duty, ending;
    The day retires, the twilight flies;
    O man, secure life's noblest prize.

HOW BLEST ARE THEY, IN CHRIST, WHO DIE!

"PEACE was the last word of little Jane, and peace seemed to be inscribed on the farewell scene at the grave where they laid her down to rest."

HOW blest are they, in Christ, who die,
　　While guardian angels linger nigh!
The dreary days of pain are o'er;
　　And life ebbs out,
As billows die on the shore.

Death wears no terror on its brow;
It comes like summer airs that blow
　　Across the earth at evening hour,
　　　Or moonlight beams,
　　That glide along the peaceful bower.

While angel-bands the requiem sing,
The joyful soul is on the wing.
　　The captive free; life's labor done, —
　　　Clad in white robes,
　　The saint appears before the throne.

Peace reigns beside the silent bed, —
Peace, where the happy soul has fled;
　　The Lord hath taken what He gave.
　　　The soul hath rest;
　　And peace is written on the grave.

TO DIE IS GAIN.

DURING a severe illness in July, 1892, Dr. Smith wrote the following lines upon small scraps of paper, as he had strength. They were preserved and printed by his son, very tender memories attaching to the family experiences of that summer. Believing that they will bear spiritual comfort to many in other households, the compiler of this volume has the assent of their author to this present use.

TO feel the mild, delicious clime,
   Where summer never fades;
To breathe the glorious atmosphere,
   Which sickness ne'er invades;

To reach at last that happy land,
   Where tears are never known;
To see the wondrous face of Him
   Who sits upon the throne;

All the great souls of all the years,
   In Heaven's high courts to meet;
All kindred spirits, glorified,
   To join, in converse sweet;

To burst the chrysalis, and soar
   On love's triumphant wing;
To swell the hymns of mighty praise,
   The ransomed armies sing;

To wear the robes of saints in light;
   To shine as shines the sun;
To hear the Saviour's welcome voice
   Pronounce the glad "well done!"

And, O, the crowning height of bliss,
  Where all the glories blend,
To know the bliss, the light, the love,
  Shall never, never, end !

Beyond the shades of sin and woe,
  With joyful speed to fly,
And in God's loving arms to rest, —
  Oh, it is gain to die.

THE DYING CHRISTIAN.

BY the couch of the saint there are loved ones to
      weep;
There are angels to watch o'er the last weary sleep;
There 's a Saviour to soothe every feeling of grief,
And a balm for the spirit that sighs for relief.

When the soul thro' the Jordan of death deeply wades,
And the light of creation burns dimly and fades;
There 's a voice that can speak thro' the gathering
      shade, —
Saint, thy Saviour is near thee, O, be not afraid.

As the sun hastens down to his place in the west,
And the calmness of evening thrills sweet through the
      breast;
So serene is the hour, when the soul sinks to rest,
And with gladness ascends to the home of the blest.

THE GRAVE.

HOW calm and peaceful is the grave !
How bright the flowers that round it wave!
How clear the sky that o'er it shines !
How soft the scene,
When morning dawns, when day declines !

The weary there forget their woes —
The pilgrim hath a long repose ;
No earthly storms the dead awake ;
Their sleep is still
As sunset on the peaceful lake.

The rich and great are slumbering there,
Set free from earth's delusive glare.
The poor are garnered in the dust,
Alike at rest,
Till comes the rising of the just.

O day of glory, when the tomb
Shall burst, and heaven's bright morning come,
When all that in the earth repose
Shall wake to life,
And Christ shall reign o'er all His foes !

WHERE IS THY VICTORY, O GRAVE!

CHRISTIAN, awake! Let thy soul swell with
    gladness!
Prospects of glory dawn bright on thy sadness;
Rising, immortal, thy spirit shall sing, —
Grave, where 's thy victory; Death, where 's thy sting?

Sown in corruption, the frame lies decaying;
Raised in its glory, all beauty displaying,
Body and spirit united shall sing, —
Grave, where 's thy victory; Death, where 's thy sting?

Peacefully sleep till the trumpet awake thee;
He whom thou lovest will never forsake thee;
Ransomed from guilt and from death, thou shalt
    sing, —
Grave, where 's thy victory; Death, where 's thy sting?

Then, when this mortal, immortal awaking,
Triumphs, exulting, Death's dark fetters breaking;
Man in his glorified nature shall sing, —
Grave, where 's thy victory; Death, where 's thy sting?

HEAVEN.

PAIN shall not enter there.   No thought of woe
    Shall rend the tender heart.   The silent tear
No more shall wet the wasting cheek.   The eye
Shall not be dimmed with sorrow.   Nor shall aught
Be done, or thought, or said, to grieve the soul

Of harmless innocence.   The thoughtless tongue,
That fills the world with sadness, then shall be
Employed in noblest praise.   Lover and friend,
And all the dearly cherished of the heart,
Who long have rested in the tomb, shall come
And join the choral strain.   From earth aroused,
The voice of harmony that flows so sweet
Around the throne, their tongues shall ever swell.
Then, then, there shall be peace, — a settled calm,
A soft serenity, more gently mild than earth,
With all its gorgeous scenes, can hope to bring
A meet comparison.   And all that peace
Shall live and reign a long forever there,
Forever there! and this eternity
Shall make that heaven, a heaven.

MAY 31, 1832.

RE-UNION IN HEAVEN.

WHEN SHALL WE MEET AGAIN, MEET, NE'ER TO SEVER?

THE first verse belonged to an English hymn which was submitted
to Mr. Smith by Lowell Mason to complete, as the remaining verses
were of a different metre. The last verses were written to conform
in spirit and measure with the first.

WHEN shall we meet again, —
Meet, ne'er to sever?
When will Peace wreathe her chain,
Round us forever?
Our hearts will ne'er repose,
Safe from each blast that blows
In this dark vale of woes,
Never — no, never.

When shall love freely flow,
   Pure as life's river ?
When shall sweet friendship glow,
   Changeless, forever?
Where joys celestial thrill,
Where bliss each heart shall fill,
And fears of parting chill
   Never — no, never !

Up to that world of light,
   Take us, dear Saviour ;
May we all there unite,
   Happy forever.
Where kindred spirits dwell,
There may our music swell,
And time our joys dispel
   Never — no, never !

Soon shall we meet again, —
   Meet, ne'er to sever :
Soon will Peace wreathe her chain
   Round us forever :
Our hearts will then repose,
Secure from worldly woes;
Our songs of praise shall close
   Never — no, never !

A REDEEMED WORLD.

YOUR THOUSAND VOICES RAISE.

A CENTENARY HYMN.

[Tune : "*America.*"]

YOUR thousand voices raise,
    In symphony of praise,
Clear, sweet and strong;
Tell it with joy unknown,
Tell it in loftiest tone,
Jesus is King, alone, —
    The note prolong.

He came, He saw, He died, —
Jesus, the Crucified ;
    He lives, He reigns.
In Him all glories meet ;
Kings bow before His feet ;
His foes are mown like wheat ;
    His throne remains.

Born from an infant root,
Once like a feeble shoot,
    Hopeful and brave ;
The twig has grown a tree,
Known over land and sea, —
O'er what immensity
    Its branches wave !

Ride on, triumphant Lord!
A hundred years record
  Thy victories won ;
Hasten the glorious day
When all shall own Thy sway,
And earth and heaven shall say, —
  "The work is done."

MORN OF ZION'S GLORY.

FROM THE GERMAN.

MORN of Zion's glory,
    Brightly thou art breaking;
Holy joys thy light is waking.
    Morn of Zion's glory,
Ancient saints foretold thee,
Seraph-angels, glad, behold thee ;
        How they glide,
        Far and wide,
    Streams of full salvation,
    Free to every nation.

    Morn of Zion's glory,
Joyful tidings bringing,
All the wilds with flowers are springing !
    Morn of Zion's glory,
All the nations hail thee ;
Foes to God in vain assail thee ;
        Peace with men
        Dwells again
    What celestial pleasure
    Swells, a sacred treasure.

Morn of Zion's glory,
Every human dwelling
With the notes of joy is swelling;
Morn of Zion's glory!
Distant hills are ringing,
Echoed voices sweet are singing;
Haste thee on,
Like the sun,
Paths of splendor tracing,
Heathen midnight chasing.

Morn of Zion's glory,
Now the night is risen;
Now thy star is high in heaven.
Morn of Zion's glory,
Joyful hearts are bounding,
Hallelujahs high are sounding.
Peace with men
Dwells again;
Jesus reigns forever,
Jesus reigns forever!

⸻⸻

THE GREAT SALVATION.

GLORIOUS days shall be to Zion
When her conflicts are no more,
And the Saviour she relies on,
Sits enthroned in regal power.

Broken, every captive's fetter,—
All in Jesus shall be free;
Kings shall crowd to Heaven's sceptre;
All the earth shall bow the knee.

Hail, the willing nations, bending,
　　Prince of Peace, before Thy throne !
Heaven to earth, in love descending,
　　Views a world at peace, — Thine own.

In the scenes of coming glory,
　　All the ransomed hosts shall share ;
All the holy, all the lowly,
　　Shall the crown of glory wear.

Hosts from every clime and nation
　　Then shall be in Christ made one ;
Gained in full, the Great Salvation, —
　　Life and joy immortal, won.

THE SUCCESS OF THE GOSPEL ASSURED.

THE MORNING LIGHT IS BREAKING.

This Hymn, and the National Hymn, " My country, 't is of thee,"
were written while the author was at Andover Theological Seminary,
in 1832.

THE morning light is breaking;
　　The darkness disappears ;
The sons of earth are waking
　　To penitential tears.
Each breeze that sweeps the ocean,
　　Brings tidings from afar
Of nations in commotion,
　　Prepared for Zion's war.

Rich dews of grace come o'er us,
  In many a gentle shower,
And brighter scenes before us,
  Are opening every hour;
Each cry, to Heaven going,
  Abundant answers brings,
And heavenly gales are blowing,
  With peace upon their wings.

See heathen nations bending
  Before the God we love !
And thousand hearts ascending
  In gratitude above ;
While sinners, now confessing,
  The Gospel call obey,
And seek the Saviour's blessing,—
  A nation in a day.

Blest river of salvation,
  Pursue thy onward way ;
Flow, thou, to every nation,
  Nor in thy richness stay ;
Stay not, till all the lowly
  Triumphant reach their home ;
Stay not, till all the holy
  Proclaim, " The Lord is come!"

JESUS EVER REIGNS.

FROM THE GERMAN.

UP, ye nations, raise
    Songs of grateful praise ;
Let creation round,
Ring the joyful sound ;
Let each happy voice,
In the Lord rejoice ;
Jesus, now adore,
Sovereign, evermore ;
He who loved our souls,
He whose mercy rolls
O'er our guilty stains, —
Jesus ever reigns.

Now His pains are o'er,
Who our sorrows bore ;
Now He mounts the throne,
Worthy, He alone,
Evermore to wear,
Wreaths of glory there ;
See the rainbow shine,
Pledge of love divine ;
See it o'er His head,
Rays of splendor shed !
Earthly glory wanes ;
Jesus ever reigns.

Thou, of David's race,
Thou, the Prince of Peace,
Thou, Almighty Word,
Thou, Incarnate Lord,

Worthy art, to be
Praised in melody,
Poured from thousand tongues,
Swelled in thousand songs.
Worthy is Thy name,
Sin-atoning Lamb,
Thou, who once wast slain,
Evermore to reign.

Lord, our praise we bring, —
Praise to Christ, our King ;
Praise to Him whose love
Leads our souls above ;
Praise to Him whose power
Guards us hour by hour.
Sing, ye choirs on high ;
Angel bands, reply,
Mortals, old and young, —
Let each joyful tongue,
Join the lofty strains, —
Jesus ever reigns.

THE LORD IS COME.

L IGHT o'er the darkened hills
  Breaks forth at last, and fills
    The glowing sky ;
See, a new dayspring born
Kindles a holy morn,
Beaming on lands forlorn,
    While shadows fly.

Glory to God on high,
Wide let the echo fly !
   His flag, unfurled,
Shall tell new wonders done,
Shall boast new triumphs won, —
His, the Immortal crown,
   The conquered world.

Welcome the glorious morn,
Welcome the hosts, new-born,
   Praise and adore.
Dispersed the heathen's gloom,
Thousands to Christ have come ;
In Christ there still is room
   For thousands more.

Hail, mighty Conqueror, hail !
Thy promise will not fail ;
   Thy crown assume.
Speak from Thy throne on high,
Bid the glad tidings fly,
And heaven and earth reply,
   " The Lord is come ! "

TRIUMPHS OF THE GOSPEL.

WHAT waves of music roll,
    What songs of joy come swelling,
Among the angel bands,
    Along heaven's sacred dwelling,
When penitents return,
    When dying souls revive,
Forsake the way of death,
    And learn for God to live !

Among the saints on earth,
    What praise and adoration
To God the Saviour wake,
    When lost ones seek salvation !
The sacramental host,
    That spreads from sea to sea,
While the glad numbers grow,
    Sing their fresh Jubilee.

Hail, day of holy joy !
    Though earth's last days are wasting,
When happy converts come,
    Like doves, to Jesus hasting !
Ride on, Thou conquering Prince,
    Till all the world obey,
And all the ransomed earth
    Yield to Thy blessed sway.

SPEED ON THY VICTORY, MIGHTY KING!

For the Young Men's Social Union, Boston, March 19, 1895.

SPEED on Thy victory, mighty King,
    The world awaits Thy call!
Swiftly Thy glorious kingdom bring,
    And reign Thou, Lord of all.

All things are Thine, — the earth we tread,
    The stars, the sky, the sea ;
And we are in Thy image made, —
    Our all belongs to Thee.

So, conquering Prince, o'er all the world,
    Bid sin and tumult cease,
And Thy blest banner float, unfurled,
    Above a world at peace.

Gather fresh crowns, of priceless worth, —
    Triumphant Saviour, Thou, —
Till the fair crown of all the earth
    Shall glitter on Thy brow.

THE PRINCE OF SALVATION IN TRIUMPH
IS RIDING.

THE Prince of Salvation in triumph is riding,
    And glory attends Him along His bright way;
The news of His grace on the breezes are gliding,
    And mortals are owning His sway.

The rays of the gospel-star, — see how they brighten!
    With splendors unknown the horizon they fill;
The wretched they soothe, and the dark they enlighten,
    And gladness their beamings distil.

Ride on, in Thy greatness, Thou conquering Saviour!
    Let thousands of thousands submit to Thy reign,
Like doves at their windows, entreat for Thy favor,
    And follow Thy glorious train.

Then sweetly shall ring from each sanctified nation,
    The voices of myriads tuned to Thy praise,
And heaven shall re-echo the song of salvation,
    In rich and melodious lays.

AMERICA'S CHRISTIAN CENTENNIAL.

WRITTEN under the conviction that the progress of Christ's Kingdom during the First Century of American Independence was typical of its supreme extension during the new century, just begun.

A HUNDRED years,— how vast the sweep
    Of scenes that fill the mighty past !
The sires that sowed, the sons that reap ;
    The trembling first, the hopeful last !

A hundred years,— through peace and strife,
    The envy of a hundred lands;
The nation, nurtured into life,
    Founded in faith, in glory stands.

A hundred years, — what names of power
    With fadeless bloom our history wreathe ;
Like petals of some fragrant flower,
    A sweet aroma still they breathe.

A hundred years, — o'er lands afar,
    Where once at heathen shrines they fell
Thousands have hailed the rising star,
    Thy radiant star, Immanuel.

A hundred years, — from sea to sea
    Freedom's unsullied banners wave ;
No tyrant bids us bow the knee,
    No zealot rules, nor toils a slave.

A hundred years, — what scenes unknown
  In wondrous vista lie outspread !
Harvests from seed in weakness sown,
  Life, springing from the mighty dead.

A hundred years, — we wait His word
  Whose fiat bade creation be,
Who spake, and echoing chaos heard,
  And light broke forth in majesty.

A hundred years, — unshrinking still,
  We wait the Master's high behest ;
In filial trust, the Master's will
  Appoints our toil, provides our rest.

A hundred years, perchance, may end,
  And sin from all its thrones be hurled,
And earth in humble reverence bend
  To Him who rules a ransomed world.

A hundred years, and earth, redeemed,
  Shall see her idol temples fall,
And He, whose star o'er Bethlehem beamed,
  Sit, crowned, triumphant, Lord of all.

THE DOXOLOGY OF REDEMPTION.

REDEEMED from death ! redeemed from sin !
  Redeemed from ills without, within !
Redeemed ! what new light gilds the skies !
What glories on the soul arise !

Glory to Him whose love unknown
Reached man's abyss from Heaven's high throne;
Like some new star its radiance beamed,
A new key rang, — redeemed! redeemed!

As ocean's billows swell and break,
The mighty tide of praise shall wake;
Thy love, Lord, like the unmeasured sea,
Shall waft a world, redeemed, to Thee.

Redeemed! creation, joyful, brings
Its tribute to the King of kings;
Redeemed! earth's million voices raise
One sounding anthem to His praise.

Part IV.

Miscellaneous Hymns and Odes.

MISCELLANEOUS HYMNS AND ODES.

INTERVIEWS WITH NATURE.

THE FLAG IN NATURE.

ALL Nature sings wildly the song of the free;
The red, white, and blue float o'er land and o'er
sea, —
The white, in each billow that breaks on the shore;
The blue, in the arching that canopies o'er
The land of our birth, in its glory outspread;
And sunset dyes deepen and glow into red.
Day fades into night, and the red stripe retires;
But stars, o'er the blue, light their sentinel fires.
And though night be gloomy, with clouds overspread,
Each star holds its place in the field overhead;
When scatter the clouds, and the tempest is through,
We count every star in the field of the blue.

FLOWERS.

BREATHS from the upper world ; Eden revived ;
 God's smiles on earth, made visible to men ;
Light, prisoned up in form ; honey, enhived ;
 Fair Paradise, once lost, restored again.

Beauty and love, enshrined in bell and cup ;
 Earth's innocents, that climb around our bowers ;
Meek, brilliant eyes, that look so sweetly up,
 Like raindrops, sparkling after summer showers.

Jewels to earth, as stars are to the skies,
 Polished and set, by more than human skill ;
Lessons that speak, though silent, to the eyes, —
 Vocal in vale and plain, on ridge and hill.

Volumes of truth, that speak the mighty God,
 Wise, loving, pitying, glorious, ever near,
That bid us trust the ever great and good,
 Whose mercy wakes and crowns the rolling year.

Symbols of man's short life, too frail to stay ;
 Living, to die, — a sweet, but passing story ;
Dying, to live when spring renews its day, —
 The precious emblems of immortal glory.

THE POET AT HOME. FEB. 22, 1895.

FLOWERS IN WINTER.

FAIR flowers that bloom so richly,
  As if the summer's breath
Were wafted o'er their birthplace,
  And not the chill of death!
I hail the joyful emblem, —
  Fit cheer for hours of gloom, —
Earth has its wintry trials,
  But 't is not all a tomb.

I listen in the evening
  To the sighing of the gale;
I watch the heaping snowdrifts,
  And hear the rattling hail;
And I think, with grateful spirit,
  What a glorious God is ours,
Who is mighty in the tempest,
  And gentle in the flowers.

The piercing blasts are blowing;
  But every smiling cup
Breathes forth such charming fragrance,
  And looks so sweetly up,
I forget the shortened daylight,
  And the wintry chill and gloom,
And heaven seems hovering near me,
  With its everlasting bloom.

And I see amid the darkness
  Of the path that mortals tread,
In the land of grief and partings,
  Of the mourning and the dead,

How God, with loving mercy,
  Softening the painful blow,
Leaves joy, to gild our sorrow,
  Like flowers in time of snow.

The cherished forms that faltered,
  And we laid them down to rest,
In their still retreats are sleeping,
  With the peace of Jesus blest;
Like the blossom from the tuber,
  Like the harvest from the grain,
They will spring, — the time approaches, —
  To their lovely life again.

They are living still in beauty,
  Where the soft airs ever last,
Where they never feel the fury
  Of the winter's bitter blast;
Nor frosts, with chilling fingers,
  Nor griefs, with scalding tear,
Where summer ever lingers,
  And flowers bloom all the year.

A SONG OF SPRING.

WELCOME, the opening buds of spring;
  Welcome, the dew and rain;
Welcome, the merry birds that sing;
  Welcome, the bursting grain.

Welcome, the balmy airs that breathe,
  The rainbows, and the showers;
Welcome, the early flowers that wreathe
  Their beauty round our bowers.

Wild from a thousand warbling throats
  Melodious music rings;
Matin and vesper swells and floats, —
  Nature's sweet offerings.

Each bird that soars, each bud that breaks
  In beauty from its cell,
Tuneful, or still, one accent wakes, —
  " God has done all things well."

Let tree and wood, let vale and hill,
  Swell the sweet, grateful song,
And wave, and rock, and rippling rill,
  The echoing strain prolong.

THE LITTLE CRICKET.

YOU sweet little cricket,
  Amid the night dew,
While the moon shines so brightly,
  I 'll listen to you.
I love your dull chirping,
  Your shrill monotone;
You soothe, with your music,
  This bosom so lone.

Your voice, like the breezes
  That mournfully play,
When the red leaves of autumn
  Look gaudy and gay,
Tells of joys now departed,
  No more to return,
Of summer hopes blasted,
  Of fair flowers torn.

Sweet cricket, thy music
Will quickly be still,
When the tempests of winter
Roar loud on the hill;
But I go when the storm comes,
Where all my friends dwell, —
No more shall my heart say
To gladness farewell!

JULY 25, 1831.

WILD STRAWBERRIES.

IN the thick and grassy wood,
Where the sunny streaks are breaking,
And the birds their songs are waking,
Where the mossy flowers repose,
There the pretty strawberry grows.

Pretty strawberry, fresh and sweet,
Say who made your cheek so shining,
Like the crimson sun declining,
And who made your pleasant smell, —
Tell me, pretty strawberry, tell?

It was God who made you so;
God, your ruddy color brightens,
And your charming odor heightens.
Leafy pines, and firs so straight,
Whisper, "Children, God is great."

THE CANARY AT SEA.

On the Cunard Steamer Abyssinia, far from land, a canary bird made its home as contentedly as if in its native forest. The poet has given to the incident that spiritual lesson which has marked his life-work as a lover of Nature, in close companionship with Nature's Master, the Creator of all.

SWEET wanderer o'er the sea,
　　Where wild winds moan,
And billowy waves, like pulses, beat
　　Their monotone, —
How tread thy little feet, so gay,
　　Devoid of fear?
How is thy heart so brave and bold,—
　　A stranger here?

The summer bloom, the verdant fields,
　　Are far away;
No leafy bower, no warbled tone,
　　Invites thy stay.
Sea here, sea there, sea everywhere,
　　Wave chasing wave, —
In peril's hour, O, who has power
　　To shield or save?

Enough for thee, the strong-rigged bark,
　　In calm and storm,
Will shelter and protect from harm
　　Thy tiny form;
Cling to the refuge, and be safe
　　From wave and gale,
And o'er the ocean's boundless waste
　　Securely sail.

Wanderers o'er life's uncertain course, —
  A dangerous sea, —
Our only refuge, Son of God,
    We find in Thee ;
Led captive by no lower aim,
  To Thee we cling,
And rest in perfect faith and hope
    Beneath Thy wing.

Sweet, simple bird, of watchful eye
  And lithest limb,
Thy trust is in this gallant ship ;
  But ours, in Him.
Thy hope may founder through some leak,
  Or stormy gale ;
Ours, anchored to the throne of God,
  Can never fail.

October 24, 1880.

TREE-PLANTING, OR ARBOR DAY.

JOY for the sturdy trees,
    Fanned by each fragrant breeze,
  Lovely they stand.
The song-birds o'er them trill ;
They shade each tinkling rill ;
They crown each swelling hill,
    Lowly or grand.

Plant them by stream and way,
Plant them where children play,
    And toilers rest ;

In every verdant vale,
On every sunny swale ; —
Whether to grow or fail,
  God knoweth best.

Select the strong, the fair ;
Plant them with earnest care, —
  No toil is vain ;
Plant in a fitter place,
Where, like a lovely face
Set in some sweeter grace,
  Change may prove gain.

God will His blessing send ;
All things on Him depend, —
  His loving care
Clings to each leaf and flower,
Like ivy to its tower, —
His presence and His power
  Are everywhere.

THE ELOQUENCE OF NATURE.

GO ye, and read at length the mystic lore
    Where some Niagara's dark waters roar.
Draw nearer; tremble at the amazing plan;
See how they scorn the pygmy works of man.
Admire the swelling, grand, foreboding hush,
Where they are gathering for the awful rush
That bears them thundering down the dizzy steep,
To mingle, boiling, in the foamy deep.
List to the rumbling of the mighty floods, —
Their eloquence is but the type of God's;
Or, note the tempest's wrath, the lightning's glare,
The rainbow's image on the cloudy air, —
Bright, beautiful, divine, too fair to stay,
Where all created beauty fades away.
Think how the whirlwind's wrath, the thunder's pride,
Terrific, echoing from the mountain's side —
Suns, planets, comets, on their pathway rolled,
Like brilliant, burning, moving orbs of gold;
The summer's radiant glow, mild autumn's ray, —
All, all, the great Creator's might display.
Each flower that sheds its fragrance on the air
Shows some divinest signet fastened there;
Exalts the soul above this meanest clod,
And bids us see and hear a present God,
Whose voice of majesty no words confine, —
An eloquence eternal, deep, divine.

RUSTIC SCENES.

FROM THE GERMAN.

———◆———

MY HUMBLE HOME.

HUMBLE is my little cottage;
　　Yet it is the seat of bliss.
Anger never dwells among us,
　　Only peace and happiness;
Kindness there you always see,
And the sweetest harmony.

———oo✕oo———

PLEASURES OF NATURE.

HOW sweet 't is to play,
　　In the green fields in May,
　　Beneath the tall trees,
Or after school hours,
To pluck the sweet flowers,
　　And feel the fresh breeze!

How pleasant to look
In the murmuring brook,
　　And hear its soft sound!
How happy are we!
How nimble and free,
　　We skip o'er the ground!

Now gone is the light;
Now comes the dark night;
All still is the vale.
We 'll go to our rest,
Nor wake till redbreast,
Renews his soft tale.

THE PLEASURES OF INNOCENCE.

BLISS is hovering, smiling, everywhere, —
Hovering o'er the verdant mountain,
Smiling in the glassy fountain;
Bliss is hovering, smiling, everywhere.

Tender love is active everywhere, —
Active in the shady bower,
In the little modest flower;
Tender love is active everywhere.

Innocence unseen is ever near;
In the tall tree-top it lingers,
In the nest of feathered singers, —
Innocence unseen is ever near.

Pleasure echoes, echoes far and near;
From the green bank decked with flowers,
Sunny hills, and pleasant bowers, —
Pleasure echoes, echoes far and near.

Up and weave us now a flowery crown;
See the blossoms all unfolding,
Each its beauteous station holding, —
Up and weave us now a flowery crown.

Go ye forth and join the May-day throng;
  Sings the cuckoo by the river,
  In the breeze the young leaves quiver, —
Go ye forth and join the May-day throng.

⸺∘○⊰⊱○∘⸺

MY DELIGHT.

THROUGH the grassy fields to run,
  And to see the pleasant sun,
    And soft twilight ;
Through the meadow and the grove,
With my nimble feet to rove, —
    Is my delight.

From the lofty hill to view,
The fair sky so bright and blue,
    And clouds of white ;
And some lovely song to sing,
While I hear the echo ring, —
    Is my delight.

When so happy and so gay,
Through the flowery meads I stray,
    All fair and bright,
There to pluck a rose for you,
Bright and sparkling with the dew,
    Is my delight.

In the bower of shady trees,
Shaken by the gentle breeze,
    By morning light,
Little Robin there to hear,
Singing praises without fear,
    Is my delight.

ON WAKING IN THE MORNING.

AROUSE up, ye sleepers, the morning has come!
The sun has awakened the insects' soft hum;
The sheep to the fields go,
The men to the meadow,
And all to their labor till daylight grows low.

Oh, lose not the brightness of morning's young beams;
The beauties of Nature are sweeter than dreams.
Your downy bed leaving,
Go forth till the evening
Its fragrant air breathes, and the night-warblers sing.

THE RAIN.

SEE, the rain is falling
On the mountain's side;
From the clouds dispensing
Blessings far and wide!
How the cooling shower
Brightens every flower,
Makes the sun-parched land
With fresh blooms expand.

Now the rain is over,
See the painted bow,
O'er the distant hilltop,
All its colors show.
God is ever faithful;
Let us all be grateful,
For the rain and dew,
And the cloudless blue.

PRAYER BEFORE SCHOOL.

FOR our life, so young and pleasing,
        Father, we
        Sing to Thee
Praises never ceasing.

Let us, filled with pious feeling,
        Waked from rest,
        Neatly drest,
Humbly now be kneeling.

Give us, Lord, a zeal for learning ;
        Mercy we
        Seek from Thee ;
Make our minds discerning.

May we, through the love of Jesus,
        Feel Thy power,
        Every hour,
From sin to release us.

THE SPRING IS COME.

THE spring is come! and vales and mountains
    Are clothed anew in lovely green,
And purling streams and mossy fountains,
    And blooming flowers adorn the scene ;
        Oh, listen to the insect hum, —
        The spring, the spring is come!

The spring is come ! New life is gleaming,
  In the fresh earth and brilliant sky ;
The warm sun on the earth is beaming ;
  And heaven is full of melody.
    And listen to the insect hum, —
    The spring, the spring is come !

The spring is come ! Away with dulness !
  Go to the rich and verdant fields ;
While morning glows in all its fulness,
    Go taste the joys the spring-time yields,
    And listen to the insect hum, —
    The spring, the spring is come !

THE GARDEN.

COME, children, and now to the garden we 'll go,
  Where cowslips and snow-drops and buttercups
    grow.

The blossoms we 'll pluck with a childish delight,
And get us a bunch of the red and the white.

We 'll plant the dark roots, the young shoots we 'll
    stick down,
To weave us next May-day a flowery crown.

Again at our school, when the dear bell shall ring,
Our tasks we will learn and our songs we will sing.

SPRING FLOWERS.

KIND, the spring appears;
  Softest smiles it wears.
Lovely flowers are springing;
Happy birds are singing,
  On the fair green trees,
  Waving in the breeze.

Blooming on the ground,
  Many flowers are found;
But so modest keeping,
On the green banks sleeping,
  By the rivulet,
  Seek the violet.

How it fills the air,
  With its fragrance there!
Lovely, little flower!
Bending to the shower,
  May we learn of thee
  Sweet humility.

THE THREE FLOWERS.

THERE bloom three young flowers, so sweet and
        fair,
  In Nature's wild, flourishing garden,
On mountains and hillsides, in forests and vales,
  As if playing watcher and warden;
Your beauties, sweet flowers, are rich and divine;
They bloom in the field; in the nosegay they shine.

The buttercup, first, all spring-time so bright,
  Like glittering beads, strung in order;
Its blossoms like dew-drops, the daughters of night,
  Gem the fields, and the green roadsides border;
Wherever its clear yellow flowers you see,
Its honey-cup swells with the food of the bee.

The violet, next, in its liveliest blue,
  In green, clasping leaflets half-covered,
The spring-meadow fills with its fragrant perfume,
  Where the red-breast, by morning-light, hovered;
The image of mildness and modesty, too,
Is the violet-flower, of heavenly hue.

And then, where the sparkling fountain gleams,
  Beneath the noon-sunlight so splendid,
The flower-de-luce, with its triple bell, smiles,
  Till the days of the spring-time are ended;
'T is sacred to friendship and sacred to love,
The emblem of union in heaven above.

A SONG IN THE WOODS.

IN the cool and leafy grove,
  Hand in hand we love to rove,
While in every shady tree,
Birds tune up their melody;
Let us join their happy song,
And the harmony prolong.

Of the mighty oaks we'll sing,
And the flowers that near them spring;
Of the trees above our head,
And the grass on which we tread;
Of the little verdant hills,
Purling brooks, and running rills.

Listen how the rustling leaves,
Ever quivering in the breeze,
Send forth each a separate sound
To the echoing woods around, —
Sounds of praise to Him who made
Pine-clad hills and forest-glade.

See around the brilliant flowers,
Freshened by the evening showers,
Bright by morning, bright by night,
When comes, and when fades, the light
In the cool and leafy grove,
Hand in hand we love to rove.

THE HUNTSMAN'S SONG.

TRARAH! Trarah!
  The morning hoar-frost on the cold earth glistens;
  The bleak wind whistles so fresh and cold,
  The huntsman arouses and listens;
  The horn is winding so clear and shrill,
  It calls him abroad to the sunny hill;
      Trarah! Trarah!
      The sunny hill,
    Trarah! Trarah! Trarah!

      Trarah! Trarah!
The winter's breeze makes strong his very marrow.
  Up fly the birds — and his eye is clear;
  He seizes the sharp gleaming arrow,
  And scours the hillside where waved the corn,
  Led on by the voice of the hunting-horn.
      Trarah! Trarah!
      The hunting-horn,
    Trarah! Trarah! Trarah!

      Trarah! Trarah!
It calls away, — the sound of sport and pleasure.
  The hounds are ready; away we go!
  The evening our frolic shall measure.
  The horn is winding; the game is here;
  And the echo salutes us far and near, —
      Trarah! Trarah!
      The game is here;
    Trarah! Trarah! Trarah!

INVITATION TO THE COUNTRY.

THE winter winds are gone ;
   Fresh dews and summer showers,
Green grass and blooming flowers,
   Brighten the pleasant lawn.

Come, see the springing corn ;
Come, hear the soft birds singing ;
Come, hear their music ringing
   At crimson eve and morn.

Come to the land of song, —
The land of sweetest fragrance
Where pleasure throws its radiance,
   And music floats along.

Up to the hill-tops come,
Where bloom the tasselled flowers,
And spring, with freshened flowers,
   Raises its insect hum.

THE LITTLE WEAVER.

I AM a little weaver, and pleasant are my days ;
My little wheel keeps whirling, and round me kitty
   plays.
My life so calm and happy, so bright and active is,
There is no joy I wish for to crown my cup of bliss.

My songs are never silent but in the peaceful night;
I always rise to labor when day is growing light;
But though I am so busy, I 'm sure I do not care;
They rather should be pitied, who always idle are.

And while my wheel keeps whirling, the hours they
      seem not long;
I feel all day so happy, so lively is my song.
My work, it never wearies, but gives me health, you see;
And I am always cheerful, — oh, don't you envy me?

I care not for the dainties and all the fancy things,
Which from beyond the ocean the rich man's vessel
      brings;
My turnips and potatoes I am content to eat;
Nor will I ever murmur for want of food more sweet.

THE LITTLE STAR.

A STAR shines in the heavens,
   With soft and tender light;
How pleasant is its radiance!
   'T is gone — and now 't is bright.

I knew the place, at evening,
   Where over me it stood,
Where doves all day were cooing,
   Over the thick green wood.

I looked to see it twinkle,
   Up in the brilliant blue;
For to its mighty station,
   It soon would come, I knew.

OUR PLEASANT VILLAGE.

OH, see how bright and sweetly shines
  Our village in the evening,
While crimson clouds and streaks of gold
  Their fairy forms are weaving !
How peaceful is the dewy air !
No place on earth is half so fair.

Look, how the polished window-panes
  The parting sunbeams lighten ;
And autumn's scarlet-colored leaves,
  Touched by the red rays, brighten.
Oh, see our pretty village there !
No place on earth is half so fair.

And now the burning sun is gone ;
  It only tips the towers
That rise above the temple roof ;
  And now the darkness lowers.
But still our village glimmers there ;
No place on earth is half so fair.

SALUTATION TO THE VILLAGE.

LITTLE vale, with fairy meadows !
  Trees, that spread your leafy hands !
Flowers, clothed in softest beauty,
  Lovelier than eastern lands !
Village ! home of every treasure,
Thee we sing in strains of pleasure ;
Village in the silent vale,
Lovely village ! thee we hail !

How thy pleasant evening-shadows
  Make our troubled passions cease ;
And thy bright and purling rivers
  Fill our souls with hallowed peace.
Village ! tender thoughts promoting,
Like the clouds in azure floating ;
Village in the silent vale,
Lovely village ! thee we hail !

In thy green and sunny pathways,
  Near thy bright and glassy streams,
Free from care we love to wander,
  Cheered by summer's radiant beams :
Scenes of sweetest recollection,
Sacred to the soul's reflection,
Village in the silent vale,
Lovely village ! thee we hail !

FAREWELL TO THE VILLAGE.

SILENT vale ! where love and pleasure
    Ever round our cottage flowed ;
Beauteous as the western evening,
    Lovely as the sunlit cloud ;
Peaceful as the vesper bell, —
Thee we bid a long farewell.
    Fare thee well ! Fare thee well !

Fare ye well, ye ancient beeches,
    Which have shielded oft our head ;
Still be green, ye sunny meadows ;
    Fields with brightest flowers bespread, —
Scenes, where oft the reapers' song
Swelled in echoes sweet and strong.
    All farewell ! All farewell !

Pleasant village ! oft thy beauties
    Shall revive within our breast,
And the lovely recollection
    Soothe, like visits from the blest.
Often to our tearful eyes
Shall thy cherished image rise.
    Fare thee well ! Fare thee well !

HAIL, BETHLEHEM'S STAR!

THE gloomy night is fleeing fast,
    The morning star appears;
Its glowing rays a splendor cast
    On morning's dewy tears.
Come, let us join in cheerful praises,
While Nature her sweet pæan raises;
    The morning star appears.

Fair star ! thy charms have ne'er declined
    Since first thy beams were given, —
Like golden chains that firmly bind
    The distant earth and heaven.
Oh, praise the Lord, as on the morning
When angels sang the lovely dawning
    Of Bethlehem's star in heaven !

Let thousand voices swell the strain;
    Let praises loudly ring;
Let melody the soul enchain,
    And all creation sing.
Hail, Bethlehem's star, thy light, abiding,
Thro' stormy life our path still guiding,
    To heaven our feet shall bring.

NATIVE LAND, SO LOVELY.

E VENING winds are breathing,
 Through the forest green ;
Crimson clouds are wreathing,
 In the sky, serene.

Trees, so tall and branching,
 Relics of the past,
In the soft breeze waving,
 Roaring in the blast,

Bloom in future ages,
 Bloom in Freedom's light;
Though the tempest rages,
 Stand in all your might.

Native land, so lovely,
 Bright thy beauties are ;
Long may noon beam o'er thee,
 Let thy night be far.

On thy rising glories,
 Let the clear light glow,
Clearer than the mid-day,
 On the spotless snow.

SUMMER EVENING.

THE summer evening
    Bright wreaths is weaving,
Round vale and hill;
The dewy flowers
Perfume the bowers,
    And all is still.

The moon shines brightly,
The birds rest lightly
    Among the trees.
The reapers, singing,
Are homeward bringing
    Their yellow sheaves.

Now day is over,
The little rover
    Must be at rest.
Till purple morning
Awakes the dawning,
    In glory drest.

VERSES FOR SPECIAL OCCASIONS.

FREEDOM ADVANCES.

WRITTEN January 1, 1829, while a student in Harvard College, as
"A Carrier's Address" for the "Christian Watchman," under the con-
viction that civil and religious liberty had gained a new impulse in
Europe and the East.

THE zephyrs are hushed, and the storm winds are
    blowing;
The rude car of winter sweeps madly along;
The bright crystal streamlet no longer is flowing;
   And the woodland has echoed the last warbled
    song : —
But seraphim bands all their lyres are waking;
  The tempests are wafting a heavenly song;
The streams of salvation their barriers are breaking;
The heathenish nations their gods are forsaking, —
  All earth is uniting the strain to prolong!

I slept, — and thick darkness around me was stealing;
  The light of the gospel had faded away;
And lordly oppression her sceptre was wielding, —
  A merciless tyrant, a merciless sway!
I woke, — and around me the dark clouds were flying;
  A fair star had risen to lead on the day;
The mourners in Zion no longer were sighing, —
But wreaths of salvation her daughters were twining,
  And onward advanced the triumphal array!

Thus, thus wakes the morn, — the mists are retreating;
  The noon-day approaches beyond the blue wave.
Round Heaven's fair banners the nations are meet-
      ing, —
  The poor and unlearned, the rich and the brave;
The far distant gun of the Moslem is rolling.
  The tyrant is fallen, — all dark is his grave!
The deep, heavy knell of oppression is tolling,
And religion beams forth, every passion controlling.
  Peace, peace to the mourners and joy to the slave!

And, hark! the shrill trump of the gospel is sounding;
  The angel in heaven pursues his career;
The heart of the widow with gladness is bounding;
  And the fatherless child weeps the penitent's tear.
And thou — wilt thou aid in the work of salvation, —
  Give thy bread to the hungry; the heart-broken
    cheer?
Wilt thou send the blest story from nation to nation,
And improve the brief day of thy mortal probation?
  Then, well cries the Watchman, — A Happy New
    Year!

WOMAN.

READ at a social gathering in Boston, where a Christian woman very
acceptably occupied the chair, as presiding officer.

WHAT were this globe, with mountain, plain, and
    wood,
Grand in their gorgeousness, and great as good,
The mighty ocean with its ceaseless flow,
Expansive sky above and sea below, —
Were all this grandeur in the world alone,
Without a veil of beauty o'er it thrown,

As o'er the trellis creeps the slender vine,
As o'er old ruins verdant ivies twine,
As near the crags, the humble wild flower sleeps,
Or gentle ripples smile on ocean deeps?

What were the storm, that darkens all the air,
When thunders roll and flashing lightnings glare?
Did not, with voice of love, God's matchless will
Quell the wild tumult, and say, " Peace, be still!"
And bid the rainbow with its lovely form
Wreathe by its light the background of the storm?

The vale is sweeter, for the o'er-hanging hill;
The beauty shows the grandeur, grander still.
What were this hour of joy and festive cheer,
Though faces meet us which our hearts revere;
What were this scene, brilliant with church and
      state, —
If, met in conclave, for some grave debate,
Man sat, alone, sombre and grave and wise,
Like old gnarled oak beneath the breezy skies?

We love the strength that rules, the light that guides,
The higher will that judges and decides, —
Blessed be God! — we own the chairman's power;
But still, to-night, 't is woman rules the hour.

WOMAN, A "SIDE-ISSUE."

Read at the Social Union, Boston, October 26, 1868.

It has been said, " Whatever be the beauty and charms of woman, let her not value herself too highly.   For it is undeniable that, in the work of creation, man was the principal, and woman only a ' side-issue.' "

YES, a " side-issue," so you say,
   Like a self-vaunting Turk :
Woman was but an after-thought ;
   But man, God's noblest work.

But no side-issue here to-night,
   As once in Eden's bowers ;
For woman holds the highest place
   In this fair feast of ours.

Creation's lords with lofty air
   Their higher work fulfil ;
But woman, in a gentler sphere,
   Labors with loving will.

We boast our greatness, wisdom, wealth,
   Proud of our rank as men ;
But for our mothers, where had we,
   Creation's lordlings, been ?

When God resolved His chosen race
   To pluck from Pharaoh's hand,
The ark that saved the infant chief
   Was by a woman planned.

When Sisera's champions led the fight,
  Armed with the warrior's mail,
He failed; and through his heathen head,
  A woman drove the nail.

When Joshua sent to search the land
  Where heathen banners waved,
No hostile hand could reach the spies
  A woman's wit had saved.

The prophet near the brook lay hid,
  By hungry ravens fed;
Till woman built his little room,
  And feasted him with bread.

Weary and hungry, Jesus sat
  At noon beside the well;
And listening ears absorbed each word
  Of love that from Him fell.

Samaria's nobles, boastful, dreamed
  Of worldly wit and lore;
A woman blessed His words that day;
  A woman owned His power.

One meekly sat at Jesus' feet,
  His gracious words to hear;
And one received Him, tired and faint,
  With love and festal cheer, —

O blessed women, never shall
  Their deeds forgotten be!
E'en the ascending Conqueror fixed
  His gaze on Bethany.

With tearful eyes and loving heart,
 Furnished with ointment sweet,
A woman bathed, perfumed, and kissed
 The Saviour's sacred feet.

Who but a woman on His head
 The precious fragrance strewed ?
" Trouble her not," the Master said,
 "She hath done what she could."

And, meanly, one his Lord betrayed
 With cruelty inhuman ;
And one denied His blessed name, —
 Both men, but never woman.

Rudely the rough procession trod,
 With smirk and shout and yell,
The pathway where the Son of God
 Beneath His burden fell.

Where were the men ? They in that hour
 Hid, trembling and afraid ;
Only the women near their Lord
 Lingered and wept and prayed.

When, dying on the shameful cross,
 In agony He hung,
The precious word " mother " was heard
 Last lingering on His tongue.

Up, curious Peter ! seek the place
 Of the Great Captive's tomb ;
Run, loving John, before the rays
 Of morn the skies illume !

They rose, they ran ; with joy they saw
  The garb the Saviour wore, —
But women at the sacred spot
  Had worshipped long before.

When first a church on Europe's soil
  Like a new sunlight burst,
And grew apace, on its fair roll
  A woman's name stood first.

When science would new worlds evoke,
  Beyond the mighty sea,
Spain's nobles doubted if at all
  Such wondrous things could be.

Men locked the treasury of state,
  " No funds to spare to-day !"
She sold her jewelled rings to send
  Columbus on his way.

Brave Isabella ! she alone
  Saw glimmerings in the skies ;
America was sought and found, —
  A woman's enterprise !

There sleeps upon a lonely isle,
  Far o'er the southern wave,
The proto-martyr of our work,
  The heathen world to save.

That silent sleeper's gentle name
  Still breathes like sweet perfume ;
The sacred dust of woman fills
  That lonely, glorious tomb.

Where were our honored, martyred chief,
    Who, through the stormy wave,
Safely conveyed the ship of state,
    Patient and wise and brave;

Whose sun has set, whose star gone down, —
    When shall we see such other?
But what had honored Lincoln been
    But for his Christian mother?

And what were he whose deeds of might
    On every banner flaunt,
But for the pious woman's name
    Who made him U. S. Grant.

Talk of " side-issues," if you please;
    Cry " woman " — " Need n't heed her !"
But history and love reply,
    " Oh, no, she is the leader."

Not a " side-issue " here to-night,
    As once in Eden's bowers;
But woman holds the highest place
    At this fair feast of ours.

THE GOOD AND GREAT MAN.

HYMN for the Soldier's Corps of the G. A. R., Chicago, Ill.,
May 15, 1887.

WHO is the truly good and great?
    Who, worthy of the highest fame?
And who, among the sons of men,
    Shall hold the most distinguished name?

The man whose heart and hands are pure;
    Who rules his thoughts, who rules his will;
Resists temptation's fiercest flood,
    Unsullied keeps his honor still;

Who heeds the cry of want and woe,
    Who gently soothes the sufferer's pain;
Pities the tempted ones who fall,
    And sets them on their feet again;

Who walks 'neath heaven's o'er-arching dome
    Purely as angels' feet might tread;
And love and faith combine to weave
    A glorious halo round his head;

Who, earnest, keeps, with reverent step,
    The ways the pious fathers trod;
Who shuns the intoxicating cup,
    And loves his country and his God, —

He shall enjoy the highest praise
    To mortals due, to mortals given;
Be owned, an honor to his race,
    And wear the crown of life in heaven.

DANGEROUS PRECOCITY.

YOUTHS of few summers — boys, still dolts at
        school,
Leaping the rigors of parental rule —
Deem all control a bore, and vote it harsh;
Ape foreign style, and sport the curled mustache;
Plunge with a zest, in nonsense and in sin, —
Hair-oil without, and hair-brained skulls within:
The pomp, external, affluently shed,
Proclaims they have within an empty head.
How eloquently weakness tells its tale!
Like ships that tower aloft, with wind in every sail.

The gentle sex, grown wise as Nature's lords,
Must learn the magic of some mystic words
From learned juntos, and aspire to speak
Some hidden mystery, in classic Greek.
They wear the secret charm upon the breast,
Like evening's star upon the blushing west.
Too frank, too good, the luscious truth to hide,
They choose to wear the symbol all outside;
And when these blooming bowers of hope they leave,
Commit the secret to their sister Eve.

"A LITTLE UPPISH." [1]

"A LITTLE uppish," — Well, it is
    The style of modern days;
For young America delights
    In such peculiar ways.

The boy escaped from female garb,
    Aged just twenty moons,
Feels very " uppish," when he sports
    His boots and pantaloons.

The girl in hoops and waterfalls,
    Just entering her " teens,"
Is " uppish," as if born to sit
    With duchesses and queens.

And when the child, become a bride,
    Sits on the household throne,
Her dear liege lord she sometimes snubs,
    Alas, too " uppish " grown.

May not a young and offshoot church
    Be good as any other ?
Oh, yes; when, " uppish " grown, she thinks
    She's wiser than her mother.

Who wonders that the offshoot stands
    With such rich grace endued ?
She feels the thrill in all her veins
    Of her strong mother's blood.

[1] Read at a Social Union, Springfield, Mass., when a young offshoot
church was characterized, by Rev. Dr. G. B. Ide, pastor of the mother
church, as " a little uppish."

"A little uppish!"   Gently speak,
  'T is but a fault of youth;
And grace will cure it, wait a while,
  Through the blest power of truth.

Thank God, such faults are but of earth!
  Thank God, they pass away,
As clouds of night and gloom withdraw
  Before the opening day!

THESE MODERN TIMES.

LIFE in these modern days strange freaks assumes;
  Old truth retires, and feeble falsehood comes;
Fiction and fancy, all the live-long day,
And airy nothings, are the things that pay.

The loudest, lightest, for the worthiest pass, —
As rise balloons, because their filled with gas.
Men scorn the wisdom of the hoary sage,
And eloquently boast this learned age: —

An age of shallow wit and weak pretence,
Whose greatest want is want of common sense;
The gaping crowd admires each changing scene,
As some new wonder, — for the crowd is green.

Fashions and follies bear the masses by,
And silks and ribbons, with their rainbow dye,
Or flutter in the air, a graceful show,
Or sweep the dusty thoroughfares below.

Along the street their gaudy pageants glide,
Gay as the butterflies of summertide, —
With equal beauty, equal lightness fraught,
As little burdened with the weight of thought.

Perchance, but spendthrifts on an empty purse ;
Perchance, the victims, too, of something worse.
An eloquence of manner often tells,
Some things have naught but tongues, besides church
      bells.

SEPTEMBER, 1838.

A MERRY HOUR.

A. E. SLOAN, Esq., of Cincinnati, delivered a course of three lectures, entitled "Merry Hours." In advance of the course he selected the names of several persons and things which would be incidentally introduced in the lectures, and requested Dr. Smith to write for him, for his use, the prelude to each lecture. The notice was very sudden ; but the impromptu responses are given below, as illustrations of the versatility of the poet, in "Mirthful Moments."

HUMOROUS FRAGMENTS, No. 1.

L END your ears, gentle friends, throw your busi-
      ness aside,
"Tom Pidger" is going to trot out "his bride ;"
On my word, you shall learn, drawn true to the life,
'Mid the frolic and fun, what makes "a good wife ; "
Or lawyer's, or " minister's," even your own, —
(Aside) if your willing to yield her your throne.

If you 've done " Saratoga," and drunk of its water,
On a trip with your wife, or your merry-tongued
      daughter;

If you 've been at the seashore, where morals grow
    lax ;
Or learned " early rising " from witty " J. Saxe," —
I 'll warrant you need, after such relaxation,
Some muscular fun, before your vocation
You ply, like an engine, through snow, sleet, and rain,
And buckle to labor and business again.
So smooth out the creases that furrow your brow,
While, juicy as apples just plucked from the bough,
I strive, gentle friends, to the best of my power,
To give, as per program, a right " merry hour."

HUMOROUS FRAGMENTS, No. 2.

If I should open here at once, and empty all my
    budget,
Like some rich mine of gold, condensed in one enor-
    mous nugget, —
Talk in one breath of courtship, love, and ardor pa-
    triotic,
Mixing, like old Egyptian priests, hieratic and de-
    motic, —
Your sides would shake, your brain would ache amid
    the varied clatter,
And echoes ring from all the hall, " Good, sir, what is
    the matter ? "

So, mindful of your case, I choose to give you in
    detail, —
Just as your daily letters, friend, come one by one by
    mail, —
How " Mr. Winkle " sought " the springs " where wit
    and beauty fed ;
And " Pickwick at the Ipswich Inn " once missed his
    way to bed ;

And Wendell Holmes, the autocrat, — his wit put
  under ban, —
Resolved, "I never more shall dare be witty as I
  can."
Perhaps, to try another strain, and prove its potent
  magic,
My rendering of "Clarence' Dream," will give you a
  touch of tragic.
So here you have a program true, — not baseless as
  false rumor, —
Apply your ears and you shall hear "fragments of wit
  and humor."

Humorous Fragments, No. 3.

The light and dark, the grave and gay, make up the
  round of life ;
Pathetic scenes and mirthful hours, — now rest, now
  battle's strife.
Chiefly in merry mood my steps from scene to scene
  shall roam ;
A tear may dampen on your lids for the " dear folks
  at home ; "
You needs must hear how " Harry Fifth " manœuvred
  for " his wife ; "
And roguish Kate, with cunning grace, worried the
  Prince's life.
There 's something sweet in early " love ; " I think
  you 've found it so ;
Some, in its budding promise yet, — some knew it long
  ago.
Sometimes the sly, winged Cupid puts a sting within
  your marrow ;
But oftener smitten hearts declare, there 's honey on
  his arrow.

Soho! you speak of "Yankee Land," a noble country,
    truly ;
I quite agree with you, my friend, I mean to praise it
    duly.
Amid the wealth of sea and soil, republic, kingdom,
    throne,
This gem of all the nations gleams, a diamond set
    alone.
You thought of courtship when I spoke just now of
    Henry V. ;
Now leave the *ship* and keep the *court*, take land in-
    stead of sea.

Call up your jury, Sheriff B., and summon in the
    Court ;
" Bardell and Pickwick's " case is reached, — so read
    the clerk's report.
This fills the docket, gentle friends : these petals make
    the flower ;
Unfolding, one by one, their scent will fill the " merry
    hour."
Unconsciously the sunlit sands will trickle through
    the glass,
While wit high carnival maintains, and " Mirthful
    Moments " pass.

ELOQUENCE.

EXTRACTS from poem read before the Philhermenian Society, of Brown University, R. I., September, 1838; and before the Erosophian Adelphi, of Waterville College, Maine, August, 1840.

WHAT, then, is eloquence?   No mere parade
    Of gorgeous words, in gorgeous forms arrayed;
No pomp of style, no art by masters taught;
Not graceful gesture, not profoundest thought,
Nor reason's power, nor feeling most intense, —
Expound the matchless power of eloquence!
What more are these than rudimental parts, —
Disjecta membra of the art of arts?
Show me the man whose words in torrents rush,
While tides of feeling from his full soul gush;
Simple and clear in style, in action strong,
With Nature's purest utterance on his tongue;
Deep, rich in thought, majestically bright,
In illustration, like meridian light;
Persuasive, gentle, graphic, great, sublime, —
A giant midst the pygmies of his time;
In whom, unconscious, Nature's beauty gleams,
And art itself, but perfect Nature seems;
Able to wield the fiercest mob at will,
Like Him whose voice bade the rough sea be still,
And every billow settled at His word,
The ocean yielding homage to its Lord; —
That man is eloquent; a coal divine,
Brought by some seraph from the eternal shrine,
Has touched his lips, set loose his noble mind
From clogs that hold the mass of human kind,
Made him soar upward, gloriously free,
And breathe the soulful air of liberty.

But not in him alone the gift resides ;
Pure eloquence has many a home besides :
Not fettered down, 't is true, by stated rules,
Chastened and trained, like logic, in the schools,
Not forced, like rhetoric, to be an art, —
But breathing life and power from Nature's heart.
Wildly, but sweet, its lovely cadence floats,
Well worthy to be viewed as Heaven-taught notes.
Where can a spot in Nature's ample round,
Filled with Jehovah's workmanship, be found, —
A spot where myriad suns converge their rays,
And worlds to worlds respond their Maker's praise,
Or where in meaner ranks creation throngs,
And countless thousands chant their gladsome songs,
While the minutest worm is called to share —
Sublime compassion ! — its Creator's care,
Where, where a spot, through Nature's vast extent,
But God has made superbly eloquent !

See where Imagination mounts its throne,
And boasts a rich creation, all its own,
Bold, mighty, clear, magnificent, complete, —
There all ideals of perfection meet !
If the real world is eloquent with truth,
In art and nature, hoary age and youth,
Which, though it grieves us, still demands an ear, —
And woe betide the man who scorns to hear ; —
Imagination, in its rainbows drest,
Utters its eloquence in every breast ;
Puts on all charms, assumes all gay attire ;
Makes tears of blood, or breath of living fire ;
Raises the beggar to a kingly throne,
Or nods, and thousands tread the monarch down ;
Bids the dark ocean heave its waves on high,
Or whispers, and the stormy tempests die !

Touched by its power, we start from troubled sleep,
Tremble and quiver, and long vigils keep;
Again, it lulls us to an angel's rest, —
Pure, sweet, and tranquil as the evening west;
Moved by the scenes it feigns, our hearts have bled,
Grief rose in floods, tears were in torrents shed;
Bound by the magic of its mighty spell,
We wept in agony, when all was well!
Oh, say, what mistress else has strength to bind
The secret movements of the free-born mind?
What energy besides can melt and mould
The human spirit like to liquid gold?
What agent rule us by a law so stern,
Which oft disgusts us, while we o'er it yearn?
Say, what within, beyond, the realm of sense,
Boasts with more right the power of Eloquence.

SOUL-LIBERTY, THE WATCHWORD OF THE WORLD.

THE following verses were originally written, as will appear during the perusal, to honor the "Early Baptists of New England." They have a larger range of tribute than belongs to any individual branch of the Church of Christ. They reflect those elements of character which pervaded the early Christians of America, and made American Independence possible.

SING, Muse of history, sing the deathless fame
    Of heroes honored by a spotless name;
From selfish aims and low ambition pure,
Born for a work which ever shall endure.
Brave men and true, with fearless steps they trod,
Soul-liberty their aim, — their leader, God.

Slaves to no creed, chained by no iron rule,
Bound by no ritual, servants of no school,
Pledged to no standing order, all their plan
To trust God's truth to God, man's rights to man, —
They held no precept but the Saviour's word,
Called no one " Master " but their glorious Lord.
They claimed no right the conscience to restrain,
Deemed human rites both useless things and vain,
Taught infant baptism, — when the babes believed,
And their young hearts the Saviour's grace received;
Believed in sprinkling — of Christ's precious blood —
And urged their converts to that cleansing flood.
But, dead to sin, they chose the mystic grave,
Memorial blest of Him who came to save;
Then taught the world, by charity divine,
How Christ's sweet spirit in the life can shine;
All men embrace within its mighty span,
Grant each his right, and honor man as man.

Careless of steepled grace and Gothic pile,
Their earliest church on yonder sea-girt isle
In faith they planted, and bedewed with tears
The infant slip, the joy of later years.
When scourged by power, the cruel stripes they
        bore;
Eased by God's succor, made their converts more.
When doomed to exile, wider still they spread
The faith they loved, the truth for which they bled.
Their zeal for God, by fire and dungeons tried,
Grew when they suffered, triumphed when they died.
Free as the water, rippling on their strand,
Reaching and kissing every distant land,
So the broad truths they taught, hemmed in no more,
Seek every land, and find each distant shore.

The church they founded here, oppressed and tried,
For which they suffered, and in which they died,
Stood for Christ's truth, brought freedom to the
    oppressed,
Joy to the prisoner, — to the troubled, rest ;
Like some fair beacon, marked the blessed way,
And shed its welcome light across the bay.
They passed from earth, the champions in the fight,
Their hearts undaunted, and their armor bright ;
Servants of men not they, but fearing God ;
And countless thousands in their steps have trod.

As gentle clouds that drink the morning dew
Float in the light, and bathe in heaven's bright blue,
But, noonday past, in gold and crimson, rest,
Like gorgeous mountains, in the glowing west,
While day departs in peaceful beauty die,
Leaving their tranquil glow along the sky, —
So lived Christ's witnesses, friends of Christ's truth,
As men endowed with an unfailing youth,
And dying, left, like daylight's golden train,
Blest memories in which they live again.

O men of God, O men of faith and prayer,
Whose souls craved freedom as the lungs crave air,
Blest for your work, whose fruits, like harvests, wave,
Blest for the noble heritage ye gave,
In filial love, in manly strength and cheer,
In queenly charms and beauty, gathered here,
Honors sincere around your brows we wreathe,
And blessings on your memories we breathe ;
Be ours the honor and the bliss to wear
With grateful joy and pride your mantles rare,
Till o'er each bannered height shall swing, unfurled,
" Soul-liberty," — the watchword of the world.

THE UNFETTERED CONSCIENCE.

In 1665 the authorities of the Town of Boston nailed up the doors
of the First Baptist Church, and forbade its use. The order was soon
after revoked.

At the 200th Anniversary of the historic event above noticed, the
following lines were read, to illustrate that heroism, founded upon
religious convictions, which largely distinguished the Founders of the
Great American Republic.

AYE, " close the doors, and nail them fast,"
      " Shut out the faithful few "
Who nailed their banners to the mast,
      To Christ and conscience true ;
Their motto, " What the Scripture saith,"
      With souls serene and brave,
And held unshrinkingly the faith
      The Word and Spirit gave.

Aye, " Nail the doors," — bleak winds of March
      Roared round the little flock ;
But, peaceful as the heaven's blue arch,
      Their zeal defied the shock ;
Not theirs, made weak by coward fear,
      The truth they loved, to yield ;
Not theirs, compelled by scoff and jeer,
      To hasten from the field.

One Sabbath, scattered through the town,
      Barred from their house of prayer,
Crushed by the ruler's scorn and frown,
      The people's taunt and stare ;

The next, to God and duty true,
  Met in their lowly shed,
They worshipped Him in tears, who knew
  Not where to lay His head.

Aye, "Nail the doors," — the rulers deemed
  Their act had power to bind
The sacred rights of men redeemed,
  To crush the freeborn mind ;
But who shall bind the beams of light
  The sun at midday flings ?
Or check the eagle's heavenward flight
  By cobwebs on his wings ?

Prisons and fines, and pain and death,
  In vain assert control
O'er that free thing, the Almighty breath,
  God's image in the soul ;
Tyrants of earth, with mace and crown,
  May make an empire cower ;
The soul — an empire of its own —
  Defies their utmost power.

Can man o'er noontide's glory bring
  A pall of blackest night ?
Or grains of dust upon his wing
  Impede the seraph's flight ?
God's thought, unchecked by human rule,
  Shall hold its mighty sway ;
God's law shall found its lofty school,
  And love make all obey.

Aye, "Nail the doors," — the mighty wrong
  The erring hammer wrought, --
A seed, that day, — harvests, ere long, —
  With wondrous fruits was fraught ;

As ships, in ballast, oft depart,
  Yet, when they homeward sail,
Bring wealth uncounted to the mart,
  Nor heed the stormy gale.

Aye, "Nail the doors," — yet God's true light
  From God's blest Word will shine;
Conscience and truth will have their right, —
  "'T is human," 't is divine;
Hold in your leash the billowy sea,
  Fetter the waves of sound,
Man's soul, — God's truth, — divinely free,
  By man cannot be bound.

BE JOYFUL.

Breakfast Hymn, for the American Tract Society, May, 1864.

JOY! — for the precious seed that springs
  In fields which God, the Lord, hath blessed;
Joy! — for the sower, where he sings
  On the bright hills of heavenly rest!

Joy! — for the fields where men have strewed,
  In faith and love, salvation's leaves!
Joy! — for the reaper, safe with God,
  And honored with his ripened sheaves!

Joy for the fathers! once they wrought
  'Mid scenes of sorrow, blood, and strife;
Gladly we choose the paths they sought,
  And track their steps, to endless life.

Joy for the fallen ! glory won,
  No more the dust of earth they tread;
The work proceeds, — and God's dear Son
  Shall triumph, where their feet have bled.

Joy for the Saviour ! sin, o'er-thrown
  At last, no more fierce fight shall wage.
Joy for Immanuel ! wear the crown,
  Immortal Prince, — from age to age !

THE CHRISTMAS TREE.

IN all this bright and pleasant land
  Of sunshine, dew, and flowers,
Has sprung to life no Christmas tree
  More fair than this of ours.

Up from the strengthening earth no sap
  Flows out from stem to stem,
But beauty crowns each bending branch,
  A Christmas diadem.

No faded blossoms drooping hang,
  No withered twig is seen;
Love set, and love adorned, the tree, —
  And love is ever green.

And every little leaflet clings
  Closely to every other,
Like nestling bird to nestling bird,
  Like child to loving mother.

Brought from the field where once it grew, —
    Alive, without a root;
'T is not a fruit tree, but it yields
    The most amazing fruit.

What would you find upon the tree?
    Cake, candy, book, or pistol?
Perhaps not all, but love, as dear
    As any love in Bristol.

Then welcome to the festal hall;
    Come to our Christmas tree;
Come where the branches drop their gifts,
    Like the blest gospel, free.

In all this bright and pleasant land
    Of sunshine, dew, and flowers,
Has sprung to life no Christmas tree,
    More fair than this of ours.

BRISTOL, R. I., Christmas, 1870.

SIBYLLINE LEAVES.

READ at a dinner of the Harvard Class of 1829.

"WILL you buy my leaves, O monarch?
    They teem with wondrous lore
Of things ordained to happen,
    Casting their shades before;
The precious truths are written
    In volumes three times three;
Come, monarch, pay the sesterces
    And take the books from me."

“Away! I scorn thee, Sibyl,”
  The haughty Tarquin cried,
“Thou hast no power to open
  What God hath sworn to hide;”
The Sibyl took her volumes
  And proudly stalked away;
“Three shall be burned,” she muttered,
  “Six shall bring equal pay.”

The curling flames blazed brightly,
  Three volumes ceased to be;
“Now, six, O haughty Tarquin,
  Await thy high decree:
Three precious tomes have perished,
  That told Rome’s coming fate;
Say, wilt thou take the six I hold,
  And save the glorious state?”

Again refused the monarch, —
  Three volumes burned again,
Like dry leaves in the forest,
  Where comes no dew nor rain.
And stood again the Sibyl
  Before proud Tarquin’s door;
“Three volumes now I offer thee,
  Their worth, — nor less, nor more.”

And Rome’s great king relented, —
  “ ’T is much, O hag, to pay,
But sesterces, whate’er you wish,
  Sibyl, are yours to-day;
These honored leaves shall rule the state
  Saved by your words prophetic,
From *Thule ultima* remote,
  To empires trans-Gangetic.”

The bark we launched in years long past
    On the world's stormy sea,
Sailed with no Sibyl leaves to tell
    How strange its fates should be.
But deeds are better far than words, —
    Acts, than prophetic pen ;
Prouder than hopes of things to be,
    Are high deeds that have been.

No Sibyl in mysterious lore
    Things secret e'er reveals,
And only life, with solemn pomp,
    The book of Fate unseals ;
Thou saidst, O Sibyl, volumes three
    Filled with thy lore divine,
Were worth as many sesterces
    As were the volumes nine.

But one grand life, whose noble deeds
    File by, as men in battle, —
Borne strongly to its glorious end,
    Amid the world's vain rattle, —
Is worth a thousand promises
    Dreamed by a brain ascetic ;
Our glory is in acts, not words, —
    Deeds done, not deeds prophetic.

DORCAS.[1]

"This woman was full of good works and almsdeeds which she did."
Acts ix. 36.

THE coats and garments, deftly made
   By Dorcas for the poor,
Excel in beauty all the robes
   That monarchs ever wore.
These, from the sphere of mortal things,
   Like breaths of wind have passed;
The record of her humble work,
   Forevermore will last.

The gold and gems of royal courts,
   Glittered their fleeting day;
The shining jewels men admire,
   Were fair, — but where are they?
The coats and garments Dorcas made
   To bless the humble poor,
Are treasured with the holy things
   Which ever shall endure.

For when the Judge, with glory crowned,
   Takes His immortal throne,
And such as did His will on earth,
   His loving voice shall own,
They, in the sufferers whom they helped,
   Their Lord Himself shall see, —
"In that ye did it unto these,
   Ye did it unto me."

[1] My sister's eighty-ninth birthday, March 17, 1895.

It is not out of place to add, for example's sake, that during a few months previous to the date of this brotherly tribute, the subject of the verses sent to the needy poor children of the South, more than two hundred useful articles, all of which were her own handiwork. — ED.

OUR YEARS ROLL ON.

A " Carrier's Address " written January 1, 1832, while a student at Andover, Mass., and recalled to mind by the poet, with a loving confidence that when years on earth shall end, a blessed immortality lies beyond.

The choice of this poem, written shortly before the hymn, " My Country, 't is of thee," has been adopted, with the poet's approval, as the closing selection of this volume.   The experience of a long life has confirmed his early estimate of duty, as " Our years roll on."

O*UR years roll on ;* and fleeting years are they,
    Brief as the rainbow on the dropping spray
Of some wild waterfall, that foams afar,
Where Nature's rudest rocks and forests are.
With heaven's bright hues the falling raindrops burn ;
They hurry onward ; others, in their turn,
Shine just as bright, and glow as soft and clear ;
But while we look, their beauties disappear.

Our years roll on ; and varied years are they.
Here smile the buds of hope ; there dwells decay.
Now friends are here ; but quickly they depart,
And death unwinds the strings that bind the heart.
Pleasure and pain their changing courses keep,
Sure as our waking hours succeed to sleep ;
From wave to wave we mount, till changing tires,
And life — the close of changing scenes — expires.

Our years roll on ; and blessed years are they,
Cheered with the righteous Sun's reviving ray.
The streams of rich salvation round us flow,
And thousand hearts their precious virtue know.

Tidings of souls renewed and sins forgiven
Come floating by, on every wind of heaven;
The sway of sin begins at length to wane;
And o'er the world the Saviour comes to reign.

Our years roll on; and active years are they.
O'er flowery banks we may not take our way;
We may not linger where soft numbers swell,
Nor over-love the things we love so well.
'T is ours to work for God; 't is ours to go
Through earth's wide field, the precious seed to sow.
We may not rest till life's bright years decline;
Then, like the sun in heaven, our names shall shine.

Our years roll on; our years must pass away.
Our youth's companions, tell us, where are they?
And where are thousands whom we knew before, —
Thousands, whose faces we shall see no more?
Among the dead their dwelling is to-day.
Hear we their voice, " Ye living, watch and pray !"
Hear and obey; then we no scene may fear;
But each revolving sun shall bring a happy year.